DEVIL'S ROCK

DEVIL'S ROCK

CHRIS SPEYER

BLOOMSBURY

LONDON BERLIN NEW YORK

Bloomsbury Publishing, London, Berlin and New York

First published in Great Britain in 2009 by Bloomsbury Publishing Plc
36 Soho Square, London, W1D 3QY

A CIP catalogue record of this book is available from the British Library

ISBN 978 0 7475 9752 0

The paper this book is printed on is certified independently in accordance
with the rules of the FSC. It is ancient-forest friendly.
The printer holds chain of custody.

FSC
Mixed Sources
Product group from well-managed
forests and other controlled sources
Cert no. SGS - COC - 2061
www.fsc.org
© 1996 Forest Stewardship Council

Typeset by Dorchester Typesetting Group Ltd
Printed in Great Britain by Clays Ltd, St Ives Plc

1 3 5 7 9 10 8 6 4 2

www.bloomsbury.com

*For my parents who taught me to sail
and for Ming who is learning*

CHAPTER 1

The jagged reef that straggles out to the east of Devil's Rock was only just breaking the surface of the water, its vicious tips disappearing completely beneath the swell when a wave rolled over them. Zaki, riding on the yacht *Morveren*'s bowsprit, watched the foam streaming through the gaps in the glistening fangs as each wave surged across the outlying reef and heaved itself up the side of the brooding black rock that guards the entrance to the River Orme.

'Start the engine!' Zaki's father shouted over the roar of the breaking waves.

'I think we can make it!' Michael was on the helm. He was forcing the yacht to claw its way into the wind, trying to make the entrance before the tide turned against them.

'No you can't. Not on this tack,' snapped Zaki's father. 'Start the engine!'

Zaki knew his brother would put off starting the engine until the last possible moment. He'd take the boat into a harbour and on to its mooring under sail, if he possibly could. Michael saw starting the engine as an admission of defeat.

'Plenty of time,' Michael pleaded.

'Ten minutes before the tide turns. Start the engine, Michael.'

Few boats ever venture into the River Orme. With its rock-strewn mouth gaping wide to the prevailing winds and a tongue of treacherous sand protruding from its constricted throat, the entrance is an uninviting prospect. Most sailors are put off by the curt description in the local cruising guide: 'Dangerous in all but the most settled conditions.' Some more intrepid skippers will approach to within sight of the outlying rocks, see the breaking waves on the sandbank, and turn back out to sea.

For Zaki and Michael, this was their river, its ferocious mouth guarding its inner secrets, protecting a world of pools, beaches and streams that they alone were meant to explore.

Zaki had been longing to visit the Orme all summer but the weather had frustrated them. It had been a summer of storms and torrential rain, the wind stubbornly blowing from the west or the south-west, and even Zaki's father, who'd been sailing in and out of the Orme all his life, wouldn't risk taking *Morveren* through the reefs in an onshore wind. This morning the forecast had promised northerlies for the next two days, and with them the chance to return to Devil's Rock.

Zaki felt a shudder run through the boat as the old diesel engine thudded into life. Zaki scrambled off the bowsprit and half swung, half danced across the rocking deck. 'Do you want the mainsail down?' he asked.

'We'll get the sails down; you steer her in,' said his father.

Zaki took a quick breath. He'd been allowed to steer the boat for as long as he could remember. But he'd never taken her into the Orme. Never threaded her through the terrifying maze of rocks and sandbanks that led to the inner sanctuary. Michael had done it, but then Michael was four years older. Zaki looked across at his brother, who was meticulously coiling a rope. Michael grinned. The grin said, 'Dare you!' He stepped away from the helm.

'She's all yours.'

'Can you see the dead tree on the cliff?' Zaki's father asked.

Zaki knew why he had to find the tree. You lined the tree up with the craggy edge of Devil's Rock. You kept the two in line and you found the narrow gap in the outer reef.

His father turned to Michael, 'Let's get the main down.'

Feet braced wide for balance, Zaki at the helm was just tall enough to see over the cabin roof. The anxiety that had swept through him a moment before drained away as he felt the boat's tiller in his hand tugging and pushing like a living thing. He was born to do this, more at home on the rocking deck of a boat than he ever felt on the land.

'Now,' he said quietly to the boat. 'Now, *Morveren*, let's see where we go.'

A wave rolled under the yacht, lifting her stern and then her bow, so that her bowsprit pointed for a moment towards the top of the cliff. There was the dead tree, trunk and branches standing out pale and grey against the wooded hill that sloped to the cliff edge. It was as though boy and boat had lifted their eyes together and searched out the all-important landmark.

His father had taught him how to read charts and tide tables, how to plan a passage and plot their course, but Zaki believed that, left to herself, the old boat could find her way into any creek or harbour on the south-west coast. *Morveren* had been his grandfather's boat, built by Zaki's grandfather long before Zaki was born, always a part of the family, a constant through all the changes of Zaki's early childhood – the house moves, the different schools, the move from Devon to London and back to Devon again. He lived two lives, the life on *Morveren* and the life ashore. When he stepped aboard *Morveren* the complications of life on shore quickly slipped away to be replaced by the slow, easy rhythms of boat-life.

Zaki eased the tiller over so that the dead tree and the edge of Devil's Rock came into line. He pushed the throttle forward a touch and *Morveren* picked up speed. Not a good idea to dawdle while attempting to thread through the narrow gap in the reef; a rogue wave from the wrong direction and they would be on the rocks.

Michael and his father busied themselves with the mainsail; neither offered words of advice or warning but Zaki knew they were keeping a close eye on everything he did.

Just four boat lengths to go and the swell running from behind. Perfect. Now they were in a trough between waves. The next wave would lift and carry them through the gap in the reef.

'Keep her steady,' Zaki coached himself – slip off course now and the wave could slew the stern on to the waiting fangs; too much speed and the wave would carry them on to Devil's Rock.

Boy and boat were one as they were lifted on the green, humped back of the following wave. Now they were surging forward, riding the wave, Zaki steering by feel rather than sight, keeping the boat on the wave – one boat length to go – into the gap with foam-flecked rocks passing on either side. Then Zaki let out a long breath as the swell slid from under the boat and raced away to fling itself against the unyielding mass of Devil's Rock. They had made it through!

But no time to relax. Time to find the next landmark.

To the east of the rock, inside the reef, there appeared to be open water, but Zaki knew he must steer clear of the long sandbank that lurked just below the surface, almost entirely closing off the entrance to the Orme.

Zaki swung the boat through ninety degrees and searched for the ruined cottage on the opposite shore that would give him a bearing clear of the protruding sandbar and The Orphans, a clutter of awkwardly placed, half-submerged rocks.

Morveren rolled heavily in the cross swell and it took all Zaki's strength to hold the boat on course.

Where was the cottage? Even on a calm day like today,

each wave threatened to carry the boat sideways on to Devil's Rock.

Ah! There! He could make out the remains of the stone chimney and tumbledown walls up on the hillside. A shiver ran down Zaki's spine as he imagined attempting to make this entrance in a heavy sea. A bit more power from the engine and soon they were safely past The Orphans and under the cliffs on the eastern side.

Zaki turned the boat upstream, keeping within a few metres of the shore, where he knew, was deep water. 'Looks like the tide's turned.' His father's voice broke through the bubble that seemed to have surrounded Zaki since he began the run into the bay.

The current in the channel hadn't yet reached any great strength, but it was already enough to slow their progress. Zaki looked around, seeing the gulls that swooped between the rock and the cliffs, hearing their cries above the sounds of the waves and the thud-thud of the boat's engine.

'You look pleased with yourself,' his father said.

But it wasn't just pride in his piloting skills that was making Zaki smile, it was the magical power of this place; that dark, towering rock that had dragged the boat towards it, the spray from the breaking waves, caught white in the sunlight, the granite cliffs streaked with red, and above and beyond them the intense green of the wooded hills. A wild, dangerous, thrilling place to be.

Beyond the bar, the creek opened out into a wide, smooth inlet, wooded on one side with a sandy beach curving around the other, the chaos of the outer bay

6

giving way to a scene so quiet that it would be easy to believe time, in this place, stood still.

Zaki turned to his brother and father. 'What do you think?'

'Well, you didn't hit any rocks.' Michael grinned.

'No, stupid, I mean where do you think we should anchor?'

'What about where we always do?' suggested Michael.

Their father pointed to a spot where the water turned a deeper blue.

Michael and their father looked at each other but neither moved to the foredeck to stand ready by the anchor well.

'You or me?' Michael asked their father.

'Oh, you do it.'

'All right,' said Michael and went forward.

Zaki glanced at their father, who was staring down into the water. Was something wrong?

'Dragon Pool, Dad! I never thought we'd get here this year!' said Zaki, trying with his own enthusiasm to push away the flat listlessness that had crept into his father's voice.

'No,' said his father, rousing himself, 'No, neither did I.'

'Oy!!' came the shout from the foredeck. 'Where do you think you're going?'

With a start Zaki realised he hadn't been paying attention to where they were going. They were heading into the shallows.

'Keep an eye on the depth,' cautioned his father. 'The

sandbars in here move around. They won't be in the same place they were last year.'

'I know – I know.'

Zaki glanced guiltily at the depth gage and saw that the bottom was rising steeply. Trying to be too clever, he thought, dropping the boat into neutral and turning upstream, into deeper water.

The current, now flowing against the boat, acted as a brake. Built from hardwood planking, *Morveren* was heavy, making her a good sea-boat, but it also meant she took her time stopping.

'She's an old lady', Grandad would say, 'Ask her politely and she'll do anything you want. But she likes to take her time over things.'

Zaki hoped he'd judged it right. If he had, *Morveren* would come to a stop in the centre of the deepest part of the bay, then drift backwards as Michael dropped the anchor, the weight of the boat pulling on the chain and digging the anchor securely into the bottom.

Zaki whispered to the boat, 'Stop . . . stop . . . stop now.'

Morveren decided to oblige, slowing gently and stopping right over the deep blue spot that their father had indicated.

'Let her go!' their father shouted.

'I'm trying! Chain's bunched up!' shouted Michael.

'Where's your mum when we need her?' their father joked, a little bitterly.

Zaki looked across to the shore and saw that the boat was beginning to drift backwards.

'Should I go and help him?'

Just then, the rattle of the chain told them that Michael had freed the twisted links and the anchor was on its way to the bottom.

Dropping the anchor had always been their mum's job. She took pride in being able to make the anchor hold in any sort of seabed, weed, silt or sand. Zaki imagined her standing on the foredeck now, instead of Michael.

Mum, Dad, his big brother and the boat. Together. Contained. That's how it had always been; how it was meant to be. The boat was their language – ropes passed from hand to hand; four bodies moving together as the boat changed course; dancing around each other on the foredeck when they changed sails, laughter and teasing banter, then, tired at the end of the day, curling into one or other of his parents in the warmth of the cabin.

'Do you think it's holding?' called Michael.

Zaki's father put the engine into reverse. The anchor chain lifted, dripping, from the water.

'Seems fine.' Zaki's father cut the engine and an empty silence gathered around the boat into which small sounds slowly trickled: the lapping of the waves, the tap-tap of a loose rope against the mast; the distant cries of gulls in the outer bay.

'Lunch?'

''Bout time. I'm starving!' said Michael.

Father and starving brother disappeared into the cabin, leaving Zaki alone with the bay.

Had anything changed? Were there signs that others had been here? Trespassers?

Zaki scanned the shoreline. There were no footprints on the beach. There was some litter at the high-tide line – the usual plastic bottles and broken pieces of polystyrene that no beach, however remote, escapes. No, there was no evidence that their world had been invaded.

Ahead, the inlet narrowed to become a twisting creek – their Amazon, where pygmies with poison darts lurked behind the oak trees. To his left the ebbing tide was just revealing the low, rocky ledge with its tide-pools, those miniature underwater worlds from which twitching, transparent shrimps could be scooped in nets, and crabs tempted from their hiding places by the soft flesh of limpets tied to thin strings. To his right, on the beach, lay the giant trunk of the fallen tree that had given the inlet its family name – Dragon Pool. The remains of the tree's roots made a snaking tail. A knotted branch arched up to form a fierce head supported on a long neck. Two more branches provided the forelegs. They had ridden that dragon, Zaki and Michael – clung to its back while its great, beating wings carried them high over snow-capped mountains. Swooped from the skies, their war cries echoing around the bay, as the dragon's fiery breath incinerated the castles of evil wizards. At the highest tides, when only the dragon's head and tail protruded above the water, they would climb its neck and leap from its head screaming 'Ahhhhhh!' – every nerve in their bodies anticipating the shock of the icy water.

'You coming down, or do you want your sandwich out there?'

'Should we rig the legs yet?' Zaki asked.

Zaki's father climbed a little higher out of the hatchway.

'Plenty of water still and we're in the deepest bit. We'll do it after lunch.'

At low tide, Dragon Pool would empty to become a wide expanse of hillocked sand, pockmarked with the little blowholes and curling casts of lugworms that had burrowed to safety. At the lowest tides, only sun-warmed pools trapped between humps of sand and the narrow channel created by the flow of the Orme remained.

Any boat wishing to stay at low tide needed to be able to stand upright on the sand. *Morveren*, with her deep keel, would lie on her side if she weren't held up by her 'legs'. Grandad had taken this into account when he built her. Two lengths of timber with iron feet lived in a cradle on the cabin-top. When needed, they were bolted to the sides of the boat, the bottoms pivoting down to rest on the sand. Each leg was held rigid by ropes that ran from the feet up to the bow and stern of the boat. When the water drained away, *Morveren* would stand on her keel and legs looking like a small-scale Noah's Ark waiting for the animals to troop two by two across the beach.

It was Grandad who learnt the trick of entering the Orme when, as a boy, he worked on the local fishing boats that occasionally used the estuary for over-night shelter. He taught Zaki's father, who, in turn, was passing the knowledge on to Zaki and Michael. These days the fishing had moved further offshore and the boats were bigger. Fishermen no longer bothered with the little Orme.

There were stories, Grandad said, that in the old days wreckers used the Orme, luring ships on to Devil's Rock to plunder their cargoes. The river got a bad reputation. Even in his youth all honest people avoided it – all apart from that woman who lived alone in the old cottage. And Zaki remembered his grandad adding, 'Who could say if she were honest? Never spoke to nobody.'

Like a relative who had fallen from favour and was shunned by the family, the little Orme became ostracised, the world had turned its back and crept away. No road came within miles of the river-mouth; even the coastal footpath looped inland to cross the river at a little-used ford four miles upstream. The hills around the river were no longer farmed, but left to woodland, and there was no mention of its picture-postcard beauty in the tourist guides.

Zaki climbed down into the cabin to join the others.

'What were you doing?' asked Michael.

'You know . . . just looking,' said Zaki, taking a mouthful of sandwich.

'Tide's not out till six. You want to take the dinghy out?' Asked their father. 'You could sail up the river, or around the pool. Got a few hours.'

'Not really,' said Michael.

'I want to,' said Zaki.

He looked at his brother who was stretched out on the bunk opposite. Headphones on, he was sliding into his own world, into himself, into a Michael-shaped chrysalis where he could dissolve the old Michael and become someone else, someone Zaki didn't know.

'What are you going to do?' asked Zaki.

'Dunno. Read a book . . . Dunno.'

'Come on, Michael,' said their father. 'This may be the only time we'll come to Dragon Pool this season. Big tide, you might get the dinghy past the ford.'

'I wish you'd stop calling it that,' said Michael.

'Calling what, what?'

'Dragon Pool – it's not its proper name.'

'It's what we've always called it,' said their father.

'It's what Mum always calls it!' said Zaki.

'Well, she's not here, is she?!' And Michael rolled on to his other side, facing away from them.

'When you've finished your lunch, Zaki, I'll give you a hand with the dinghy,' said their father. 'And, Michael, I'll need help with the legs later.'

The chrysalis rocked slightly to show that the thing inside had heard.

The sandwich in Zaki's mouth refused to be swallowed.

It had always been Michael who had led the expeditions up the Amazon. It was Michael who had the idea to make bows and arrows in case the fierce tribes lurking in the woods launched an attack on the brave explorers. It was Michael who engineered the dams to hold back the incoming tide, urging on the frantic shovelling of sand until the crumbling walls were finally breached and their castles overrun by the sea. Hours, days, lifetimes had been spent with Michael crouched over rock pools, or floating, heads back, arms out, spreadeagled in the water, the blue sky flooding into them, as they drifted on the current from the Jumping-off-Stone to Sand Island.

But that Michael was inside his chrysalis, being transformed by the music that pulsed through little wires into his ears.

Zaki spent the afternoon alone in the dinghy, the boat's little red sails zigzagging across an estuary that looked utterly familiar but today felt utterly different.

He sailed imaginary races, beating his way through a fleet of invisible competitors to streak first across the finishing line.

The rock pools remained unvisited, the Amazon unexplored.

Every now and then he would send the dinghy scudding across the water to spin around *Morveren* but Michael only emerged on deck to help his father rig the legs and then descended out of sight without even acknowledging the victorious wave from the winner of the Dragon Pool Regatta.

That night, in the fore cabin, there was no whispered rehashing of the day's exploits and no plans were laid for the next day's adventures.

CHAPTER 2

Low tide; the boat standing as still and solid on its keel and legs as a house on its foundations. Was it the lack of movement that woke Zaki? Even in the calmest weather a boat at anchor moves slightly, swings with the fluctuations in the current, turns to find where the wind blows from. Cradled inside, the crew sleeps, secure in the knowledge that their ship, like a mother, is awake, watching over them.

Zaki lay, his sleeping bag drawn up to his chin, listening. He had been whispered to sleep by the little ripples that jostled against the hull of the boat, now all was silent.

The V-shaped fore cabin that Zaki shared with his brother contained two raised bunks with lockers underneath and a narrow shelf above for books and other personal odds and ends. As the lockers were mostly given over to spare sails, storage space was at a premium and Zaki had to fight to keep Michael's 'junk' from invading his shelf. Michael claimed that eleven-year-olds did not need as much space as fifteen-year-olds.

What time was it?

Above Zaki's head the hatch cover was propped slightly open. A little light entered through the gap. Must be nearly morning.

Zaki wriggled his shoulders and arms free and tilted his watch to catch the light. Quarter to five.

All that was visible of Michael in the other bunk was an untidy tuft of hair protruding from the mouth of his sleeping bag.

The air in the cabin was cold. Zaki felt along the narrow shelf for clothes, found a fleece and his shorts, freed his legs from the sleeping bag and dressed quickly.

What now?

Wake Michael?

Last year he would have.

Better let him sleep.

Standing on his bunk, Zaki eased the hatch cover back and put his head out. A few faded stars were visible in a pale sky. A little colour was creeping across the very tops of the hills. The estuary valley was still in darkness.

He quietly closed the hatch, got down off the bunk and opened the door to the larger, rear cabin that doubled as the saloon and their parents' sleeping quarters. In the centre of the cabin was a table flanked by two settees that served for seating and lounging during the day and sleeping at night. His father was fast asleep on one of them.

At nine metres over all, *Morveren* was not a large yacht by modern standards. Below decks she was cosy, as Zaki's grandad liked to say, or a little cramped, depending on your point of view. On the starboard side of the companionway, the steep steps that led to the main hatch, was the galley with its sink and spirit stove, opposite which, on the port side, was the chart table. No space in the saloon was wasted; there were shelves beside the chart table to hold tide atlases and coastal pilots, the logbook, books on seamanship and ocean-lore and a selection of Grandad's favourite whodunnits. Around the galley were more shelves for mugs and glasses, bowls and plates, all cleverly designed with fiddles and pegs so that nothing could fall out no matter how *Morveren* pitched or rocked. Although the woodwork had darkened with repeated varnishings down through the years, there was an elegance about the yacht's interior that bore witness to Grandad's skill as a boatbuilder and cabinetmaker.

Aft of the chart table a narrow gap gave access to Grandad's bunk, which ran back under the cockpit. When Michael and Zaki were little, Grandad had come on holidays with them, but he had now declared himself too old for long passages and only came out for the occasional day's sailing.

Zaki crept past his sleeping father and lifted the sloping top of the chart table, revealing folded charts, parallel rules, a hand-bearing compass, binoculars and a spare spark plug for the dinghy's outboard motor. He found what he was looking for, a slim, silver torch, and slipped it into the pocket of his fleece.

Quietly, he climbed up the companionway steps. The deck was wet and slippery. Peering over the side, he saw that a thin mist surrounded the boat.

He made his way to the back of the boat; climbed

17

down the boarding ladder and dropped the last few feet on to the sand, into the mist. He looked up at the boat's stern, where a painted mermaid swam under its name – 'Morveren' – maid of the sea.

How strange to be standing where the sea has so recently been; knowing that in a few hours this place would, once again, be deep underwater. Through the mist, Zaki could make out the anchor chain looping down from *Morveren*'s bow. He followed it along the ground until he came to the half-buried anchor.

He had a clear two hours before the tide began edging back across the sand. He set off for the rock ledge.

Last year, at low tide, they had found the rock pools full of pulsating jellyfish, the small ones pink and transparent, the centres of the largest purple and dangerous. They had dared each other to touch them. Perhaps he would discover some other remarkable stranded sea creatures. Then Michael would have to come and see for himself.

He stamped his bare feet into the soft, wet sand, leaving deep, dark footprints that quickly filled with water.

As he crossed the empty inlet, the sky brightened and colour crept down from the hilltops. A thin mist still clung to the estuary floor and, looking back, Zaki saw that *Morveren* appeared to float on a ghostly sea. There was no sign of life on deck.

He continued on his way. Then stopped, bewildered. Where was the sandbank you climbed to reach the rock ledge? Gone. Swept away. In its place a four-metre drop from the ledge to a bed of shingle.

He set off along the bottom of the little cliff to find a way of climbing up. He was a good climber but could see no obvious hand or footholds. The boulder up ahead might offer some possibilities. The nearside of the boulder was smooth and slippery with weed. He walked around it to inspect the other side. Behind the boulder was a dark, low hole in the cliff. A cave. Cave-mouth and boulder were so similar in size and shape that the boulder might have served as a door for the cave, if you had a handy giant to roll it into place. This side of the boulder was almost entirely free of weeds and shells but still too smooth to climb.

Zaki ran his hand over the surface of the stone and wondered why it had remained so clean. Perhaps it had been buried in the sand that used to be banked up against the cliff, and only recently exposed.

He could see that a little sand had collected in the cave entrance, making a small mound. Beyond the mound was impenetrable darkness. Zaki remembered the torch in his fleece pocket, took it out and turned it on. The entrance was little more than his own height but when he shone the torch in and up he could see that the ceiling sloped upwards. The walls of the cave were surprisingly smooth and, like the back of the boulder, free of marine life.

Zaki stepped inside. How deep was the cave? He shone his torch into the darkness. There was no back wall that he could see. Like the ceiling, the shingle floor of the cave sloped upwards. If he followed the passage, would he emerge through another hole in the rock ledge above, or did the cave penetrate deep into the hillside? He edged further in, then stopped.

What was the time? He didn't want to be caught by the returning tide.

Shining the torch on his watch he saw that it was only five thirty. He had plenty of time. Still, it was unsettling to think that in a few hours this tunnel would be full of water. The thought made him hurry forward. Best to have a quick look and get out.

What if he had misread the tide tables? No. It had been high tide when *Morveren* entered the estuary, and low tide around six in the evening. Tides get later each day. The tide should still be falling. Dead low in about an hour. Loads of time.

'Nothing to worry about,' he told that bit of himself that remained unconvinced. The primitive animal – that gut instinct that distrusts clocks and calculations.

'There's really nothing to worry about.'

The deeper he went, the more the cave sloped upwards. It certainly wasn't going to come out through the rock ledge; he must already be inside the hill. The air in the cave seemed a little drier now and the shingle floor of the first part of the passage had given way to solid rock. Zaki stretched a hand out to the side but the wall was no longer in reach. Dropping the torch beam he saw that the rock floor ahead had been cut into a flight of rough steps. Someone at some time had gone to a lot of trouble. This was more than just a cave, perhaps it was a secret passage! A smugglers' den? Wait until he showed this to Michael! This was better than rock pools!

Zaki pressed on quickly.

The first flight of steps led up to a long flat section and then more steps. He must be above the level of the rock ledge – above the high-tide line. This part of the cave would never flood.

Reaching the top step, he shone the torch ahead. A wall! The light reflected back at him off solid stone. Was this the end?

Maybe the passage led off to the left or right?

He shone the torch in both directions. Nothing but stone.

He was in a chamber, and not a particularly large chamber – six or seven metres across and almost circular. The floor, he noticed, was covered in clean, dry sand.

At first he felt disappointment. A smugglers' passage should have led to a hidden panel in an ancient inn or to a trap door in the crypt of the village church.

But, of course, there were no villages for miles.

He began to explore the walls. Perhaps there was a cleverly pivoted rock that would swing aside when pushed.

Working his way around the walls, searching for cracks, he failed to notice the rock platform that jutted out below knee level until he caught his shin, hard, on the jagged corner. The shock made him let go of his torch, which fell on to the platform, and rolled a short distance before coming to rest against something white.

Zaki reached for the torch, but snatched his hand back in horror. The white object was a bone. He stumbled back never taking his eyes off the object in the torchlight. Laid out on the stone ledge was a complete, human skeleton. His heart slamming against his ribs, Zaki struggled for breath. What else lurked in the darkness that now seemed to press in around him?

CHAPTER 3

The torch, lying on the stone ledge, caught the side of the skull in its beam, accentuating the dark hollows of the eye sockets. As he watched, something moved in one of the sockets and Zaki opened his mouth as the scream leapt into the back of his throat. A black, glistening beetle dropped from the socket and scuttled into the darkness.

Zaki tore his gaze away from the skull's unblinking stare and forced himself to take in the rest of the skeleton. It wasn't very big. This was a child!

Clammy, chilling fear flooded through him. Someone had killed a child. His age, maybe younger . . . or the child had died here. Abduction. Murder. He was always hearing those words in the local news. On the radio, on television.

Get out! He had to get out! He made a lurching dash for the place where the passage should begin, but in the moment of panic all sense of direction had been erased and he yelled with sudden pain as he collided with unyielding rock.

He sat up in the sand, his back against the cave wall,

nursing his left shoulder, which had taken the full force of his fall. 'It's just a skeleton,' he told himself. 'Bones can't hurt. Probably been there for centuries.' This could be an ancient burial chamber. He'd read about those. The body carried here from somewhere else. Perhaps the child of an important family. This explanation made Zaki feel better. The thought that whatever had happened here had happened a long time ago made the darkness seem less threatening. Slowly, he got to his feet and crossed the chamber to stand by the stone platform. The pain in his left shoulder was intense, but he found he could reduce it by putting his hand in his fleece pocket so that his fleece, and not his shoulder, took the weight of his arm.

Gingerly, he leant forward and picked up the torch, taking care not to touch the bones, and then he forced himself to examine the skeleton. The ribs and pelvic bones poked out through the threadbare remains of a simple dress.

The dress suggested a girl, but didn't boys wear tunics in the really old days? The fabric looked fairly modern so he supposed it couldn't be all that old. Who was she? If it was a she. But . . . was there an arm missing? Zaki took a step back and swung the torch beam on to the floor. There were the missing bones; three large bones and the little bones of the fingers and wrist scattered and pressed into the sand where he had, unknowingly, stepped on them. 'Sorry,' he muttered – but what was he saying? She was dead! Still, it seemed wrong to have trodden on the bones – sacrilegious, a desecration, and now he was somehow involved, he had changed something, disturbed her rest.

The body must have lain with one arm hanging over the edge of the platform. Not a formal burial, then. Whoever it was most likely died here.

Among the little bones in the sand, Zaki noticed there was something else; a narrow metal band, a bracelet perhaps. He knelt down next to it. It felt wrong to disturb her remains but it might give a clue to who she was. He glanced up at the skeleton, seeking permission. The skull, lying on its side, stared out across the chamber as, perhaps, the dying child had stared, hoping for rescue, or waiting for death.

'It's just so I know who you are,' Zaki said. Pain stabbed through his left shoulder as he eased his hand out of his pocket to hold the torch, then he picked the little metal band out of the sand and twisted it around in the torchlight. The metal was green with corrosion. The inner surface was flat and the outer surface slightly curved with a pattern of inscriptions running all the way round it. Some sort of writing, maybe. He tried it on and found it just fitted over his own hand and hung, loosely, on his wrist.

'I'm not stealing it, but I think I should show it to somebody. I'll bring it back.'

Zaki closed his eyes as a throbbing ache spread down his arm from his injured shoulder. Had he broken something when he hit the cave wall? His stomach tightened and he thought for a moment that he would be sick. He sank slowly on to the sand. Was the light from the torch getting dimmer? Perhaps he should turn it off and save the batteries.

He felt giddy, almost as if something was taking him over.

Now the darkness seemed comforting.

He switched off the torch and let the darkness enfold him. It was soft and dense.

He lay back on the sand and breathed the darkness in and out. It brushed his face. It poured into his ears. It made no difference whether his eyes were open or shut. He was safe. Cradled. He heard his own voice say 'Mum, I've hurt my shoulder,' and he thought a hand stroked his hair.

Someone, something would take care of him.

There was light now.

Somebody coming?

Bright light – but where? His eyes were shut. Was it inside his head? Getting brighter.

And voices talking, talking, talking, talking! A man's voice then a child's, then a man's, talking, talking, shouting, screaming! Voices shouting! Voices screaming! Talking, shouting, screaming – all at once – all together.

'Who's there?' Zaki called.

Smoke – he could smell smoke. The air grew thick with it, making him cough. Perhaps the light came from a fire. No – not a fire – inside him. The light was inside him.

And faces – lots of faces – crowding – drums beating – eyes full of fear. Who are you? Now just one face – a monstrous face – eyes of fire – teeth stained with blood!

Who are you? Why are you staring? What have I done?

I didn't hurt you.

I didn't hurt you!

I'm the one that's hurt.

Can't you see? I'm the one that's hurt!

Help me!

Help me!!

Gone.

Hiding – can't see them any more – but I know they're there.

Climbed into my head – they all climbed into my head – it's all inside me – everything.

Zaki lay on the sand. The light that had been so bright shrank and shrank and shrank until it was a tiny, glinting speck in the vast, empty darkness. He clung to the vanishing gleam. Focused on it. If he lost it, there would be nothing.

The speck flickered and was gone.

All was black. All was still.

Zaki waited. What now?

In the stillness Zaki became conscious of a familiar sound. Water. Lapping water. The sound of water nearby.

Water! The tide! Water in the mouth of the cave!

How long had he been in here? Can't have been that long? The tide hadn't even turned when he came in. Should have been hours before the water reached the cave.

Zaki rolled on to his right side, then slowly on to his knees. In the disorientating darkness he had the strange sensation that he was now upside down. His head swam and he had to lower it on to the ground between his knees.

When he felt a little steadier, he groped around in the sand for his torch. There it was; a familiar, reassuring shape. His thumb found the switch and clicked it on. The narrow beam sprang out across the cave's sandy floor. To his immense relief the battery wasn't flat. Zaki swept the light around the chamber, over the rock platform and the white bones, across the walls, until he found the entrance to the passage. No sign of water, but he could clearly hear little waves washing against stones, the sound amplified and sharpened by the rocky tunnel. He crouched, listening, like a tiny fly caught in a giant's ear.

Go! Move! Get out! The same fear that told his mind he must act kept his crouching body frozen in panic. An age seemed to pass before the messages from his desperate brain reached his cramped muscles. Slowly he straightened. Pain from his shoulder shot down his arm. His heavy legs clumsily obeyed the command to walk and he stumbled into the passage and down the rough-hewn steps.

At the second set of steps he stopped. The torchlight flashed back at him off the surface of a dark sheet of moving water. Trapped! The sea had entered the tunnel and flooded the first section. How had this happened?

Only then did Zaki think to look at his watch. Ten fifteen! He'd been in the cave for over four hours. How? How? He must have been unconscious – fallen asleep – but, four hours?

How far would the water rise? He was pretty certain that it never reached the main chamber. At worst he could wait until the tide went down again: six, maybe seven hours; a long time, but there was plenty of air. Then he thought of his father. His father would be mad with worry. Would have no idea where he was. What would he be doing now? What would he say when he found out what he had done? And Michael? What would Michael think? They'd be searching for him for sure.

Should he shout? Try to let them know that he was OK?

'Dad!'

'Dad!' I'm in here!'

'I'm in here!'

'I'm in a cave!'

His voice rang back off the cave walls. They'd never hear him through the water and rocks.

Would his father have called the coastguard on the radio? No. He couldn't. No VHF reception in the estuary.

How could he have been so stupid?!

Now shame pushed fear aside.

He needed to think. Calm down. Get a grip.

Zaki turned off the torch to save the batteries, put it in his pocket and sat on the top step, his right hand cupped over his aching left shoulder. With the torch off, he could see that the water was not dark but glowed a greeny-blue. Sunlight outside was reflecting off the sandy bottom and filtering through the water into the cave. For a moment he was mesmerised by the

29

flickering turquoise light that played across the cave walls.

'It's not that deep,' he told himself. 'I could dive down and swim out.'

But how much of the tunnel was flooded? How far were these first steps from the entrance? He couldn't remember. It was as though days, rather than hours, had passed since he stepped into the cave.

'The longer I sit here, the deeper the water will get.'

Zaki forced himself to his feet and started down the steps into the water. It was cold and, as it crept up his bare legs, he began to shiver, but he kept going. Soon the water was up to his chest. A few more steps and he would be swimming. He pushed off from the bottom and floated out into the luminous water. He swam with a lopsided breaststroke, unable to do more than paddle with his left arm. The further he went the smaller the distance between the water and the cave ceiling became until, treading water, there was just room to keep his nose and mouth above the surface in the narrow air-gap. Rising panic and the chill of the water constricted his chest, reducing every intake of breath to a short gasp. His fleece was heavy and waterlogged, dragging him down – he should have taken it off. Go back? He saw again his father's anxious face. Dive. He had to dive. Three breaths, then go. Stay down as long as possible. Just hope it's not too far.

Zaki fought to fill his lungs with air. It was as though his body, knowing the risk was too great, was refusing to cooperate. With the third breath, he plunged down, kicked up with his legs and struck out along the flooded tunnel. He was swimming towards the sunlight. Keep going – he just had to keep going. Now his lungs, that had refused air when it was available, were desperate for breath. The drag of his clothing, like a malicious hand, held him back, trying to drown him. The weakness in his left arm made it hard to keep from floating up against the cave roof and soon the coordinated strokes, arms and legs together, with which he began gave way to shorter, desperate kicking. He couldn't do it. He could see the sunlight but he couldn't get to it. His head struck the roof, his fleece snagged on the rough surface of the rock. This was it. A sob bubbled out of him and choking salt filled his nose and mouth.

He knew he was drowning – then hands took hold of his clothing and tugged him clear of the snagging ceiling. As he rolled over in the water, a flash of white arm passed his face and he was gripped firmly beneath the shoulders. The arm that held him was thin but strong and pulled him against the owner's body. Swiftly, he was propelled through the water – out and up – and suddenly he was gasping and coughing in the clean, fresh air and the dazzle of sunlight.

I'm alive! I'm alive! It was all he could think between retching coughs.

'The rock – get hold of the rock,' a girl's voice commanded.

Blinded by the sunlight, Zaki groped with his hands as his rescuer pushed him on to the top of the now submerged boulder by the cave-mouth.

Zaki clung to the boulder. He squeezed shut his eyes to try to clear his vision; when he opened them, the girl's face was inches from his own. Her hair was cropped short, the roughly cut curls sticking up in spikes around her head. Her mouth was set in a firm, no-nonsense line and the look in her grey, widely spaced eyes was not sympathetic.

'What did you find? Did you touch anything?'

Then her eyes fell on the bracelet on Zaki's wrist.

'Give me the bracelet. It's not yours.'

When Zaki failed to move, she seized his arm and twisted the bracelet over his hand then thrust it on to her own arm.

'Don't tell anyone what you have seen. Do you understand?

Zaki stared at her in bewilderment.

'Do you understand? You mustn't tell.'

Zaki managed to nod.

'No one. You understand?'

'All right, I understand.'

'No. That's not good enough. You have to promise. Promise. Promise me you won't tell.'

'Yes, I promise. I promise.'

'Good. But don't forget you have promised.'

She looked towards *Morveren* and then sank down into the water.

'Hold on to the rock. They'll come for you now,' she ordered.

Before he could say anything else, she was gone.

Too exhausted to wonder who had saved him, or how

32

she had known he was in the cave, Zaki lay on the rock, too exhausted to move, half in the water, half out. Gradually he became aware of voices shouting his name, shouting instructions, telling him to 'Stay where you are!' – not to move – his father's voice – and Michael's. An outboard engine revved and whined then his father and brother in the inflatable were beside him.

'Are you hurt?' his father asked, the anxiety tight in his voice. Getting no reply he turned to Michael.

'We'll have to get him into the dinghy, then we can take a look at him. But be careful, we don't know what's happened to him.'

His father climbed out on to the rock as Michael held the inflatable steady.

'Can you sit up?'

'Think so,' Zaki mumbled.

'Anything hurting?'

'Shoulder.'

Gently, his father and brother helped him to slide over the rubber side of the inflatable and down on to the floor. His father followed him. Then, kneeling beside him, he tried to ease open his sodden fleece to examine his shoulder.

'How did you get on to that rock? Did you fall? What were you doing?'

Zaki shook his head. It was all too confusing.

His father's fingers became clumsy with the effort of being gentle and, dropping his hands into his lap, he looked searchingly into Zaki's face.

'Zaki?'

Zaki closed his eyes.

'Zaki! Where the HELL have you been?!'

His father's sudden anger together with the relief of being alive and the exhaustion overwhelmed Zaki. His body shook and tears began to stream down his face. No words could possibly get out.

'Dad,' Michael leant forward from his place by the outboard. 'Dad, let's get him back to *Morveren*.'

'Yeah,' nodded his father. 'OK.'

CHAPTER 4

Zaki now lay in Grandad's bunk padded around with cushions. Its narrowness and his present immobility brought to his mind the image of a body in a coffin and underlined the narrowness of his recent escape.

Having got him back aboard, Zaki's father had helped him into dry clothing and examined his shoulder. It was already turning interesting shades of red, blue and yellow with swelling over the collarbone which made his father think that, if it wasn't broken, it was most likely cracked.

Of course there were more questions about where he'd been. 'Why were you gone so long?' his father wanted to know. 'How did you hurt your shoulder?'

At first, Zaki's own genuine confusion prevented him from saying much, but his father persisted. 'We've been searching for you for hours. I've had Michael up and down the river a dozen times in the dinghy, then you turn up on that rock! Didn't you realise we'd be worried?'

Zaki desperately wanted to talk about what had happened; to share his adventure; to ask his father for advice. But his promise to the girl made him hold back.

Hadn't she saved his life – dragged him out of the cave just as he was about to drown? Didn't he owe her something? Maybe she was in some sort of trouble, some sort of danger, and he could make it worse for her by betraying her. Did she need help? Then, the ghastly thought hit him – had she killed the child in the cave?

After a moment of horrified contemplation, Zaki pushed this possibility from his mind – no she couldn't have! Could she? The body had been there too long. And if she had, why would she save him, knowing he had discovered her secret? No – it must be more complicated than that. But where did she go? Where was she now?

Zaki decided that, for the moment at least, he would not say anything about the cave. It was obvious from his father's questions that he knew nothing of its existence; that the tide had already hidden the cave entrance by the time the search for him began. Instead, he invented a plausible explanation for his long absence. He said that he had set off at low tide up the river, along the bed of the estuary, that he hadn't noticed the time and been cut off by the incoming tide. He had then been forced to return through the woods; scrambled down on to the rock ledge, where he had slipped when trying to hail them and fallen onto the boulder, injuring his shoulder and bruising his shin.

He pictured this fabricated journey as he spoke and became half convinced that this really was what had happened. The real events were so much more bizarre; like a nightmare – a secret passage, a skeleton, the strange images that filled his head in the dark cave, three or more hours that were lost and couldn't be account for, near-drowning and the mysterious girl who had rescued him and then vanished. If he did tell anyone the real story, would they believe him? He doubted it very much. He wished he still had the bracelet – a solid object to prove that it had all happened, something to hang on to. But the bracelet was gone with the girl and he didn't suppose he'd see either of them again.

The story he told appeared to satisfy his father, who decided that Zaki's shoulder needed to be seen by a doctor as soon as possible and this meant getting out of the Orme straight away, while there was still enough tide to cross the bar and clear the outer reef. So Zaki was tucked into Grandad's bunk, where he would be in no danger of rolling out when *Morveren* was under way.

It was a relief to be left alone. He listened to his father and Michael up on deck making preparations for departure: the inflatable being packed away; the sailing dinghy being hoisted aboard; their footsteps crossing and recrossing above him. Then the diesel starting, thudding loudly in the engine compartment next to his bunk, and the rattle of the anchor chain.

The plan had been to spend two nights in the estuary before heading home to *Morveren*'s mooring off East Portlemouth. Normally, Zaki would have wheedled and begged, 'Couldn't we stay another night?' – 'Do we have to go home so soon?' Today, he was glad to be going. It was as though a close friend had turned against him. He had looked forward to this trip all holiday and it had gone so terribly wrong. Of course, if Michael had done stuff with him . . . If Michael . . . But Michael was no fun any more. And Mum . . . Something twisted very tight in his stomach. He didn't want to think about any of it. He would do what he always did at home when he wanted to take his mind off things; he would close his eyes and count the number of objects he could remember in *Morveren's* cabin. He knew this cabin so intimately that he had often been able to recall and place over two hundred items including brass hinges and visible screw heads. So that he couldn't accuse himself of cheating, he wouldn't count anything that could be seen from Grandad's bunk.

Zaki was mentally enumerating the contents of the chart table when *Morveren* passed through the outer reef and reached open water. He felt the change in the boat's motion as she met a gentle swell. There were footsteps on deck followed shortly by the chatter of the rope winch and the crack and flap of the mainsail as it was run up the mast. The rigging creaked as sheets were tightened and also when *Morveren* leant over as her sails caught the wind. The engine fell silent and Zaki could hear the wash and slap of water against the hull. *Morveren* settled into a steady, easy motion, like a long-distance runner settling into her stride. Zaki had just remembered to count the spare sparkplug in the chart table when he drifted off to sleep.

Emptiness. An immense, blue void, bright and clear as the sky on a crisp, cloudless winter's day. Nothing, until the appearance of a tiny speck, like a full stop in infinity.

The speck gets larger and larger – soon it is the size of a house, a mountain, a planet hurtling towards him. It is black, so black that it drinks up all the light – soon he will be crushed. Then it blinks open – an eye. He plunges through it. He is underwater – a flick of his tail and he can shoot forward – he is at home here, in his element. Movement behind him seizes his attention – instinctively he thrashes with his whole body. He is the prey, the other is the hunter, razor-sharp teeth open to swallow him; he swims up, up, striving for the surface that floats above him, striving for safety, flinging himself from water into air as teeth snap shut. Suddenly he is free, airborne, looking down. Each beat of his outstretched wings lifts him higher – a tilt of the tail and he slips sideways, riding the wind. High above him the hawk hangs on air, haloed by the sun, then drops, talons reaching, beak outstretched, sharp as an arrow. The chase is on again and when the hawk strikes he tumbles, falling through treetops, past whipping branches into the shelter of the undergrowth. He cowers among the gorse – he is a hare – his long ears twitch and turn to catch each sound. His nose picks up the scent of fox. He is up and running, weaving, dodging, doubling back, leaping over heather. The fox is on his heels, matching turn for turn, twist for twist, leap for leap, flying behind him like a flag connected by an invisible thread. Nowhere to hide – this is certain death! Teeth knife into his shoulder – he snatches breath to scream!

'Zaki . . . Zaki!'

Zaki opened his eyes.

39

'Bad dream?'

Zaki struggled out of the nightmare to find he was drenched in sweat. He looked up at his father, who had come halfway down the companionway, into the cabin.

'Try to sit up and drink some water.'

Stepping down into the cabin, his father helped him to sit up in the bunk and handed him a plastic bottle of drinking water.

Zaki could tell from the boat's motion that they were still at sea.

'Where are we?' he asked, after taking a swig from the bottle.

'We're off Bolt Head. Not far to go now,' replied his father. 'We've had a nice reach up the coast. You missed a good sail.'

'Can I come up on deck?' asked Zaki.

'How's the shoulder?'

'It hurts, but I need some air.' Zaki grimaced as he slid out of the bunk.

'We'd better put that arm in a sling,' said his father, 'keep the weight off the shoulder.'

Zaki's father improvised a sling out of an old scarf, a scarf that Zaki's mother had left on board. The perfume from the sunscreen she used on holidays had penetrated its fibres and was released as his father arranged the soft, silky fabric around Zaki's neck. He closed his eyes and, in that moment, it was his mother, not his father, who adjusted the sling, her familiar scent comforting and upsetting him all at the same time.

'We won't get a lifejacket over that, so don't go falling

overboard,' said his father. 'You go up, I'm going to start stowing everything we don't want to take ashore.'

Zaki climbed up the steps and out into the cockpit. Michael, on the helm, gave him a cheery smile as he emerged.

'Urgh! You look awful! You've gone all green.'

'Thanks,' said Zaki.

'You're not going to be sick, are you? Because if you are, do it downwind.'

His brother's banter, together with the refreshing breeze, began to dispel the nausea he had felt in the confines of the cabin. He settled himself next to Michael, hanging on to the cockpit edge with his good hand. It was perfect sailing weather: a steady wind blowing out of a clear, blue sky; a gentle swell with white horses brightening the tops of the waves. '*Morveren*'s going like a train,' said Zaki, borrowing one of his grandad's favourite expressions.

Michael grinned. With the wind sweeping the mop of dark hair off his freckled face, he looked like the old Michael, Zaki's best friend, the one he could talk to about anything.

'I had the weirdest dream.'

'Yeah? What was that?' asked Michael.

'I kept being chased by things. First I was a fish, with an otter after me, then I was a bird, then a rabbit, or something, and other things kept wanting to eat me.'

'Who'd want to eat you, you smelly little toerag?'

'Well, it was really weird. And there was this great big eye.'

41

'You've been watching too many scary movies,' said Michael. 'Can you make yourself useful and have a look under the sail? Tell me if there are any boats downwind that I can't see.'

Zaki scrambled down, taking a little more care than usual, his left side stiff and sore. There were a few open boats fishing for mackerel a fair distance off and a crab pot buoy just downwind.

'Don't change course until you pass the crab pot,' called Zaki.

'What crab pot?' shouted Michael.

'That one!' Zaki called back, as the buoy bobbed past, only a few metres clear.

'Thanks for the warning,' said Michael. 'Anything else you're not gong to tell me about until it's too late?'

'No. All clear,' said Zaki.

'As you're going to be next to useless pulling ropes, you'd better steer,' said Michael, as Zaki clambered, one-armed, back up to the windward side. They swapped places, Zaki taking over the helm.

Rounding Bolt Head always seemed to be the slowest part of any journey *Morveren* made west of Salcombe. No matter how well they planned the passage, the tide was always against them.

Unlike the other great headlands of the West Country coast – Start Point, Prawl Point and the Lizard, which stab their jagged blades out into the Channel – Bolt Head appears to have been chopped off square and blunt by a mighty guillotine, leaving a precipice that runs for several miles like a massive granite curtain, torn in the middle by Soar Mill Cove, with its narrow beach in a deep cleft.

'If you come up on to the wind now, we should make the entrance,' called Michael.

Zaki brought *Morveren* round to point at the tip of the headland as Michael hauled on the main sheet and then winched in the jib.

Since the tide was approaching dead low, Zaki chose to play it safe and lined *Morveren* up with the red and white way marks that guide boats over the Salcombe bar and, as they passed the starboard Wolf Rock buoy, their father joined the boys on deck to get the sails down and furled away.

As is usual for a sunny day in the summer holidays, Salcombe Harbour was busy with day boats and dinghies, launches and tenders, and Zaki was kept on his toes keeping clear of the small craft races and giving way to ferries and fishing boats. The harbour master came by in his launch but, recognising *Morveren* as a local boat, he gave them a wave and motored off to assist a large family adrift in a small flat-bottomed boat with outboard motor problems.

No sooner were they moored than Grandad's old blue launch nosed alongside. Jenna, Grandad's black and white collie, gave two welcoming barks then scrambled from one end of the launch and back, wagging her tail, eager to greet everyone. Grandad tossed a mooring line to Michael. Zaki loved to watch the effortless way the old man moved around on a boat, never hurried, never losing his balance; ropes always falling exactly where he intended, judging boat speed and distance with unerring precision.

'What you done to your arm, boy?'

'Fell,' said Zaki, a little shamefaced.

'Wasn't expecting you back for a day or two.'

'Think we should get the doctor to take a look at him,' said Zaki's father.

'Doctor, eh? Don't sound too clever.'

'Anyway, they're back to school next week. Won't do them any harm to look at a book or two before they start back.'

'Oh, Dad! Did you have to mention school?' groaned Michael.

'Here, if you're ready, you can start handin' down your bits and pieces,' said Grandad.

'How did you know to meet us?' asked Zaki.

'Telepathy,' said Grandad, with a wink.

'Dad called him on the mobile,' said Michael.

'What we call mobile telepathy,' said Grandad.

Zaki winced as he attempted to lift a holdall over the yacht's rail.

'Come on, young'un, get in the boat. You look about ready to hand in your knife and fork.'

Grandad steadied Zaki as he climbed over the side and down into the launch. The constant ache from his shoulder had worn him out and his head felt a little dizzy. Jenna came to sit beside him. She beat her tail against the wooden seat and licked his face. Zaki pushed her nose away and rested his head against the dog's warm fur. It was a relief to do nothing while the others handed the bags and gear down to Grandad, who stowed everything in an orderly pile on the floor of the launch.

Zaki gazed vacantly at the other local boats on the surrounding moorings. He knew most of the boats; these were town moorings, which seldom changed hands, often staying in families from one generation to the next. The remains of a white, plastic rubbish bag, trapped by the wind against the stern rail of a neighbouring yacht, caught his eye. The tattered edges of the bag flapped in the wind. As he watched, a small, dark hole appeared in the centre of the flailing plastic; more an absence than a presence of anything, a still, black point about which the white plastic fluttered. Something was happening around the hole, the stillness was spreading outwards, reordering the whiteness of the plastic, giving new definition to the edges of the hole. Then the hole blinked and became an eye; an eye that was regarding him with sharp attention. The shock of the transformation made Zaki catch his breath and he felt the dog beside him stiffen. Zaki glanced round to see if anyone else was watching this metamorphosis, but when he looked back, the plastic bag had gone and, instead, a large, white gull balanced on the stern rail, its eye still fixed on him. Jenna erupted in an outburst of furious barking. The gull opened its wings and, with a few powerful beats, climbed into the evening sky.

'Quiet!' growled Grandad.

The barking stopped but occasional tremors continued to run through the dog's body.

'What set her off?' asked Grandad.

'Didn't you see?' began Zaki. 'There was a bag and then it turned into . . .' He trailed off, realising the ridiculous impossibility of what he was about to say.

'You're lookin' terribly queasy,' said Grandad, his face serious, 'we best be getting you home.'

A single chandlery and half a dozen small, ramshackle, wooden sheds, their slipways reaching down to the water's edge, were all that remained of Salcombe's once busy marine industry, most of the buildings on the waterfront having long since been converted to boutiques or pulled down to make way for holiday apartments. The faded sign on Grandad's shed said simply 'Isaac Luxton – Boatbuilder', although most of the work now was in maintenance and restoration.

There was just enough water left in the channel for Grandad to bring the launch to the foot of the slipway, where the holiday gear was unloaded, carried through the shed and piled into the back of Grandad's battered Volvo estate for the drive to Kingsbridge.

Once settled in the back seat of the car with Michael and the dog, Zaki propped his head against a sail bag and slept all the way home.

CHAPTER 5

'Not much we can do for a cracked collarbone, I'm afraid,' said the young duty doctor as she showed Zaki the X-ray with its ghostly image of his chest, shoulder and upper arm.

'There – you can see the crack. It's pretty insignificant.'

Zaki could see a very fine, dark line, like a hair, running in from the edge of the bone.

'Nothing's out of place, so it should heal up OK.' She turned to Zaki's father. 'But no sport for a few weeks. He needs to be careful he doesn't bash it again.' And to Zaki, 'We can't put your shoulder in plaster, so it's up to you to look after it.'

Zaki nodded. He was still studying the X-ray. He could see the left half of his chest with its curving ribs, the shoulder joint and the big bone at the top of his arm. He thought of the child's bones in the sand, on the floor of the cave. Once the flesh had rotted, there had been nothing to hold the bones together, to keep the arm attached to the body. How long had that taken?

'What's that bone called?' he asked, pointing to the arm.

'That's your humerus. Although it wouldn't be funny if you broke it.'

She was nice, this doctor. She looked tired, but she explained everything carefully and didn't rush them.

'How long do bones last?'

If he could think of the right question, he might be able to work out how long the child's skeleton had been in the cave.

'Come on, Zaki,' said his father, 'I'm sure the doctor's got plenty of other people to see.'

'Last?' asked the doctor. 'You mean inside you?'

'I mean, once you're dead.'

'I'm not a pathologist, but I guess that would depend on what age you were when you died.' The doctor filled in a card and clipped it to the X-ray image. She looked up. 'As you get older, the mineral content of your bones decreases, so they become more fragile. I would think a young person's bones would last longer than an older person's. But it would also depend where the bones were. Why? Do you have a skeleton in the cupboard?' She smiled her tired smile.

'If they were in a cave, for instance?'

The doctor glanced at Zaki's father, who shrugged and said, 'I'm sorry; I haven't a clue what he's on about.'

'Can't answer that one,' said the doctor. 'Probably a very long time. Now, remember what I said about sport.'

Zaki was having difficulty getting his shirt back on. Anything that required him to lift his arm was painful. His father came across to help him.

'We'll need to take another look at it in a few weeks –

48

make sure it's mending properly. Ask reception to make you an appointment for three weeks' time.' The doctor ushered them out into the corridor, where they hesitated, trying to remember whether they had come from the left or the right.

'Left for reception,' said the doctor.

'Thanks,' said Zaki's father. 'Thanks very much.'

'Good luck with the skeleton,' said the doctor.

Zaki looked at her in surprise, then realised she was referring to her own joke and, of course, knew nothing about the child in the cave. He turned and followed his father down the brightly lit hospital corridor with its lino floor that squeaked against the soles of his shoes.

Zaki was keen to talk to his grandad. He wanted to find out if there were any stories about a cave or secret passage leading off from the Orme estuary. Maybe his grandad had even seen the cave during his time on the fishing boats. His dad had said the sandbanks kept moving. Could it be that the cave entrance was only covered up quite recently?

The opportunity to talk to his grandfather came that very afternoon. His father, who was anxious to get back to work on Number 43 Sandy Lane, figured that, as the hospital visit had meant Zaki missing most of the first day of the new school term, he might as well miss the rest of it and spend the afternoon with his grandad at the boat shed.

Number 43 was the house his father was renovating. It was how he had made his living since giving up his city job and bringing the family back to Devon; buying houses that were neglected, sad and damp, fixing them up, calling them something like 'Fisherman's Cottage' and selling them to outsiders. They were holiday houses – second homes, mostly – 'grockle cottages,' the locals sneeringly called them. In the past, they had lived in each house while it was being rebuilt and then, just as it stopped being a building site and began to resemble a proper home, they had sold it and moved into another ruin. Fortunately, they couldn't live in Number 43 – it had no roof – so they were allowed to stay on in Moor Lane and call it home for the present, or at least until Number 43 was habitable.

There was no sign of Grandad in the boat shed. There were the usual smells of freshly planed wood and varnish, smells that so permeated Grandad's clothing that they travelled with him wherever he went and would hang in the air of a room for some time after he left it. The back door of the shed was ajar and competing estuary smells of weed and mud entered on the little gusts that swung the door on its rusty hinges.

In the centre of the shed stood the bare spine of the open, wooden rowing boat that Grandad had just begun building. Another skeleton, thought Zaki, running his hand over the silky-smooth timber.

He made his way through the clutter of the shed and out on to the slipway behind to see if the launch was there. If it wasn't, Grandad would be somewhere out on the water. It was and Grandad was kneeling on the boat's floor, his back a round hump, as he peered into the engine compartment. Jenna sat, patiently panting, watching her master. Hearing Zaki approach, she barked once and began to wag her tail.

'Engine not working?' asked Zaki.

'Will be, soon as I get all these bits back in their proper manner,' said Grandad, without looking up from what he was doing.

Zaki knew better than to distract his grandfather during the tricky business of reassembling the engine. Instead, he made himself comfortable on a bollard and watched two men on the jetty opposite loading crab pots on to a brightly painted fishing boat. He felt something rub against his leg and, glancing down, saw a pale grey cat.

'Hello, puss,' he said, scratching the cat behind an ear. 'Who do you belong to? I haven't seen you before.'

The cat sat by Zaki's foot and regarded him with an unblinking stare and then, as though satisfied that it now knew all there was to know about him, stretched and sauntered across to the other side of the slipway to watch the grey mullet feeding on the weed-covered mooring lines.

Eventually, Grandad heaved himself up off the floor of the launch and started the engine. He let it run for a couple of minutes and then shut it off.

'What was the problem?' asked Zaki.

'Sucked up a bit o' weed.' Grandad put the spanners back into his toolbox and wiped the grease off his hands with a piece of rag. 'What did the doctor say?'

'Said it was cracked. They took an X-ray.'

'Teach you to be more careful, you great gawk,' said Grandad.

Zaki followed his grandfather back into the shed. The grey cat followed Zaki, and Jenna, as though wary of the cat, followed her, tail down, a few metres behind.

'Whose cat's that?' asked Zaki.

'She's been hanging around the last few days. Never seen her before. If you're makin' us a cuppa, you can give her a dollop of milk.'

Zaki took the hint, put the kettle on and poured some milk into a cleanish plastic bowl for the cat, then, seeing the dog looking jealous, made a fuss of her until, satisfied that she was still loved, she went to lie down in her box under the workbench.

When the tea was made, Zaki and Grandad settled themselves on the dusty camp chairs that lived in one corner of the shed.

'See your father's allowin' you to neglect your edification again,' said Grandad. 'What's your mother going to say?'

Zaki studied the steam rising from his tea. He wished his grandfather hadn't raised the subject of his mother.

'Does she know about your arm?'

'Don't think so,' said Zaki. 'She didn't phone at the weekend.'

'Couldn't you phone her?'

'Dad says she's really busy and we shouldn't worry her.'

Grandad frowned. 'So, when's she comin' home?'

'Don't know. She says soon, but she says it's difficult

to know when.'

He felt that what his mother was doing wasn't fair. She shouldn't have stayed away so long. 'This job in Switzerland is just temporary,' she'd said. Temporary. That was only a short time, wasn't it? That's what he'd thought. That's how they'd made it sound. Now, whenever he tried to talk to his father he'd say something like 'We did all discuss it before your mum took the job', as though they'd offered him a choice – like 'Do you want your mum to go away or not?' Well, nobody had ever asked him that.

'Expect you miss her, don't you?' said Grandad.

'There aren't any jobs like that here in Devon,' said Zaki, feeling compelled by family loyalty to defend his parents. 'Dad says it's an opportunity. They had to borrow a lot to buy number forty-three and this'll put us back on our feet.'

'Been quite a long time, though,' said Grandad.

It had been a long time. It had been much too long for Zaki.

The cat jumped up on to Zaki's lap, almost spilling his tea.

'That cat's taken to you,' said Grandad.

Zaki seized the chance to change the subject.

'You know the Orme . . .' he began.

'I ought to, number of times I've been in there.'

'Did you ever hear about a cave or a smugglers' passage, or anything like that?'

'Why do you ask?

'I just thought, since smugglers used the river, you

know – there might be one.'

'There was somethin'.' Grandad took a pencil from his shirt pocket and stirred his tea thoughtfully. He took another sip from his mug. 'Did you sugar this?'

Zaki nodded.

'Could've been sweeter.'

'About the Orme,' Zaki prompted.

'There was a lot of smugglin' went on . . .'

'And?'

'Excise turned a blind eye to most of it. I'm talkin' maybe a hundred and fifty, two hundred year ago. Course it still goes on today.'

'And the cave?'

'I'm comin' to that. Would you like a biscuit?'

'Thanks.'

Grandad fetched the biscuits, blew the dust off the packet and offered them to Zaki, who took two.

'There was a man named Maunder, so the story goes – time of my great-great-grandfather. This Maunder wasn't from round this way, but 'e was the ringleader. Led the others on, so to speak, from smugglin' to wreckin'. There was always wrecks on this coast, plenty of 'em. Did you ever consider why they called that great stone off the Orme Devil's Rock? Some say it's because in a certain light you can see the devil's face in it. But I never seen a face. More likely it's on account of the number of souls it's taken to hell. It's an easy thing, if you're runnin' from a storm on a black night, to mistake one harbour entrance for another and plenty of skippers mistook the Devil for the Mew Stone and turned into the

54

Orme thinkin' they was off the mouth of the Yealm, especially when some fiend lit a beacon to mislead 'em.

'What came ashore from a wreck was considered property of they that found it. They was meant to pay duty on salvage but nobody took too much notice of that, it was the landowners, not excise, caused the problems for the wreckers. The landowners laid claim to anything that washed up on their foreshore and the land around the Orme was owned, at that time, by a family called Stapleton, and Robert Stapleton took exception to Maunder and his gang clearin' out the wrecks on his property.'

Grandad dipped his biscuit in his tea and Zaki stroked the cat while he waited for him to continue.

'Grandad?'

'Hold your horses, boy – I'm tryin' to call to mind what happened next.'

Grandad nodded slowly as though agreeing with an invisible storyteller.

'It seems Stapleton and Maunder fought for a bit, but then they joins forces and it's hard to say which of 'em was more evil. Seafarers have a natural loyalty to other seafarers, but Maunder's lot took to killin' any poor soul, seaman or passenger, who survived a wreck and the bodies was buried in Stapleton's fields. That's why nobody will farm the land by the Orme. They're afraid of turning up bodies when they're ploughin'.'

'What about the cave?'

'Well, villains'll always fall out, won't they? And Maunder and Stapleton were no exception. They say

Maunder dug a secret hidey-hole somewhere there-abouts so he'd get most of the plunder hidden before Stapleton could arrive at the wreck.'

'Does anyone know where it is?'

'Not as far I know. Maunder disappeared – killed by Stapleton most likely. Then Stapleton handed the rest o' the gang over to the authorities. The men were hanged and the women an' children were transported.

'What happened to Stapleton?'

'Lost the family estate gambling. Maybe he found Maunder's hidey-hole, maybe 'e didn't.'

'So you never saw this cave when you were on the fishing boats?'

'No, none of us ever saw it. Maunder and the others, they all lived a long time ago remember, and it's probably all just an old yarn.'

'Do you think it's just a story?'

'Maybe yes, maybe no.'

'Did you ever look for the cave?'

'No I did not. And neither should you.'

'Why not?'

'What's buried is best left buried, boy, that's why not.'

'But what if someone . . . Ow!' Zaki was going to say 'found it by mistake', but just at that moment the cat on his lap dug her claws into his leg.

His grandfather was looking at him hard and he realised that, if he continued, the old man would guess, perhaps had already guessed, that he'd found the cave.

'Would there be treasure, do you think?' asked Zaki, trying to make it sound like idle curiosity.

'Shouldn't think so. The cargoes those days was mostly food, wool, some wine and spirits p'rhaps – nothing of much value by today's standards. Maunder would have sold it as quick as he could.'

Zaki was certain there was more to the story than his grandfather was telling, but he couldn't press it any further without admitting that he'd found the cave and, in doing so, breaking his promise to the mysterious girl who'd pulled him to safety. It was a problem. Zaki decided to change the subject. He'd get his grandfather talking about the wreckers another time.

'Has anyone bought *Queen of the Dart* yet?' The *Queen of the Dart* was a motor yacht that Grandad had restored and for which he was hoping to find a buyer, but no one had shown any interest. It was becoming a family joke.

'Not yet. Why? You thinkin' of buying her?'

'Me?!' exclaimed Zaki in mock horror. 'You know I only like boats with sails.'

'Sensible lad. Wish I'd never taken that boat on. Looks like I'm stuck with her.'

Grandad eased himself out of his chair and took the mugs to rinse in the paint-spattered sink.

'Well, best be getting on. Can't spend the whole after-noon chatting. You goin' to be any use to me with that shoulder?'

'What do you need to do?'

'I was hopin' to get some planks on the bottom of that rowing boat.'

Zaki spent the rest of the afternoon helping his grandfather as best he could. They said little to each other, concentrating on what needed to be done, but Grandad would pause occasionally to straighten his back and praise the virtues of wooden craft. 'Did you know the Vikings built their longboats this way?' he asked when the first plank was in place, and then, half an hour later, 'Light and strong, light and strong, that's the advantage of a boat like this.'

Watching the easy skill with which the old man handled the tools and materials, Zaki wondered how long it took to learn to be a boatbuilder. Could he join his grandad when he was old enough to leave school and one day take over the boat shed? After all, he shared his grandad's name, Isaac Luxton, even if everyone did call him Zaki. Maybe one day he would be Isaac Luxton, boatbuilder.

At a quarter to six, Grandad downed tools, hung up his apron and shut the back door of the shed. Jenna recognised the signs and went to stand, wagging her tail, by the front door. When the door was opened, the cat made a dash past the dog and seemed to disappear.

'Is your dad picking you up, or am I expected to drive you home?' asked Grandad.

'You know Dad.'

'In yer get.'

Zaki let Jenna into the back of the car before getting in the front.

'If you put the radio on, we might catch the shipping forecast,' said Grandad as he started the motor. The forecast with its litany of place names – Forties, Cromarty, Forth, Tyne, Dogger, Fisher, German Bight – seemed to Zaki to belong to Grandad in the same way as the smell of wood and varnish, and, as Zaki watched him steer the old Volvo through the twisting lanes above Batson Creek, he could imagine him at the wheel of a trawler battling its way through a force 8 gale in sea areas Fastnet, Shannon or Rockall.

Grandad pulled up in front of the house in Moor Lane.

'I'll not stop, the ol' dog'll be wantin' her dinner.'

'Thanks for the lift, Grandad.'

'Watch that arm, boy.'

As the car pulled away, Zaki was astonished to see the grey cat waiting by the gate. She must have sneaked into the car, thought Zaki. How else could she have got here?

The cat followed him into the house, and immediately made herself at home in the kitchen.

'Where'd that cat come from?' asked Michael, who was spreading a thick layer of peanut butter on to a piece of toast.

'Grandad's.'

'Grandad doesn't have a cat.'

'You asked me where it came from, not whose it was.'

'All right, smart arse, whose is it?'

'I don't know, do I.'

'Well, I don't know what Dad's going to say.'

'Isn't he home yet?

'Not yet.'

'I'm starving.'

'Make yourself some toast, that's what I'm doing.'

'But I've got a bad arm.'

'Aw, diddums! All right – have this piece. I suppose I can make myself another!'

'Thanks, Michael. You're a pal.'

'Yeah, aren't I.'

Zaki waited to see if Michael would say anything about the first day of school but, having made another piece of toast, Michael headed upstairs. His bedroom door slammed and soon Zaki heard him playing his guitar. He had begun mixing bass runs in with the strummed rhythms and, although he would never say it to his brother, Zaki had to admit Michael's playing was sounding surprisingly good.

CHAPTER 6

The grass, long and wet, clung to his ankles. He wanted to leave, to run, but the grass was holding him back. He shouldn't be in this field. This was the field where they buried the bodies. The ground heaved by his feet. A hand reached up to grasp his leg.

Zaki woke, his heart pounding, but as the dream image faded he became aware of two eyes that glowed in the soft morning light filtering through the window curtains. The cat was sitting on the table beside his bed, looking down at him, her pupils large and dark.

'Oh, it's you,' said Zaki.

The cat tucked her forepaws under her chest, closed her eyes and seemed to doze, sphinx-like, inscrutable, as though, now Zaki was awake, she no longer needed to be on watch.

The relief of waking and finding the horror that had gone before was just a bad dream was quickly followed by the stomach-clenching realisation that today was his first day at a new school, THE BIG SCHOOL. Of course, he comforted himself, Michael would be there – Michael knew his way around; Michael would show him what to do – it wasn't like it was the complete unknown. And friends from his primary school were going up with him – yeah, Craig would be there – but he still wished he could crawl back under the sheets, put today off, claim his arm hurt too much. Yeah, and he'd gone and missed the first day when everyone found out where their classrooms were. Was he meant to take PE kit? No, he couldn't do PE 'cause of his arm. His primary school had been small and friendly; he'd been one of the big kids. Now he'd be one of the smallest. If his mum had been here, she would have phoned up and found out what the timetable was. Why was his dad so useless at that sort of thing!? Didn't he understand anything?

People would want to know about his arm, of course – how it happened. If only he could tell the real story! The cave, the skeleton, almost getting drowned – and the girl. He had to tell somebody, there had to be someone he could talk to about it. A thing like that can't just happen and then you never talk to anyone about it – it would drive you crazy. It was driving him crazy.

He put on the blue school sweatshirt and black trousers that Michael had grown out of – at least they didn't look new. Getting his left arm through the sleeve was a painful business, but the fact that the sweatshirt was a little too big for him made it easier. As he dressed, he thought about the story Grandad had told him. So there was a smugglers' cave. It must have been the one he found, but that didn't explain the skeleton. And what about the girl? Why didn't she want him to tell? He was still puzzling over it all as he went downstairs.

'What's that cat doing here?' asked his father, as Zaki entered the kitchen.

Zaki looked round to see that the cat was sitting, nonchalantly, at the foot of the stairs.

'It was at the boat shed.'

'That wasn't the question, Zaki. I asked what it's doing here.'

'I don't know. It just is.'

'It just is! Zaki, why did you bring it home?'

'I didn't. It must have followed me.'

'Grandad drove you. How could it have followed you?'

'I don't know. Maybe it got in the car.'

'How could it have got in the car without you knowing? Zaki, you can't go bringing stray animals into the house. It probably has fleas. I suppose it's been in your room all night. Did you let it sleep on the bed?'

'No! And I didn't bring it in! It just came in! Ask Michael!'

'Well, it's not staying in the house while you're at school, and after school it's going back where it came from. Is that clear?'

'Dad,' said Zaki, 'it's nothing to do with me – honestly! Grandad's been feeding it.'

'That doesn't give you an excuse to bring it home.'

'I told you. I didn't. It just . . .'

'Eat your breakfast. You don't want to be late for your first day at your new school.' And his father went upstairs to tell Michael not to spend the whole morning under the shower.

* * *

As Zaki and Michael left the house – Michael, breakfast toast in hand – the cat shot past them. Zaki watched it run across the small front lawn and saw that as it ran it seemed to tumble, becoming a grey spinning blur in the centre of which something glittered. The glitter became an eye, a small, bright, round eye that blinked. Zaki stopped and stared. The grey blur around the eye twisted and shrank as though drawn inwards by the eye, coalescing quickly into a new form, a bird, a grey pigeon, that flew up to perch on the telegraph wire.

'Come on, Zaki!' shouted Michael. 'We'll be late. What are you gawping at?'

'I have to find the cat,' Zaki said, dropping his bag and running to the spot where the cat had seemed to have disappeared.

'Leave it, Zaki. It'll be all right.'

'No, something strange happened.' Zaki stood on the spot where the cat had last been, looking all around. The pigeon regarded him from the overhead wire.

'Something strange is always happening to you, Zaki. If you're going to mess about, I'm going without you.'

Reluctantly, Zaki followed his brother.

Although it was only a short walk from Moor Lane to school, by the time they got there the playground was ominously empty and silent. They were late and classes had already started, so there was no chance for Zaki to find anyone he knew to ask where he was meant to be. Michael said it was Zaki's fault anyway – that they would have been on time if he hadn't made all that fuss about the cat.

'Nobody ever showed me around when I started school,' said Michael. 'I had to find everything out for myself, so why can't you?'

Left on his own, Zaki had to suffer the humiliation of being shown to his classroom by the school secretary, and thirty-two faces turning as one when she ushered him through the classroom door. On seeing him, almost every face lit up with the delighted fascination of a cannibal witnessing a human sacrifice, and there was obvious disappointment when the teacher, whom he later discovered to be called Mrs Palmer, failed to do anything more to embarrass him but merely waited for him to find a vacant seat before continuing the lesson. Zaki saw that there was a seat by Craig. Perhaps his friend, who was now indicating the vacancy with little nods of his head, had saved it for him.

There were whispers of 'Hey, Zaki, what you been doing?' and 'What happened to your arm?' as he made his way between the tables, but Zaki, conscious of the teacher's eyes on his back, thought it best not to respond. Once in his seat, he searched the whiteboard for clues to the subject of the lesson. 'Myth in Ancient Societies – Ceridwen and Taliesin,' he read and felt very little the wiser.

Mrs Palmer resumed where she had left off. 'Ceridwen was a witch,' she said, tapping with a finger on the white-board, 'who had a son called Morfran. Morfran was ugly and stupid, so the witch decided to make him wise by brewing up a great spell in her cauldron of wisdom.

65

The cauldron had to be stirred for a year and a day and that job she gave to a boy called Gwion. On the last day of the spell, three drops splashed from the cauldron on to Gwion's finger.' Mrs Palmer paused and looked around the class. 'What would you instinctively do if three burning hot drops had fallen on your finger?'

'What's she talking about?' Zaki whispered to Craig.

'It's some old story from Wales,' Craig whispered back.

'It's Craig, isn't it,' said Mrs Palmer with exaggerated sweetness. 'Perhaps you would like to answer my question?' But Craig was showing Zaki where to find the chapter on myths in the textbook.

'Craig!' their neighbour hissed. 'She's talking to you!'

Craig's head jerked up but Zaki kept his eyes down, hoping not to be drawn into whatever was about to take place.

'Sorry, miss. What was the question?' asked Craig, turning a deep shade of pink.

A great hoot of laughter burst from the class. This was only the second day of term and the air in the classroom was still full of the wild disorder of six teacherless weeks of running free.

'Clearly, Craig has more important things to think about, so I will tell you what Gwion did,' continued Mrs Palmer. 'He put his scalded finger in his mouth and so received all the wisdom that was intended for the witch's son. Of course Ceridwen was furious that Gwion got the wisdom that was intended for her son, so she began to chase him, but Gwion dived into a river and used his new knowledge to change himself into a fish. The witch changed herself into an otter and pursued him . . .'

The image of the frantically swimming fish with the sleek otter after it – the otter's needle-sharp teeth centimetres from the fish's tail – sprang into Zaki's head.

'It's just like my dream!' he whispered to Craig.

'I'm sorry, Isaac, I didn't catch that,' said Mrs Palmer.

A titter rippled through the room, but Zaki, unused to being called by his full name, stared into space, or rather, into the image of the watery chase that continued to be played out before his mind's eye.

'Hello! Isaac – are you with us?' called Mrs Palmer.

Zaki, becoming aware that the teacher was talking to someone, looked around to see who it was, only to find all eyes were on him.

'Miss?' said Zaki.

The class held its breath.

Mrs Palmer allowed the silence to linger. At last she said, 'Oh, are you back with us, Isaac?'

This time uproarious mirth was accompanied by stamping feet and calls of 'Hello, Isaac!' 'Are you with us, Isaac?'

When the racket had died down, Mrs Palmer said, 'Now Isaac, perhaps you could tell us what so fascinated you.'

'It's just that I had a dream,' said Zaki, 'like this story. About being chased and turning into different things.'

'Share it with us, Isaac. Share it with us,' said Mrs Palmer. 'Since your dream is obviously more interesting than anything that I have got to tell you, come up in front of the class and tell us all about it.'

'It was just a dream,' said Zaki.

But Mrs Palmer was not to be put off and Zaki found himself, once again, the sacrificial victim before thirty-two hungry pairs of eyes.

'So?' prompted Mrs Palmer. 'How did this dream go?'

'Well, miss . . .'

'Don't just tell me. Tell the whole class.'

Many of the faces in the classroom were faces he knew from primary school, others were new to him, but all stared at him eagerly, just waiting, he thought, for him to make a fool of himself.

'It didn't start like your story,' he said. 'It started with an eye that got bigger and bigger until I fell through it. Then I was underwater and I was a fish being chased by an otter.'

There were a few snickers from the back of the class. Like a tightrope walker who has stepped on to the wire, Zaki knew he had to keep going or fall.

'I swam as fast as I could towards the surface to get away, and then I went right through the surface of the water into the air and suddenly I wasn't a fish any more, I was a bird!'

Zaki saw looks being exchanged, but he could feel the same excitement building inside that he felt in the dream – the wonder of being a bird, the soaring exhilaration of flight.

'It's fantastic being a bird! The wind carries you like you're riding a wave and there's nothing underneath you, just air, but you don't fall because you've got wings and your wings are lifting you higher and higher.'

Zaki winced as a stab of pain reminded him he couldn't lift his left arm to demonstrate.

'But then there was a hawk up above me – right in the sun – a black shape like a shadow, and I knew it was after me. I dived sideways but it dropped like – like this! – claws reaching for me. I tried to get away but . . .'

Zaki glanced up and saw that a poster promoting healthy eating was slowly detaching itself from the back wall of the classroom. First the top left corner, then the right curled over and it began to roll downwards. A drawing pin glittered and became an eye and then the poster was gone and the air was full of beating wings and the harsh, screeching *keek-keek-keek* of a swooping, whirling hawk.

Chaos followed. Children dived under tables, chairs were overturned, Mrs Palmer crouched, screaming, the book of myths and legends held over her head. Zaki and a girl he didn't know were the only ones still standing, both staring in stunned amazement at the place on the back wall where the poster had been. With a violent lurch, Zaki's world tipped and spun and everything leapt into sharp focus; objects flashed past at dizzying speed. Zaki was looking down on the heads of his class-mates; he skimmed over tabletops, swerved to miss a wall, one moment the ceiling was rushing towards him and the next he was swooping down towards startled, upturned faces. The sickening, helter-skelter ride lasted for no more than a few seconds, then he was back in his own body and the hawk was flying straight at him.

Instinctively, Zaki threw up his arm to shield his face, saw the hawk's talons reaching out, then felt them grip his arm and the claws stab through his sweatshirt sleeve. In the sudden quiet, Zaki stood, frozen; the bird perched on his upheld arm, its piercing eyes glaring into his own.

'Bring it to the window.' The girl's voice was tense but steady.

Zaki saw that, by climbing on a table, the girl had managed to get a window open. Slowly, he made his way across the classroom, like a figure from a medieval hunting scene, the bird of prey, proud and fierce, gripping his outstretched arm.

The hawk's head swivelled to take in the girl. Zaki felt its grip tighten on his arm as its muscles bunched, ready for flight. A wing brushed his face, the harsh *keek-keek-keek* broke the silence and the hawk was airborne, through the window, and gone.

The next moment Mrs Palmer's hand was on Zaki's shoulder. She spun him around, bending to thrust her face, contorted with anger, close to his own.

'What sort of a stupid stunt was that?! Do you realise that people could have been seriously hurt? Do you? Hmm? How did you get that bird into the classroom? Did somebody help you? Somebody must have helped you. If it hadn't been for Anusha getting the window open . . . well, I don't know what would have happened.' Mrs Palmer straightened and glared at the class. 'I will find out who else was involved. Be sure of that! Now you are to sit in your places. You will not move or make a sound until I return.' And she marched Zaki out into the corridor. As soon as they were through the door, an excited babble erupted in the room behind them.

Mrs Palmer took a deep breath as though about to speak, thought better of it, turned and set off down the corridor. Zaki followed, feelings of anger, hurt and bewilderment chasing each other around and around inside him. When they reached the door of the head teacher's office, Mrs Palmer commanded Zaki to 'Wait!', then she knocked and entered the head's office. When she emerged she said simply, 'We've sent for your father. You will stay here until he arrives,' and returned to the classroom.

Zaki stood waiting, staring at the floor and avoiding the curious glances of teachers and children who occasionally passed by. Eventually, he heard the break bell go and the corridor filled with noise and bodies, but Zaki kept his eyes down.

'I know what happened.' She stood close to him as the pushing, chattering crowd heaved around them. 'I saw it. It was the poster. I don't know how you did it but you changed the poster into the eagle, or whatever that bird was.'

Zaki looked up. He and the girl were almost exactly the same height. Her eyes were so dark that it was difficult to see the difference between the black of the pupils and the brown of the irises. Her dark eyes seemed to intensify the seriousness of her expression. What had Mrs Palmer called her?

'How did you do it? Was it real?'

Zaki knew he should say something but when he thought about the moment that the hawk appeared all became confused.

'I don't know,' he said, 'I don't know how it happens. Things just keep appearing. Look, I don't think you should be talking to me. You'll get into trouble.' But he didn't want her to go away. It was a relief to be talking to someone; someone else who'd seen what he'd seen.

'I'll meet you after school,' she said. 'Do you take the bus?'

'No, I walk.'

'So do I. Meet you down the harbour. By the tourist information.'

'Um . . . Well, they might send me home, I suppose,' he said.

'Yeah, but we've got to talk. So come to the harbour anyway.'

She was right. 'OK,' he said. And felt better, much better. He wasn't alone any more, 'Yeah, I'll meet you – by the tourist information.'

'I know you're called Isaac,' she said. 'I'm Anusha.'

'Zaki – I'm usually called Zaki.'

'Fine – Zaki – Whatever. Meet you after school.'

The crush in the corridor had subsided and Anusha joined the stragglers heading outside for break.

A few minutes later, Craig came by, looking furtive, and wished Zaki luck. Others waved from a safe distance or pulled faces. It was clear that the story had spread like wildfire during break because the returning crowds regarded him with much more interest, but soon classes resumed and Zaki was left on his own.

Zaki's father arrived looking hot and worried. He had obviously come straight from Number 43, as he was in his work clothes and there was brick dust in his hair. He looked questioningly at Zaki while the school secretary knocked on the head teacher's door, but they were shown in before they had any time to say anything to each other.

'Please sit down, Mr Luxton,' said the head, and then added, 'you'd better sit as well, Zaki.' And, to Zaki's surprise, she smiled at him. She was a large woman, smartly dressed. Her short hair and the lines around her eyes gave her face a slightly mischievous look. She remained standing, picked a pen up off her desk and put it down again.

'I must apologise for dragging you in here,' she said to Zaki's father, 'but this a serious matter and, if what I am told is true, there's the question of animal welfare.'

'I'm sorry, but would you mind telling me what's been going on?' asked Zaki's father.

'I think the best person to tell us is Isaac,' said the head.

Both adults looked expectantly at Zaki. What was he supposed to say? That a poster at the back of the classroom had mysteriously turned into a hawk? That for a few seconds he'd been looking through the hawk's eyes and seen everything from the bird's point of view? That this wasn't the first time; that the other day he'd seen a plastic bag turn into a seagull and, only this morning, a cat turn into a pigeon! They were hardly likely to believe that, were they?

'Well, Zaki?' said his father.

'There was this bird in our classroom this morning,' said Zaki. 'The teacher thought I brought it in, but I didn't.'

'It wasn't just any bird, was it, Isaac,' said the head. 'It was a bird of prey. Quite a rare bird and, if I'm not mistaken, a protected species. Am I right, Isaac?'

'Think so, Mrs Bennett.'

'You think so. And how did this bird of prey get into the classroom?'

'I don't know. It just appeared. I didn't bring it in!'

'Mrs Bennett, could you explain why my son is being accused of bringing this bird into school?' asked Zaki's father.

'Somebody released a bird of prey in Mrs Palmer's class this morning at precisely the time when Isaac was telling the class a story about being chased by a hawk. It seems that Isaac and one or more of his friends thought it would be a bit of a laugh.'

'No!' cried Zaki, 'We didn't! I didn't! It was just there!'

'OK, Zaki,' said his father, 'OK – let's keep calm. If you say you didn't bring the bird in, then I believe you. But a bird can't just appear.'

'If no one brought it in, perhaps you can tell me how it got there,' said the head.

'Couldn't it have come in through a window?' suggested Zaki's father. 'Birds sometimes do.'

'The windows were closed,' said the head. She picked

up her pen, removed the cap and then clicked it back on again. She sighed, walked around her desk and sat down.

'Do you have any idea how it got in?' asked Zaki's father.

'No – I told you!' said Zaki.

'OK,' said his father, holding up his hands in a way that indicated he considered the subject closed.

'Mrs Palmer says the bird appeared to have been trained,' persisted the head. 'That Isaac held up his arm and the bird flew to him.'

'It was going for me! I was protecting myself! Look!' Zaki pulled up his sleeve; the claw marks were clearly visible on his forearm.

'Oh, this is ridiculous!' Zaki's father got to his feet. 'Are you seriously suggesting my son is some sort of expert in falconry?'

'I'm merely trying to establish the truth, Mr Luxton; to hear Isaac's side of the story.' The head sighed again. 'Isaac was off sick yesterday, I think? Hurt his shoulder, or something?'

'He's cracked his collarbone,' said Zaki's father.

'Perhaps he should have the rest of today off. Let this business blow over. Is there anyone at home who could look after him? I believe his mother's away.'

Zaki saw his father stiffen. 'I'm quite capable of taking care of my son, thank you,' he said.

'I wouldn't suggest for a moment that you are not,' said the head, then to Zaki, 'Well, if you or any of your friends think of anything more you want to tell me about this bird, do come and see me. You won't get into any trouble.' And she smiled, but all Zaki could think was, *She doesn't believe me.*

On the way home in the van, his father turned to him and said, 'First a cat turns up in the house that you have nothing to do with and now this bird. It does make me wonder.'

He doesn't believe me either, thought Zaki miserably. Then he remembered Anusha. There was somebody who believed him; someone who'd seen what really happened that morning, and she said she'd meet him after school. He would have to find an excuse for going out. He had to talk to her.

CHAPTER 7

When his father steered the van into the driveway at Moor Lane, Zaki half expected the grey cat to be waiting for them outside the house, but there was no sign of it, nor did it materialise inside the house. Would it be back at the boat shed? he wondered.

Over lunch, Zaki asked his father about progress with the renovations at Number 43, anything to keep him off the subject of the morning's problems at school. Zaki knew his father would be keen to get back to work, so, once they had finished eating, he said, 'I think I might take a look down the harbour. There's an old sailing trawler tied up there and they'll take her back down the river when the tide turns.' His father knew he loved old boats, so this seemed perfectly plausible.

'Fine, just keep out of trouble,' said his father, 'I'd better get back to number forty-three. They're meant to deliver the slates for the roof this afternoon. But if you're thinking of meeting Craig after school, don't go playing football; remember what the doctor said.' His father gave him a searching look.

'Don't worry, Dad, I'm not stupid,' said Zaki.

When he reached the harbour, there was still half an hour to kill before school finished, and even if Anusha hurried, Zaki figured it would take her a further fifteen minutes to get down to the harbour. Zaki hadn't invented the old trawler he'd told his father he was going to look at; he had noticed her tied up at the visitors' berth when they passed on their way home from school. He thought he might as well take a look while he waited for Anusha to arrive. He wandered down to the water's edge. 'Vigilance' said the gold letters on the boat's stern. Zaki's grandad could remember a few still fishing under sail in the 1930s and spoke with loving respect of seeing them running home, laden with fish, before a southerly gale.

But Zaki's mind wasn't on boats, it was on his meeting with Anusha. What should he tell her? Should he tell her everything? Should he tell her about the cave and the skeleton? What about the girl who rescued him and the promise he made her?

Zaki used his good arm to help clamber on to the harbour wall, swung his legs over and sat staring down into the water. His reflection bent and buckled, distorting on the rippling surface. Passing small craft sent larger waves racing to strike the harbour wall and bounce back, bringing confusion to the pattern of ripples, fragmenting his reflection, making his arms, legs, head spring away from each other and then draw back together to reunite. He watched this repeated, hypnotic disintegration and reunification of his body. The sunlight on the water flashed and sparkled and an aura radiated out from his reflected head.

Zaki looked up to rest his eyes from the dazzle of the water and saw that there was a boat making its way up the estuary under sail; another old gaff rigger, but much smaller than the sailing trawler. Was there some sort of old gaffer's convention taking place in Kingsbridge? Her hull was painted black with a white stripe at the waterline and a snub-nosed pram dinghy with a matching black hull and white stripe trailed behind her.

Zaki knew it took considerable skill to sail all the way to the top of the estuary, the narrow channel of deeper water winding its way down between wide mud flats, the twists and turns of the channel marked only by red and white striped poles. It was one thing to do it in a sailing dinghy with a lifting centreboard, as he and Michael had often done, quite another to attempt it in boat with a fixed keel. She looked like a Falmouth Working Boat, thought Zaki, the sort still used on the oyster beds of Carrick Roads. As the boat came around the next marker post, Zaki saw that there was only one person on deck and he was even more impressed by the skill of her skipper, who now left the boat to look after herself while checking the fenders and ropes were in place for mooring. The next turn would bring her into the cluster of moorings that lay just off the visitor's berth and Zaki expected to hear the motor start and see her sails come down, but to his surprise she continued on under sail, weaving between the moored boats.

This guy would even impress Michael! thought Zaki.

Emerging from the moorings, with less than fifty

metres to go, the skipper loosed the sails and now the wind no longer drove the boat along and only her momentum kept her moving forward. It was the sort of trick old-timers like Zaki's grandad used, but this skipper looked young, a kid almost, maybe his brother's age. And then, with a shock, Zaki realised it was a girl – the realisation was followed a split second later by near-certainty that he knew who she was. Spiky, cropped curls framed a tanned face with widely spaced eyes; a pair of eyes that had been centimetres from his own, while he clung to the boulder in Dragon Pool.

Normally, Zaki would have hurried over to catch mooring lines and help the skipper make fast; it was the friendly thing to do, particularly when someone was bringing a boat alongside single-handed. But instead, Zaki slid off the wall and ducked behind a large green recycling bin. Peeping around the bin, he watched the boat close the last few metres to the harbour wall.

If she'd got the speed wrong, he thought, that long bowsprit would skewer the sailing trawler. But she hadn't got it wrong – the boat slowed gently, and as the side kissed the harbour wall, the girl reached over and dropped a mooring rope round a bollard, let the line run out, then with a flick of her wrist tied off the other end. In another moment she was ashore securing her bow line. It was so expertly done that Zaki felt like applauding.

Then she dropped and furled the sails before disappearing into the cabin.

* * *

'Why are you hiding?'

Zaki spun round and found Anusha standing behind him.

'You weren't by the tourist information office, so I came looking for you.'

'Sorry,' said Zaki, not wanting to take his eyes off the boat for more than a second. 'I wasn't hiding from you.'

The girl was still below decks.

'What are you doing, then? Who are you spying on?'

'You see that boat there?'

Anusha nodded.

'There's a girl on it. And I think I know who she is. Well, I don't really know who she is. That's the thing, you see? And I want to know what she's doing here.'

Anusha examined him quizzically, her head tipped slightly to one side. 'You're not making that much sense.'

'Sorry. It's just – I don't have time to explain it all.'

'All what?'

Zaki could hear the note of irritation in her voice but he couldn't think of a simple answer.

'OK,' she said, 'if you don't want to trust me.' And she turned to leave.

'Wait! Please . . . I need your help.'

Anusha waited, arms folded, while Zaki struggled to organise his thoughts.

'On holiday . . . we were on my dad's boat and I found a cave . . . with a skeleton in it . . .'

'A what! A skeleton! Are you making this up?'

'. . . and she's got something to do with it, but I don't know what.'

Anusha sucked her lip and said nothing. Zaki knew she was having trouble believing him. Then, a wild idea came into his head.

'Listen. If she comes ashore, I want you to follow her.'

'You're kidding! Me? Why?'

'I want to know where she goes.'

'What about you?'

'I can't follow her, she might recognise me. Anyway, if she leaves the boat open, I'm going to take a look on board.'

'Isn't that against the law, or something?'

'I need to know who she is.'

'Well . . . why don't you just ask her?'

'You don't understand.'

'No – I don't.'

'The skeleton – maybe she did it – maybe she killed someone. She made me promise not to tell. She's keeping it a secret.'

'So, maybe she's a murderer, and you want me to follow her?'

'Yes,' said Zaki, thinking, when put like that, it didn't sound such a great idea. Also, he had just broken his promise to the girl who had saved his life.

'All right,' said Anusha, after a pause. 'OK, I'll follow her. But make sure you're out of her boat before she gets back. Please?'

'If she starts coming back suddenly, try to warn me.'

'How?' Anusha demanded.

'I don't know. Look! She's coming ashore.'

The girl jumped ashore. She was barefooted and had

an old canvas rucksack, the sort with leather straps that you might find in an army surplus store, slung over one shoulder. It looked empty. She took a moment to put her rucksack on properly and then strode off towards the road into town. Anusha allowed the girl to get to the corner of the waterside buildings and then hurried off after her.

Zaki waited until Anusha was out of sight, checked that nobody was watching him, then quickly crossed the dockside to where the boat was moored and climbed on board. He crouched down in the cockpit. The boat's deck was below the level of the harbour edge so that, by keeping low, he could keep out of sight of anyone ashore, unless they were standing just above the boat.

Curlew – the boat's name was painted in neat black letters across the edge of the sliding hatch over the steps down to the cabin. A good name for her, Zaki thought. With her long, downward-bending bowsprit she looked quite like the long-beaked wader she was named after.

Now, could he get into the cabin? He tried the hatch cover. A gentle push and it slid forward. Not locked. Carefully, he lifted out the washboards and laid them on the floor of the cockpit.

The cabin was dark by contrast with the sunlight outside. The sudden thought struck Zaki that she may have left the boat unlocked because there was someone else on board, someone who had remained in the cabin. Gingerly, Zaki climbed down the steps. There was no one in the small saloon. Zaki listened at the door to the forward cabin. If anyone was aboard he or she was keeping very still. There was just enough height below the deck for Zaki to be able to stand; anyone taller would need to remain stooped.

In the flickering, reflected light off the water that entered through the small brass portholes Zaki examined his surroundings. All was neat and tidy. Two narrow bunks, a drop-sided table, a spirit stove; no room for a chart table. He opened the wet-locker by the companionway and found a single set of old-fashioned oilskins hanging inside that looked to be the girl's size and a pair of sea boots. He closed the locker. A spirit lamp hung from a deck beam aft of the mast. It was the only visible form of artificial lighting. There were no electrical fittings. Whoever owned this boat was a true traditionalist; there was no radio and no modern navigation aids, no GPS, no depth, speed or wind gauges, not even electric lights. Zaki bent down and looked through the steps of the companionway; there was no motor. No wonder the girl had brought the boat in under sail! His gaze took in the fittings – wood, brass and bronze – no stainless steel. She was like a boat out of a museum, out of a different time.

'Get a move on!' Zaki told himself. He was supposed to be finding out about the girl, not the boat. But what to look for? Cautiously, he moved forward and opened the door to the forward cabin. A small crowded space, but again, everything neat and tidy. There was a locker on each side, beyond which were canvas sailbags containing spare sails, coils of cotton and hemp rope and other bits of gear.

Zaki opened the locker on the starboard side. Clothing that Zaki guessed to be the girl's, although there was nothing particularly feminine about any of it. Still, he was now pretty certain that she was sailing alone.

He closed the locker and opened the one on the port side. Behind the door were two shelves and below them a set of drawers; the shelves were full of cloth-covered writing books. It was clear from the state and style of their covers that the books had been purchased at different times. Zaki picked one at random and flicked through the pages. It was a logbook: dates, passage plans, ports of departure and arrival, weather details, notes, each entry written in the same sloping handwriting. He read the date of the last entry '6th July, 1965'. Too long ago to have been written by the girl. He replaced the log on the shelf and took down the one that looked the newest. Over half the pages were empty, so it had to be the current log, and this was borne out by the most recent entry; it was dated the previous day and gave details of a passage from Plymouth to Salcombe. It gave no reason for the journey, revealing nothing beyond the bare facts. She'd had a favourable wind and made good time, averaging, by Zaki's reckoning, around five knots. But the handwriting! . . . Zaki took down the book he'd just put away; he opened it and compared entries in the two books. Yesterday's entry was written in the same handwriting as an entry made over forty years ago. How could that be? She must have an older companion, the log keeper, perhaps the boat's real owner; some-one she'd put ashore in Salcombe before today's short trip up to Kingsbridge?

Perhaps his assumption about the clothing was wrong, perhaps it wasn't all hers. Then why one set of oilskins? Maybe the other person had worn his or her set ashore.

Zaki put away the logbooks and turned his attention to the drawers. Hurriedly opening and closing them, he quickly surveyed their contents without disturbing anything. Personal belongings, toiletries – he felt he was prying where he shouldn't, like a burglar in somebody's bedroom. In the third drawer, a locket on a golden chain lay open, but the two little pictures it contained were so faded that Zaki could only make out the vague outlines of the faces. He opened the fourth drawer and froze, staring at what he had revealed. Two bracelets, identical in size and design, except that one was tarnished and the other polished. He lifted the tarnished bracelet from where the girl had nestled it among her scarves and woollen gloves. There was the design of engraved symbols or runes that he had seen when he held it in the cave. He ran a finger over its convex outer surface and around the flat inner surface, and then slipped it over his hand and on to his wrist. So she hadn't returned it to the cave, she had kept it, and what's more it was one of a pair. The other, judging by the way it was polished, she wore herself from time to time. Lying in the drawer, it glowed like pale gold even in the dim light in the cabin. What were they made out of? Not gold, since they tarnished, but they were too pale for copper or brass. The bracelet on his wrist felt warm against his skin, as though it had been lying in the sun before he put it on. It was a comforting warmth that seemed to flow up through his arm to his injured shoulder. He pushed it further up his arm, under his sweatshirt sleeve, past the sling.

The warmth now flooded through the rest of his body, and as it spread it brought a delicious drowsiness, forcing him to sink down among the sailbags. He heard music and singing, chatter and laughter – faces crowded around him and he retreated deep into himself, where he hid for a long time, until he heard one voice, more persistent that the rest, saying, 'Zaki! Zaki!'

Anusha was there! She was in the cabin! She was shutting the drawers, closing the cupboard.

'Zaki, get up! She's coming back! Get up! Get up!'

Zaki struggled back to consciousness. It was like climbing up from the bottom of a deep well.

'I lost her. She just disappeared, so I ran back here. Then I saw her coming down the road. If we go out now, she'll see us. What are we going to do?'

Zaki scrambled to his feet. He felt dizzy but there was no time to lose. Quickly, he went to the main hatch, retrieved the washboards and, from the inside, slotted them into place, then slid the hatch cover shut.

'You've trapped us! She's sure to come in here!'

'Quick, into the forward cabin and shut the door. Perhaps we can get out of the forehatch while she stows things in the saloon.'

It was a desperate plan but Zaki could think of no alternative except trying to explain to the girl why he had been searching her boat, and he didn't fancy doing that.

No sooner had they shut themselves in the forward

cabin than they heard the girl jump lightly down on to the deck. They waited, huddled among the sailbags, listening, trying to guess what she was doing. They heard the main hatch slide open and then her footsteps on the stairs. There was the thump of the now full rucksack being dropped on the cabin floor and then she went back up on deck. There was no time to get the forehatch open and make their escape. Zaki and Anusha exchanged anxious glances and Anusha pulled a face. They could hear the girl's bare feet padding about above them and the creak of rigging.

'What's she doing?' whispered Anusha.

'She's putting the main up.'

'What does that mean?'

'It means she's getting ready to leave.'

Sure enough, the footsteps went quiet for a moment and were followed by the sound of ropes being tossed from the shore on to the deck.

'She's casting off!' hissed Zaki.

'So, what now?'

'Maybe she's not going far. It's a bit late to be setting out to sea and she's towing the dinghy. Could just be going to anchor in deeper water down the estuary.'

'Great! So we'll be stuck in the middle of the harbour!'

'I think she left someone in Salcombe. She might stop at the ferry wharf to pick them up.'

'And if she doesn't?

Zaki shrugged.

There was a soft thud as the girl landed back onboard and they could feel the boat heel gently to the wind as it swung away from the dockside.

Zaki pictured what was happening above him: the girl pushing off and hurrying back to the helm. There was the splash of a rope dropping into the water and the sound of it being hauled aboard. She'd have her hands full right now, managing the sail and steering through the moored boats.

'Can you swim?' asked Zaki.

'Oh my God! You're not serious?' Anusha saw that he was. So she said, 'Yes,' and then added, 'if I have to.'

'Sorry,' said Zaki. 'Sorry I got you into this.'

Anusha gave a little toss of her head that seemed to say, 'I must have been mad.'

The wind was light. *Curlew* was running down the estuary in almost total silence, the only sound the lap of little ripples against her bow. Zaki and Anusha no longer dared risk even whispered conversation. Minutes passed slowly and the boat continued steadily on. Zaki's faith in his theory that the girl would stop when she reached Salcombe began to fade. He gathered his courage and got to his feet. He would go and speak to her, try to explain. But before he could open the door the boat tipped suddenly and he was thrown across the cabin, jarring his injured shoulder.

'What's happening?' Anusha's eyes were wide.

'She's turned into the wind. Shhh! If she's going to anchor, she'll have to come on to the foredeck.'

Now the boat was full of noise: sails flapped, shaking the rigging, blocks rattled, ropes beat against the deck, every sound amplified down in the cabin.

Footsteps overhead were followed by the splash of the anchor and the clatter of the anchor chain. The beating sails quietened as they were lowered and furled. The footsteps retreated back to the stern and then Zaki heard the girl descend into the cabin. His eyes met Anusha's and they both held their breaths. Zaki willed Anusha not to move; her knuckles were white as she gripped a sailbag. They could hear the girl moving about in the saloon. What was she doing? Would she come forward? At last, she went back on deck and closed the main hatch. There was a pause and then the distinctive rattle of oars in rowlocks followed by the splash . . . splash . . . splash of the girl rowing steadily away in the dinghy.

'She's gone,' breathed Zaki.

'Ohhh! Thank goodness!' groaned Anusha, slowly unfolding herself from her cramped seat on the sailbag.

Zaki eased the forehatch open, enough to see out. *Curlew* was anchored amongst the local moorings on the East Portlemouth side of the harbour. Zaki could see the girl rowing across to the quayside.

'She's either going ashore, or to pick someone up. Either way, we've got at least quarter of an hour,' said Zaki.

'Let's get out of here,' urged Anusha, stepping into the saloon.

'Wait! There's her logbooks. I've read bits of them already. They'll maybe tell us where's she's been, what she's been doing.'

'Are you crazy? We can't hang about reading stuff! Anyway, she's not going to have written "I just killed so-and-so, and stuck the body in this cave", is she? Not unless she's completely bonkers!'

Anusha was already sliding back the cover of the main hatch. Zaki hesitated then opened the port-side locker. There were the logbooks. He already knew, or thought he knew that she wasn't their author. He took down the one that looked the oldest and flipped through it quickly. The handwriting was still the same, although a little less regular; there were crossings out and corrections, notes written in the margins. Then he saw the date of an entry. It was impossible! That entry was dated 1908.

'Now what are you doing?' called Anusha.

Zaki closed the locker. In the saloon he found an empty carrier bag. He dropped the logbook into it and followed Anusha up on deck. 'Keep your head down,' warned Zaki. 'She might still see us.'

They crouched in the cockpit.

'What's that?' demanded Anusha.

'One of the logs.'

'What? You mean you're going to steal it?'

'Yes,' said Zaki simply.

Anusha let out a low groan. 'Well, how are we going to get off here, anyway?'

It was a good question. It was fifty metres at least to the shore and the girl had the dinghy. Of course they could swim, but it was a ten-mile walk back to the main road from East Portlemouth, it was already getting dark and Zaki wasn't sure how well he could swim with his injured shoulder. He looked around, hoping for inspiration. His eyes fell on the familiar shape of *Morveren* tied to her mooring a little to starboard and about six boat-lengths away. If they could get to *Morveren*, they could use the sailing dinghy that was stored upside down on her deck to get across to Salcombe.

'I've got an idea,' said Zaki. 'You see that yacht there? That's our boat. If we can get to her, we can get ashore.'

'So we still have to swim,' said Anusha gloomily.

'No, we have to let out the anchor chain,' said Zaki.

The ebb tide was running quite fast, with the anchor chain let right out, they could use the flow of the tide over the rudder to swing *Curlew* across to *Morveren*. At least, that was Zaki's theory.

They waited until the solitary rower reached the pontoon and then allowed her a few more minutes to tie up her dinghy and go ashore.

'Come on,' Zaki said, 'I'll need a hand.'

Up on the bow, Zaki opened the hatch over the chain-locker; most of the chain was already out, but there looked to be a good length of anchor rope after the chain. Zaki wished he had two good arms; Anusha would have to do most of the work and *Curlew* was a heavy boat. He explained what needed to be done and together they began to pay out the anchor, easing *Curlew* back on the tide until she was lying just forward of *Morveren*. Zaki peered into the chainlocker; they were almost out of rope. 'Hold her there,' said Zaki, 'I'm going see if I can steer her across.'

He went back to the cockpit and unlashed the tiller, then pushed it over to port. *Curlew* began to swing to starboard.

'Let her out slowly!' called Zaki.

Anusha let out more rope.

'There's not much left!' she called.

Curlew's stern was now level with *Morveren*'s bow and three metres to starboard.

'That's all the rope – and I can't hold it much longer!'

Zaki lashed the tiller to port and leapt to the foredeck to help Anusha tie off the anchor rope.

Morveren was tantalisingly close, but still just out of reach.

'I'm going to try something,' said Zaki. 'If I get the boats close enough, can you see if you can get on to *Morveren*?'

'I'll try,' said Anusha.

Zaki untied the tiller. He put the helm over to starboard and *Curlew* 'sailed' on the tide away from *Morveren*. When he judged she would go no further, he put the helm over to port and she swung back towards the other boat, gathering momentum like the weight on a pendulum – closer – closer – closer . . .

'Now!' shouted Zaki.

Anusha flung herself from the stern of *Curlew* and landed with her stomach across *Morveren*'s bowsprit, where she hung precariously, arms and head dangling one side, legs dangling the other as *Curlew* swung away.

'Owww!' She kicked and wriggled until she got one leg over the spar. She sat up grinning and gave Zaki a thumbs-up, then scrambled back to *Morveren*'s foredeck.

Zaki repeated the manoeuvre and this time, as the gap closed, he tossed a rope to Anusha. With a line across, it was an easy matter to pull the boats together so that they could cross with ease from one to the other. Zaki joined Anusha on *Morveren*. They unlashed the sailing dinghy from *Morveren*'s deck, turned it over and heaved it into the water. They'd have to row; the sails were locked up in the cabin. Zaki dropped the oars into the dinghy and tied it to *Curlew*'s stern. Now came the most tiring part of the whole job, to haul *Curlew* back up her anchor rope against the ebb tide, but the thought that the girl might return at any time spurred them on and fifteen exhausting minutes later they had *Curlew* back where she had started.

Time to abandon ship. They closed up the hatches and climbed into the dinghy. Zaki tucked the pilfered logbook under the dinghy's seat. It was twenty-five to six by Zaki's watch; they should have just enough time to row across to his grandad's shed before he packed up for the night. Row? There was a flaw in his plan – how could he row with one arm?

'Can you row?' he asked hopefully.

'Not very . . . Well, I've never tried,' came the reply.

Zaki made room for Anusha on the centre seat.

'You take one oar; I'll take the other. Just try to keep in time.' Zaki cast off.

At first, they tended to go round in circles, and the ebb tide threatened to carry them out to sea. On two occasions Anusha missed the water altogether with her oar and fell backwards into the bottom of the dinghy, after which she got a terrible fit of the giggles, but eventually they settled into a steady rhythm and pulled away from the moored boats. Zaki kept them on a diagonal course, aiming up the estuary to allow for the strong current that sucked at the yellow buoys in mid-channel.

'You're doing great,' encouraged Zaki.

'Don't distract me,' came the sharp response.

After which they rowed in silence until Anusha asked, 'Did you see that cat?'

'What cat?'

'There was a cat on the boat when I came looking for you.'

'On *Curlew*?'

'Yes. I thought it must belong on board but it was gone when we got out of the cabin.'

Zaki's oar dug too deep and he lost the rhythm. 'What was it like?' he asked, but he knew the answer.

'Grey. It was sitting at the back of the boat. Almost like it was on guard.'

For six strokes Zaki made himself concentrate on the rowing, then he said, 'That cat is like the hawk in the classroom. It appears and disappears. It's been following me. It slept in my room last night. And it can change its shape.'

He could feel Anusha fighting her disbelief. She pulled at her oar with extra ferocity.

'OK,' she said at last, 'I think you better tell me everything.'

Lift the oars, lean forward, dip the oars, lean back – lift the oars, lean forward, dip the oars, lean back. They were much the same height and weight and their movements were now perfectly synchronised. Zaki's sentences, clipped short by shortness of breath, fell into the rhythm of their rowing. He began with the moment he entered the cave by Dragon Pool, told how the tide had trapped him and of his near-drowning. How the girl had rescued him and made him promise to tell no one what he had seen. How she'd taken back the bracelet.

The bracelet! With a gasp of horror, Zaki remembered he was still wearing it! She might overlook the missing logbook – but how long would it be before she discovered the theft of the bracelet?

'What is it?' Anusha asked when Zaki fell silent.

Zaki covered his alarm over the bracelet by looking round to check their progress. For some reason that he couldn't quite explain he chose not to tell Anusha he had taken it.

'We're almost there,' he said.

A few more strokes and the dinghy nosed against the slipway behind Grandad's boat shed.

By the time they had tied up the dinghy, Zaki had added the details about the grey cat and its strange transformation.

'Better hurry,' he now urged, 'Grandad likes to finish before the shipping forecast.

'Whatever that is,' said Anusha, as she followed him into the shed.

CHAPTER 8

Jenna gave one loud bark as Zaki entered the shed with Anusha close behind him. The old dog heaved herself up from her place under the side workbench and, tail wagging, came to greet them. She accepted a quick scruffing of her fur and a 'Hello, Jenna' from Zaki before pushing around him to inspect Anusha.

'Where did you spring from?' demanded Grandad, looking up from sweeping the shed floor. 'And who's this pretty little maid?' as his eyes fell on Anusha, who was now kneeling among the wood shavings, scratching Jenna under the collar.

'This is Anusha, Grandad. I was teaching her to row.'

'Hello, Mr Luxton,' said Anusha.

'You'll be all over dust and shavin's if you crawl around there, my love.'

'I don't mind,' smiled Anusha, hopping up and dusting herself off.

'Learnin' to row, eh?'

'Yes,' said Anusha, 'but it was getting late, so we had to give up. Wow! This is so beautiful! I didn't know boats were built like this.' She walked around the part-built boat, examining it inside and out.

'Not many are any more,' grunted Grandad.

Zaki could see that half the planks of the rowing boat's hull were now in place. It was a slow process, particularly if you worked on your own. Each plank had to be offered up to the one before, marked, then shaped by hand and finally fixed in place. For the hull to be watertight, the fit had to be perfect.

'We left the dinghy by the slip. Hope that's OK,' said Zaki. 'I'll take her back out to *Morveren* on the weekend.'

'Shouldn't be too much in the way. Your parents know where you are?'

'Dad won't be home yet,' said Zaki.

'I probably ought to phone my mum,' said Anusha.

'Probably you ought to,' said Grandad. 'You can call her from the house.'

They filed out of the shed and waited with Jenna while Grandad locked up. Jenna sniffed hopefully at the carrier bag containing the logbook that Zaki had 'borrowed' from *Curlew* but, having ascertained that it contained nothing edible, she lost interest.

'What you got in the bag?' enquired Grandad.

'School project,' said Anusha quickly, to cover Zaki's hesitation.

'Has that cat been back?' asked Zaki.

'Not since your last visit.'

Grandad led the way across the narrow lane and up the steep flight of steps to the cottage overlooking Batsford Creek where four generations of Luxtons, including Zaki's father, had been born and raised. Little ever changed in Grandad's house. The green oilcloth that covered the kitchen table was the same green oilcloth that Zaki could remember covering the table when he was little more than a toddler. The same chipped mugs and jugs hung from hooks, the same pictures of ships under sail hung on the walls. But, although the range was still always alight, some of the cosy warmth seemed to have left the kitchen since Zaki's grandma had died two years earlier, and the smells of cooking and baking had slowly faded, to be replaced by the workshop smells carried in by Grandad.

Jenna pushed between their legs, crossed the kitchen and threw herself down in her favourite spot with her back against the stove.

Zaki remembered the day his grandmother died. He had raced up the steps to the cottage ahead of his mother and father, eager as ever to see his grandparents. His grandmother had been ill for some time and they were visiting regularly. His grandad was sitting at the kitchen table, an unusual place for him during the day. 'How's Grandma?' Zaki had asked. His grandfather looked up and there was an emptiness in his eyes that Zaki had never seen, like a grey empty sea under a winter sky. 'We're just waitin' for the tide to go out. She's a fisherman's daughter, she'll go with the tide' his grandad said quietly. His grandmother died at low tide that evening.

'Telephone's by here. Help yourself,' Grandad said to Anusha. ''Spect you children'll be hungry if you've been rowin' all afternoon. Have a rummage in the larder, Zaki.

See if you can find some eggs. I'll get a bit of tea and toast goin'.'

It was agreed that after tea Grandad would run them back into Kingsbridge. Soon the three of them were sitting around the kitchen table eating fried eggs on thick slices of buttered toast. With the first mouthful Zaki realised he was starving and, judging by the quiet concentration with which Anusha was attacking her food, he guessed she was just as hungry.

'Grandad,' began Zaki, through egg and toast, 'do you have a chart of the Orme?'

'Should do. Why d'you ask?'

'Is there deep water anywhere in the Orme, apart from Dragon Pool?'

'Not in the river, but in one o' them creeks there's a bit of a pool by an old lime kiln. They must have dredged it once upon a time.'

'Can you show me?'

'Finish up your tea an' I'll fetch the chart down.'

When they had finished eating, Zaki cleared the table and Grandad spread out the chart.

'Look here,' Grandad said, tapping a callused finger on the chart.

'Stapleton's Creek,' read Zaki. 'Stapleton – that was the name of the landowner, wasn't it?'

'That's right. Owned the land right down to the sea. There's the lime kiln, and see? Deep water right by it. Makes sense – they would 'ave had to bring quite big boats in there with lime for the kiln.'

'What was the lime for?' asked Anusha.

'Well – they made quick lime, didn't they – to put on the fields – stopped the soil gettin' too acid. Of course, they say, Stapleton had another purpose.'

'What purpose?' asked Zaki.

'I told you about the wreckers burying the bodies in Stapleton's fields? Well, they say they buried 'em in quick lime. Helped 'em to rot down, you see.'

'Urgh! Yuck!' declared Anusha in disgust. 'Whose bodies are you talking about?'

'I'll explain later.' Zaki studied the chart; it looked quite old. 'Are these depths fathoms or metres?'

'Metres,' said Grandad.

Not too old, then. But he remembered how the sandbanks moved around in the Orme; the depths would certainly have changed since the chart was drawn. In the pool by the lime kiln there was a depth of three metres marked close in-shore. So a boat could lie in there and stay afloat even at low tide. The mouth of the creek was blocked by a mudbank that a boat would only be able to cross when the tide was high. No wonder he and Michael had never bothered with this creek, seen where it met the river, it would appear to be just a muddy little backwater.

'You can't see the lime kiln from the main river, can you, Grandad?'

'No. It's all overgrown for one thing, and for another, Stapleton's Creek tucks around behind that hill.' He tapped the chart again.

'What's all this about, boy?' Grandad looked quizzically at Zaki.

'Have you seen the little Falmouth workboat anchored

by the town moorings?'

'I've seen 'er. Pretty little craft.'

'How deep do you think her keel is?'

'Not much. Those boats was made for workin' in shallow water – not more 'n a metre.'

'So she could get up that creek at high tide?'

'Easy.'

'And she could lie there and nobody would see her?'

'Reckon she could.'

'I can see you've got the wind in your sails, boy, but I wonder if you know where you're headin'.' Grandad straightened his back and poured himself another mug of tea.

'That's the bit we call Dragon Pool,' said Zaki, showing Anusha where they usually anchored. 'When we were last there, *Curlew* could have been in the creek and we would never have known.' Anusha gave a little nod to show she understood the significance of this information.

Zaki turned back to Grandad. 'The ruined cottage . . .'

'What of it?'

'You said a woman was living there.'

'Years ago.'

'What was she like? Did you ever get a good look at her?'

'I told you before, she never spoke to nobody.'

Zaki could tell by the closed look on his grandfather's face and by the tone of voice that he had no wish to continue this conversation but Zaki was determined to press on. There was something his grandfather was keeping from him. Of course, it made no sense to connect that woman who lived in the cottage years ago and the girl, except . . . except . . .

'Was she young? Old?'

'Young,' conceded Grandad grudgingly. 'Pretty, some said.'

'So you knew people who saw her?'

'Oh ay – knew. An' little good it did them.'

'What happened?' It was Anusha who asked, her eyes alight with curiosity. Grandad placed his mug of tea on the table. He drew out a chair and sat facing Zaki and Anusha. He looked sternly from one to the other.

'There was a Plymouth boat – *Silver Harvest*, she was called – belonged to three brothers. Hard men – heavy drinkers, and out for whatever they could get. Well, everybody knew the story of Maunder and Stapleton and there was always talk of lost treasure, but no one never found it. Now these three brothers got it into their heads that the treasure must be hid in the old cottage. Happen one day there was a number o' boats in the Orme waitin' for a bit o' weather to blow over – *Silver Harvest* among 'em. The three brothers decided to go treasure huntin'. They climbed up to the cottage with pickaxes and shovels and the like and began tearing the place to pieces. The woman of the cottage surprised them at it and ordered them to stop, but they just laughed in her face and kept right on at it.'

Grandad gave a little shake of his head and took a sip of tea.

'That's awful,' said Anusha.

Grandad stared hard into his mug and when he looked

up there was something like fear in his eyes. 'Then,' he continued, 'they said she cursed them.'

'Did they find anything?' asked Zaki.

'Of course not. Why would a woman live on her own in a tumbledown cottage if she had a pile of treasure?'

'But what did they say about her, about the woman, what she was like?' asked Zaki.

'Young, no more than a girl, they said, but wild. And they weren't going to let some wild girl stand between them and the treasure. Next time they'd make sure she didn't catch 'em.'

'And?'

'There was no next time. They was all killed.'

'Killed?' gasped Anusha. 'How?'

'Different ways. One at a time.'

Zaki glanced at Anusha, who was staring, wide-eyed, at Grandad.

'The oldest brother went first. They was liftin' crab pots and he was haulin' in the line when somethin' gave the rope an almighty tug and he was pulled clean out of the boat. Before the others could grab a hold of him he was dragged underwater. When he bobbed up again he was dead – drowned.'

Grandad twisted his mug on the table.

'Middle brother was next. Everyone knew he was fond of oysters an' someone left him a present of a couple of dozen on the *Silver Harvest*. Must've been poisoned. At any rate the oysters was blamed when he took sick. Never recovered, though it took him six days to die.'

'And the youngest?' asked Zaki.

'Well, stands to reason no one'd go fishing with him. Went off on his own one day and was never seen again. They found the *Silver Harvest*; she was driftin' two miles off the mouth of the Orme.'

'They could all have been accidents,' protested Zaki.

'Could've been,' grunted Grandad.

'What happened to the woman?' asked Anusha softly.

'No one ever bothered her again. We saw her from time to time, standin' or sittin' at the top of the cliff, lookin' out to sea. Like her was waitin' for someone who never came home.'

Zaki looked down at the chart. There it was – 'Ruin (Conspic)' – Conspicuous. The cottage was on the chart because it was a conspicuous landmark. She wasn't hiding; she chose to live alone but somewhere conspicuous. And yet, no one really knew anything about her. And did his grandad really believe that she could curse people, cast spells? This was not the same person, Zaki reminded himself. If she were still alive now, she'd be an old woman, not a young girl. But there had to be a connection – didn't there?

'Do you think she ever had children?' asked Zaki.

'I told you, she lived on her own.'

'No one lives there now, do they?'

'Cottage was abandoned long ago.'

Grandad gathered the mugs and made a great clattering as he began to wash them with the plates in the sink. Anusha hopped off her chair and stood by with a tea towel.

Zaki thought about their many visits to Dragon Pool.

Had he ever seen movement up by the cottage? He didn't think so, but then you only saw the cottage as you were entering the bay. They'd never climbed up there.

'Did you ever go up to the cottage?' asked Zaki.

'I told you, we left her alone.'

'But later – when you went there with Dad?'

'There's nothin' there. A pile of old stones, nothin' else.' Grandad turned and scowled at Zaki. 'I didn't go there – I didn't let your father go there – and you're not to go there either.'

'But why?'

'Evil – that's why. Some places have got evil in 'em.'

Grandad stomped off out of the kitchen. Zaki and Anusha looked at each other and Anusha raised her eyebrows. When Grandad returned moments later with his jacket on, Jenna struggled to her feet and stood wagging her tail.

'You'll get your walk in a bit,' said Grandad. 'I'm runnin' these young'uns home first.'

Jenna dropped back down with a low groan of disappointment.

Zaki and Anusha hurried to follow Grandad out of the house.

CHAPTER 9

'I'll drop you here, if it's all the same to you. Save me turnin' the old girl round.'

Grandad pulled in at the end of Zaki's street.

Zaki was done in. It had been the longest day ever. He was grateful for the lift home but he wished his grandfather had driven him to the front door. He climbed out into the darkness, said, 'Goodnight, Grandad,' and swung the passenger door shut.

The old Volvo's suspension groaned as it heaved itself slowly out of the gutter, as if it too were tired and reluctant to make the journey home. Zaki waved to the red glow of the receding tail lights, then, head down, trudged off along the street. The houses here were set back from the road, tucked behind high hedges or front gardens full of the dark, looming shapes of shrubs and trees. In most windows the curtains were drawn and little light reached the deserted street.

'I know where you are.'

Zaki froze. The voice was unmistakable. It was infused with the same cold venom with which she had spoken after she had pulled him from the cave. The girl! But where was she? Zaki glanced frantically up and down the dark street. Had she followed him? How? Or had she been lying in wait for him? What was she going to do to him?

'I don't need to follow you.'

Zaki shrank back into a garden hedge, but its prickly surface felt too insubstantial to offer real protection. Zaki's mind conjured up a shadowy form couching behind the hedge.

Where is she, he thought, *where is she?*

She gave a chill little laugh. 'Yes, where am I?'

He jumped. She seemed to be right beside him. Had he spoken his thoughts aloud? No – then she knew what he was thinking! How could that be possible? Zaki kept completely still, listening, but his mind refused to stay quiet for long. *What do I do now?* he thought.

'You could start by giving back what you've stolen,' came the sharp reply.

The bracelet! Of course, she was after the bracelet.

'All right,' he said aloud, 'All right, I didn't mean to take it. I just put it on. I was just looking at it, and then I forgot. You can have it back. I haven't done any harm.'

'You have no idea how much harm you have done!'

What did she mean? What harm? If only he could see her.

'You really don't understand, do you.' It was more of a statement than a question, but he answered it anyway.

'No, I don't!' He was tired. He was confused.

'Look around. Can you see me?'

'No,' he said, 'but it's dark.'

108

'You can't see me, because I'm not there.'

Not there? What did she mean? He was talking to her, for goodness' sake!

'Work it out for yourself.'

It made no sense unless . . . the bracelets – she had one, he had one – they could connect – it was like telepathy. No. Impossible! But he was wearing one of the bracelets, maybe if she was wearing the other one then she could hear what he was thinking.

'Good . . . good,' she mocked, 'you're not completely stupid.'

Suddenly he felt annoyed. He pulled the bracelet off his arm and laid it carefully at his feet. There, now he could think in peace without her listening in. He waited to see if he were right. Yes, the voice was gone. He took his time deciding what he wanted to say. It gave him some satisfaction to know that he could cut her off. It was like hanging up the phone on an annoying caller. When he was ready, he picked up the bracelet and slid it back on to his left arm. Of course, he didn't need to say anything out loud; all he needed to do was think. He understood that now. *Tell me where to meet you, and I'll bring you back the bracelet.* He thought the words very clearly.

'No!' There was an edge of panic to her reply and he couldn't help glancing round, it seemed so loud, as though she had shouted in his ear. It was hard to believe all this was happening inside his head.

'No,' her voice repeated, 'you mustn't, mustn't, mustn't come near me. Do you understand?'

No, he thought back angrily, *I don't understand.*

'Perhaps you are stupid after all.'

I am trying to help, thought Zaki.

'Well, don't. I will decide what to do, then I will let you know.'

How?

But instead of her reply, another voice broke in – a deep, unearthly growl, like the grinding of boulders upon boulders at the base of a slowly moving glacier, a voice that ground out the single word, a name – 'Rhiannon!' – and again, 'Rhi-a-nn-o-n!' If the dead could speak, this, surely, was how they would sound. A voice that made Zaki's blood freeze and every hair on his body stand on end.

Then the girl's voice came again, full of fear and urgency, 'Take off the bracelet! Take off the bracelet! Do it now!'

Zaki did not wait to ask why. He never wanted to hear that terrible voice again. He tore the bracelet from his arm. His instinct was to fling it as far from him as possible, but he held it at arm's length until his fear and panic had subsided, and then placed it on the ground between his feet.

All he could hear was his own rapid breathing and the hammering of his heart. The voices were silent.

Something had used him; something that spoke out of another time and place had used his mind to reach the girl, and whatever it was, she was very much afraid of it.

Gingerly, he picked up the bracelet and put it in his pocket. He waited – there were no voices. It seemed he must be wearing the bracelet, and not simply carrying it,

110

for the girl – Rhiannon – and her tormentor to have access to his mind.

Zaki glanced around, his imagination conjuring monsters out of the dark shapes of the surrounding bushes. He was frozen to the spot, terror gnawing like a rat at his intestines.

The street was still empty. He prayed someone would come.

After what seemed hours, a car reversed out of a nearby driveway. Its headlights swept across Zaki as it turned and briefly illuminated the street ahead of him. There was the scrunch of footsteps on gravel as a man and woman came down the driveway to exchange good-byes with the driver of the car. The sudden light, the sound of cheerful voices and the presence of other people going about their normal lives broke the spell and gave Zaki the courage to hurry towards the safe familiarity of home.

The girl knew he had the bracelet; had she also noticed that one of the logbooks was missing? The logbook! Where was it? He had it when he left the boat shed, he was certain of that. He'd carried it as far as Grandad's. Had he left in the cottage? No – he'd picked it up again. The car. He'd left it in the car. He'd have to telephone Grandad in the morning – ask him to look after the 'school project' and hope he didn't take a closer look at it.

CHAPTER 10

Michael was quiet at breakfast and the silence continued during the walk to school. The air outside was cold and a pale sun shone through a fine white mist. This was not the heavy, wet sea fog that rolled up the estuary and over the town like a slow-motion wave in summer, fog with droplets so big you could see them blowing past your face; this was hazy autumn mist that smelt of wood smoke and damp leaves. With the chill from the air, a gentle sadness crept through Zaki's body, and his muscles tightened, knowing that summer was over. Even the comforting warmth of the sun that reached down to him through the mist couldn't banish the unhappy realisation that the outdoor life of the warmer months would soon be replaced by the indoor activities of winter. He envied his grandad whose link to the sea remained unbroken throughout the year; who woke every morning to a view of the estuary, walked down the steep steps, across the narrow lane and into his boat shed to spend every day building and repairing boats.

* * *

Zaki looked up at his brother walking beside him. Michael's guitar was slung over his right shoulder and one strap of his rucksack over his left.

'You've brought your guitar,' said Zaki, knowing he was stating the obvious but wanting, somehow, to get his brother talking.

'Yeah,' said Michael.

'Are you rehearsing?'

'Yeah,' said Michael.

'Got any gigs?'

'Yeah.'

They walked on in silence.

'Where are you going to play? What's the gig, I mean? asked Zaki in a last attempt to get his brother to open up.

'Hallowe'en,' said Michael.

'At the school party?'

'Yeah,' said Michael.

'Brilliant!'

Michael added nothing further and Zaki couldn't understand why his brother seemed so morose. The Hallowe'en party was a big deal at the school, a night that everyone looked forward to. To be the chosen band was really something! This knowledge, that his big brother and his band would be the stars of the party, made Zaki feel slightly better disposed towards school and a little less apprehensive about returning there after his disastrous first day. He wondered what sort of reception he would get this morning. He knew his classmates would pester him for answers and he had already decided he would simply say the hawk had nothing to do with

113

him and he had no idea how it got into the classroom. But what about Mrs Palmer? How would she treat him? And naturally, he was anxious to talk to Anusha.

He had telephoned his grandad first thing that morning and asked him to look after the 'school project'. Now he wanted to fix a time with Anusha when they could look at the logbook together and he needed to tell her about the bracelet and the voices. The memory of that second, monstrous voice sent a shudder through him and he couldn't help, even now, in the light of day, glancing round in case, by the very act of thinking of it, he might summon up the being that had spoken the girl's name and its awful shape would emerge from the morning mist.

In fact, the school day went better than Zaki had feared. There was the anticipated initial rush of questions, but as he steadfastly refused to admit to any connection with the bird, his interrogators lost interest and went off to torment easier prey. Mrs Palmer studiously ignored him throughout English and on the one occasion when he looked up from his work and caught her looking in his direction, she quickly looked away and busied herself with the papers on her desk.

When morning break came, Zaki and Anusha hung back as everyone else filed out of the classroom. They both looked up at the rear wall of the room.

'It's a different poster,' said Anusha. 'Was one about not eating chips, and that.'

'I know,' said Zaki.

114

There was a glossy new poster extolling the virtues of Britain's regional cheeses.

'Cheesy,' said Anusha.

'Ha, ha,' said Zaki.

'So, do you think it was the poster that turned into the bird?'

It did seem crazy, thought Zaki, but the poster had vanished the moment the bird appeared.

'But that's mad, isn't it!' protested Anusha. Posters don't turn into birds. How can a poster turn into a bird?'

'Listen,' said Zaki, 'there's something I haven't told you.'

Zaki glanced at the classroom door to make certain no one was about to disturb them. He removed the bracelet from his pocket and laid it on the desk between them.

'What's that?' Anusha reached to pick it up.

Quickly, Zaki caught her hand. 'Better not touch it.'

'What? Why not?'

'It has special powers.'

'You're kidding me!'

Anusha crouched down and examined the bracelet without touching it.

'You should show this to my dad. I'm pretty sure it's Indian. Where did you get it?'

Zaki hesitated and Anusha read the guilt in his eyes. Her own eyes flashed with sudden anger. 'You took it, didn't you! It was on the boat and you took it. That's why you wanted to get on to that boat! You wanted to steal this bracelet! What have you dragged me into? I'm not a thief!'

'It's not like that,' pleaded Zaki. 'I didn't mean to take it. That's not why I got on to her boat. But I'd seen the bracelet before. It was in the cave. She took it off me when she rescued me. When I saw it again on the boat, I picked it up and, in all the panic, I forgot to put it back.'

'You forgot.'

'Yeah. It's the truth.'

Her dark eyes regarded him coolly. 'So what does it do?'

'There are two of them – two bracelets, identical. She's got one and I've got one. And if we're each wearing one, she knows what I'm thinking.'

He told Anusha about what had happened after Grandad had dropped him off, about being able to talk to the girl and about the terrible voice that seemed to call the girl's name.

'But you weren't wearing the bracelet yesterday in class when the hawk appeared. You didn't nick it until we were on *Curlew*.'

'I know – but I put it on in the cave. That must have been how she knew I was there. That's how she knew I needed rescuing – maybe once you've worn it – I don't know – it changes you somehow.'

Zaki picked up the bracelet and returned it to the safety of his pocket.

'You were telling us about the bird in your dream when the hawk appeared.'

'You think I sort of dreamt it up?'

'Something like that. Look, I've got an idea. My dad's got a camcorder – perhaps I could film you while you

116

retell that dream. If it happens again, we'll have a recording – we'll have proof.'

'Proof? What for? I mean, for who?'

'I don't know. It's just an idea. I'll bring the camera tomorrow.'

They had a change of classroom after break, so they began to gather up their belongings.

'When shall we meet to look at the logbook?' Zaki asked, keen that it should be soon.

'I've got a violin lesson after school today.'

'How about tomorrow after school?'

'Yeah, fine. Come on, we'll be late for maths.' And Anusha headed for the door.

Zaki's shoulder injury forced him to do everything one-handed. Once he had finally gathered his things together, he hurried to catch up with Anusha. In his haste, he blundered into Mrs Palmer in the doorway, who was returning to the room. The shock of the collision sent stabbing, blinding pain shooting out from his cracked collarbone. He let out a cry and dropped everything he was carrying. He leant against the doorframe, feeling faint.

'You . . . !' Exploded Mrs Palmer. But then, seeing he was hurt, she continued more gently. 'Is it your shoulder?'

Zaki nodded.

'You'd better come and sit down.' She led him across to sit on the chair beside her desk and then gathered up his dropped books.

'I'm not sure you should be at school if it's that bad.

Do you want us to call your mum?'

'I'll be OK in a minute,' said Zaki. *Not much point calling my mum anyway*, he thought.

On the desk was the book of myths from which Mrs Palmer had been reading before the incident with the hawk.

'That story you read us . . .' began Zaki.

'Taliesin and Ceridwen?

'Where's it from?'

'Well, the version in here,' she flipped the book's pages, 'is from Wales, but, as I explained to the class' – she paused – 'after you left us, shapeshifting is a theme found in stories from all parts of the world.'

'Shapeshifting,' repeated Zaki.

Mrs Palmer nodded.

'Do you think it might – you know, shapeshifting – sometimes really happen?' he asked and then wished he hadn't, thinking it sounded a pretty stupid question. To his surprise, rather than brushing his question aside, Mrs Palmer looked thoughtful.

'In some ways, yes. The shamans, the holy men and women of many societies, go on spiritual journeys during which they become birds and animals. Poets inhabit the minds and bodies of others in order to write.'

'I meant . . .'

'I know what you were really asking. Can people actually change into animals? I doubt it,' she said, with a slightly patronising little laugh. 'Although some children I know wouldn't have to change very much.'

Zaki, who was beginning to think that, perhaps, Mrs

118

Palmer was all right after all, decided that probably she wasn't.

Just then the bell went for the end of break.

'Why don't you borrow the book?' suggested Mrs Palmer, adding the book of myths to Zaki's pile. 'You could do a project for me on shamanism and shapeshifting. You'll probably find plenty about it on the internet.

Zaki stood up and Mrs Palmer loaded the books on to his good arm.

'Hope your shoulder feels better.'

'It's OK now, thanks,' said Zaki, although it wasn't.

There was one big plus to having an injured shoulder – it gave Zaki the perfect excuse for not joining Craig and his mates for a kick-about in the park after school and left him free to catch the 3.45 bus to Salcombe. All day, he'd been thinking about the logbook and what it might contain, and he was anxious to get it back from Grandad. He was disappointed that Anusha couldn't come with him. She was part of this now. They were doing this together. But he didn't want to wait until tomorrow before opening the log.

CHAPTER 11

'If you're wondering where your package is,' said Grandad, 'it's by the kettle.'

Zaki pushed Jenna out of the way and crossed the boat shed. The logbook was still in the carrier bag but there was no way of telling if his grandfather had taken a look at it.

'Glad you've popped round, I could do with a hand.'

'Sure. What needs doing?' asked Zaki enthusiastically, always eager for the opportunity to work with his grandfather.

The old man was taking the next plank for the boat's hull out of the steam box where it had been softening.

'Help me clamp this one up for starters.'

The plank had to be clamped into position while it was still hot and flexible to ensure a perfect fit. Grandad made minute adjustments to the plank's position until he was satisfied and then the clamps were tightened.

'Fetch us over them copper nails.'

They worked steadily along the length of the new plank, fastening it to the one below. The tide was in and the sound of waves lapping against the slipway could be heard in the pauses between the tap-tap-tappings of Grandad's hammer. The rhythm of the work, the wood and varnish smells of the workshop, the sound of the waves, his grandfather's proximity, patient, unhurried, calmed Zaki, and soon he was concentrating entirely on what they were doing. So it came as a jolt when Grandad rested his hammer and asked, 'Your dad all right, is he?'

Zaki felt momentarily disorientated. Dad? He'd been a bit grumpy recently – was out a lot – he seemed a bit worried about something, but that wasn't unusual. Was he all right?

'I dunno – I guess so.'

Grandad went 'Hmmm, hmmm, hm,' picked up the next nail but then paused.

'Never talks about buildin' that boat?'

'What do you mean?' asked Zaki.

'Have you forgot why you all came back down 'ere from London? You were goin' to build a boat but I haven't heard much mention of it lately.'

It was true; that had been the plan. Zaki remembered the cold, winter morning in the London house, that seemed so long ago now, when his father gleefully announced they were moving back to Devon. At first, Michael had objected, said he 'didn't want to live in some hick town in the sticks!', had threatened to run away. But his parents' enthusiasm had been overwhelming; they were like a couple of kids, laughing every time they looked at each other, like they'd just decided to do something truly wicked. They were going to live by the sea – build a beautiful, big, wooden boat, then they were all going to sail around the world together!

He and Michael had climbed into their parents' bed and they had all talked and talked. His father had fetched breakfast on a tray and they had filled the bed with toast crumbs while they discussed the best time to cross the Atlantic and looked at pictures of anchorages with turquoise water and perfect, white-sand beaches in the Caribbean, while a fine drizzle fell from the grey London sky outside the bedroom window. It was such a brave, wonderful, frightening yet exciting plan. What had happened to it?

At first, after the move from London, Grandad would come over on Sunday afternoons and boat plans would be spread out on the kitchen table to be discussed. Lists of ropes, rigging, deck fittings, navigation equipment and engine parts were written, and cabin layouts and sail plans drawn and redrawn on sheet after sheet of paper. Zaki pictured his mother dressed in one of his father's old sweaters, her arms around his father, her chin resting on his shoulder, as they both leant over to examine Grandad's latest sketch. His parents looked so happy, their eyes bright and full of life. At last, all agreed they had designed the perfect long-distance cruising yacht and they began combing the small ads and the boat jumble sales for the equipment on their lists. It didn't have to be new, so long as it was in good order, and there were family outings to inspect second-hand anchors and unwanted bilge pumps. Each purchase, it seemed at the time to Zaki, brought them closer to the day when they would sail off to explore the world, maybe discover paradise. What happened?

The boat was never built. Instead, his father took to renovating houses. The boat was mentioned less and less often and 'When we build the boat' became 'If we build the boat' until, eventually, only Zaki's mother seemed to believe it could ever happen, and then even she stopped talking about it. And then she went to Switzerland. It would never happen now. Why was his grandad bringing it up? It was like poking at a bruise to see if it still hurt.

'Mortal shame,' muttered Grandad. 'Your dad always dreamt of sailin' round the world, ever since he was your age.'

'I don't think he's got enough money to build the boat now,' said Zaki.

'We could always sell this place. Be worth a bit these days to a developer.'

'No!' cried Zaki, feeling shock and horror. 'You mustn't! Please don't. Oh, please, Grandad, you mustn't ever, ever sell this place!'

The boat shed was the never-changing, still centre of Zaki's universe; his refuge. Destroy the centre and everything would be set adrift.

'Hey now,' said Grandad gently, 'Hey, I only said we could – never said we would. I'll tell you what – we'll finish up 'ere and then have a cup o' tea. You can tell me all about that school project of yours.'

'I should be getting home,' said Zaki, anxious now to be gone before his grandfather became any more interested in the contents of the carrier bag by the kettle, and before there was any more talk of selling the boat shed.

'I can run you home.'

'That's OK, thanks, Grandad, I can take the bus.'

'Suit yourself.'

They worked on in silence until they finished fixing the plank and then, after retrieving the logbook, Zaki said his goodbyes to Grandad and Jenna and set off to catch the bus back to Kingsbridge. As he left the boat shed, a grey cat scampered away down the narrow lane.

CHAPTER 12

Was his imagination playing tricks on him? All the way from the bus station by Kingsbridge harbour to Moor Lane, Zaki had the distinct feeling that there was someone or something behind him, like a slight pressure in the centre of his back, a tension between his shoulder blades. Sometimes when he turned his head he thought he detected the swift movement of a shadowy form slipping beyond the periphery of his vision. When he reached the main shopping street he loitered in front of shop windows, trying to use their reflective surfaces to catch sight of his pursuer. People passed by. Outside the chemist a young woman with a baby in a pushchair, wondering what could be so interesting, stopped to stare with him into the window, saw nothing out of the ordinary, gave him a puzzled look, shrugged and moved on.

As he entered the quiet residential streets behind the busy thoroughfare, Zaki began to walk more quickly. The thought struck him that, if Anusha were right, and he could dream things into existence, then he might, right now, be dreaming up a monster that would burst through into the real world at any moment. He tried to empty his mind but it was hopeless; the more he tried to keep his mind blank the more he saw shapes and shadows from the corners of his eyes. He tried to think about sailing *Morveren*, but that only carried his thoughts to the cave. He made himself concentrate on his grandfather's workshop, anchoring his mind by picturing the old man patiently shaping planks for the hull of the little boat. Even then, the sense of being followed never left him.

It was a relief to reach his own front garden. He walked down the narrow passage between the side of the house and the garden fence, but as he approached the back door he stopped. He could hear raised voices. It was Michael in the kitchen and he was shouting . . . Now he heard his father, not shouting, but speaking loudly and firmly . . . Then Michael again. What was it about? What were they saying? It was not unusual for his brother and father to argue, particularly recently, but not like this, not shouting. Zaki remained rooted to the spot where the sound of the voices had stopped him, not daring to take another step; it was as if beyond that point lay thin ice that could not be trusted to take his weight, that might crack and swallow him.

'You lied! You lied!' Michael's voice was on the edge of tears.

'That's not true, Michael.'

'Yes it is! It is!'

'Michael, listen . . .'

'Why? Why should I? Why should I believe anything

you tell me?'

'Michael . . .'

'You lied!'

'Michael, this isn't helping.'

'I don't care!

'Michael, please . . .'

'I hate you!

'Michael, listen to me . . .'

Zaki began to retreat. He didn't want to hear those voices, those words. One step back and then another and another and another, as though he could rewind time, creep back from this moment and then edge around it, reach the future by a different route. He found himself in the passage between the house and the fence. He pushed his back against the wall, pushed his head hard against it; by only moving his eyes he could see to the left and right. There was nobody in sight. The tarry smell of creosote spread across through the evening air from the high wooden fence that screened him from the world. He waited. He could only hear the usual neighbourhood sounds; birds twittered, someone strimmed weeds, distant traffic.

He began to count. 'When I reach a hundred,' he told himself, 'I'll go round.' He reached one hundred and decided to go on to one hundred and fifty. One hundred and fifty came and went and he counted on, one number following another like links in an endless chain running through his head. He counted until he heard the front door slam and his father calling after his brother. He listened. He didn't hear the front door reopen and close again. Had they both gone out? He crept around to the back door and opened it very carefully. All was quiet in the house, but some new thing had been released, something that now lurked in the corners, lurked in the dark spaces behind the furniture, something that made the air in the house more difficult to breath. Zaki stood just inside the kitchen door and examined the room, examined the mundane, household objects that, by being abandoned, had taken on a sinister significance; a partly chopped onion and a knife on the chopping board, the cutlery draw left open, potatoes boiling in a pan of water on the cooker, building plans for Number 43 spread out on the kitchen table. There was nothing to explain the source of the argument. Zaki took the knife from the chopping board and prodded the potatoes. They seemed to be cooked. Should he take them off? He slid the pan off the ring and turned off the cooker. Now what? Moving carefully, as though through a minefield, he made his way upstairs.

The door to his brother's room was open. Michael's guitar lay across his rumpled bed. His phone was in the middle of the floor along with his school sweatshirt and trousers and his rucksack. Zaki crossed the room and sat on the bed. He brushed a fingernail across the guitar strings, needing a noise to fill the silence but wanting above anything to hear the cheery sound of his brother's teasing banter. He was hungry but he didn't want to return to that unnaturally empty kitchen.

He was still sitting on the bed when he heard the front door open and close and his father's footsteps in the hall.

He listened – his father had definitely returned alone and he judged that he was now back in the kitchen.

Eight o'clock came and went. Hunger drove Zaki downstairs. It was growing dark in the house and the light was on in the kitchen, it streamed out through the door into the unlit hall. Zaki's father was leaning over the kitchen table, his hands resting on either side of the spread-out plans, his head hung down between his raised shoulders. Zaki stood in the doorway and waited for his father to notice him. After what seemed a long time, his father looked up. Catching sight of Zaki, he quickly straightened and tried, with a smile, to hide the worry on his face, but it continued to hover around his eyes.

'I took the potatoes off. I think they're cooked,' said Zaki to break the silence.

'Oh, yes. I expect they are. Sorry, I forgot about them.'

'I'm a bit hungry,' Zaki ventured.

'Yes,' his father said, looking around the kitchen in a vague sort of way as if hoping a meal might have materialised while he was out. 'Yes, I . . . I got distracted. There's a problem with one of the gullies on the roof.' He tapped the plans with a finger. 'What about mashed potato and some beans?'

'Fine,' said Zaki and, when his father continued to stare at the plans, he added 'Do you want me to mash the potatoes?'

'Um – yes, if you could. I'll do you some beans.'

Zaki mashed the potatoes while his father opened a tin of beans and tipped them into a saucepan.

'Where's Michael?' asked Zaki without looking up

129

from his mashing.

'He's gone to practise with his band,' his father replied after only the slightest pause.

Zaki pictured the guitar lying on Michael's bed. Whatever the truth was, his father was hiding it. Of course, his father didn't know that he had overheard the argument.

When the potatoes looked thoroughly mashed, Zaki got himself a plate from the cupboard.

'Are you going to have some?' he asked his father, reaching for a second plate.

'No, I'll have something later.' His father folded the plans to make space for Zaki on the kitchen table. He spooned beans on to Zaki's plate. The sauce ran around the mound of mashed potato, creating an island in a steaming sea. Zaki took a fork from the drawer and then sat at the table. His father hesitated before gathering up the plans and turning to leave the room.

'Can we phone Mum?' Zaki asked quickly before his father could get through the door.

For a moment his father didn't answer. In that moment, Zaki was afraid. Afraid his father would find a reason to say no; afraid he would be denied the sound of his mother's voice. He needed to hear her.

His father half turned, the smile that didn't reach his eyes, again on his face. 'Yes, if you like,' he said, the tone of voice hinting that there was something unreasonable in the request. 'I spoke to her earlier today. She knows about your shoulder.'

'I'd still like to talk to her.'

'Yeah – OK.' His father returned to the table and wrote the number with its long, international dialling code on a scrap of paper. 'You can call her when you finish your tea.'

Left alone, Zaki quickly shovelled beans and potato into his mouth. The beans were too hot, but the potato was stone cold. Mixed together they became an edible temperature.

As soon as his plate was empty, Zaki took the scrap of paper to the phone and carefully keyed in the numbers. He listened to the tone. Was it engaged or was it ringing? 'Bee . . . Bee . . . Bee . . .' Why did Swiss phones have to ring differently?

'Guten Tag. Bitte sehr?' said the woman who answered the phone.

'Mum?' Zaki asked a little cautiously, afraid he might have misdialled.

'Hello, sweetheart.' His mother's voice switched into the cheery sounds he was so used to. 'I heard about your poor shoulder. Does it hurt a lot?'

'It's not *too* bad,' Zaki replied with careful emphasis, so that his mother would know that he was suffering terribly but was being brave.

'How did you do it? Dad said you fell on a rock. Is that right?'

'It's a long story.'

'Well, you will be careful now, won't you? Don't go falling out of a tree or something. You don't want to make it worse.'

There was a pause.

'Are *you* all right, Mum?' Zaki asked, not quite knowing why.

'Of course I am! I'm fine. I've been busy, but I'm fine.' Then his mother chatted on about places she'd been and things she'd seen. Zaki listened, wanting her to keep talking and talking so that he could go on listening to the reassuring sound of her voice; he didn't really listen to the words, he just wanted to know that she was there.

'But I almost forgot!' she exclaimed, breaking off. 'You started your new school this week. How are you getting on?'

So his father hadn't told her about the business with the hawk. 'I'll tell you all about it when you come home,' he said.

There was another pause. Zaki waited, willing her to say when that would be, longing to ask the direct question – 'When are you coming back?' – but unwilling to risk the disappointment of hearing her say 'I don't know,' or 'Soon, but I'm not sure when,' or 'I'll tell you as soon as I know.'

'Well . . .' said his mother after a bit, 'I suppose I'd better be getting on.'

Zaki's heart sank. 'Do you want to talk to Dad?'

'I spoke to him earlier. Is Michael around?'

'He's out.'

'Practising with his band, I suppose?'

'I don't know.'

'I hope he's not letting it distract him from his school-work. But I'm sure your dad wouldn't let that happen.'

Could that have been what the argument had been

about? Zaki wondered. No, surely not.

'Send your brother a big hug from me, won't you,' said his mother. 'It's all right, I won't ask you to kiss him from me.'

They both laughed.

'How's Grandad?'

'He's fine. He's got a new cat.'

'Grandad doesn't like cats!'

'He only pretends he doesn't. Anyway, it's not really his cat, but he gives it milk.'

'What does Jenna think?'

'She's jealous.'

'I'm not surprised.'

Zaki tried to think of things to say that would prolong the conversation but now his mother was saying goodbye, explaining she was going out, that she had to hurry, and as soon as he managed to mumble his good-byes the phone went dead and she was gone.

Zaki sat looking at the phone. He reran the conversa-tion in his head, holding on to the faint echo of his mother's laugh. He pictured her leaning against the kitchen counter, a mug of tea cradled between both hands, laughing. It was the sort of laugh that made you smile no matter how you were feeling. Whenever Zaki thought about his mother, her laughter was the thing he could remember most clearly. Then he realised some-thing he hadn't thought about – before she left for Switzerland, she had stopped laughing. It had been gradual. When had it started? When they moved to Moor Lane? He couldn't say for certain, but now that he thought about it he couldn't remember her laughing in the months before she left. Did she stop laughing because she was going to Switzerland, or did she go to Switzerland because she had stopped laughing? she seemed to be happy now. Had they made her unhappy? Zaki wanted to ask her what they had done. He put his hand on the telephone – but she was going out, she wouldn't be there. He folded the scrap of paper with her number on it and put it in his pocket.

Zaki could hear the sound of the television in the living room. His father would be watching the news. He put his dirty dinner plate in the dishwasher before leaving the kitchen. Passing the living-room doorway, Zaki saw his father sitting in one of the armchairs; the television was on but his father was staring at the window. Zaki continued on to his bedroom, where he took his mother's telephone number from his pocket and hid it in his sock drawer, as if it were something he shouldn't have.

That night Zaki tried to stay awake, listening for the sound of his brother returning, but the events of the day had worn him out and he drifted into a troubled sleep. He was in the cave again – the skeleton had gone and in its place, on the rock ledge, crouched a dark, shadowy form. It was growing. Each time he took a breath, the thing on the ledge got bigger. He tried not to breathe but he couldn't hold his breath for ever. It would fill the cave. It would suffocate him! He wanted to escape, but he couldn't move – couldn't turn his back on that thing on the ledge. He woke. The house was quiet. He was sure the dark thing from his dream was somewhere in the room. Perhaps he was still dreaming.

CHAPTER 13

Breakfast the next morning was eaten in almost total silence. Michael had returned sometime in the night from wherever he had been and was up and dressed uncharacteristically early. Normally, Zaki would have demanded to know what his brother had been doing, maybe made some joke about a secret girlfriend, but Michael never once allowed their eyes to meet, closing himself off behind a barrier of silent hostility.

'If you're ready to go, I'll drop you at school,' their father offered. 'I've got to go that way, I need some things from the builders' merchant.'

'Thanks, Dad,' said Zaki, grateful that someone had broken the awful silence and had driven the shadows back into the corners. He raced upstairs to get his school things. He picked up the bracelet and put it in his pocket; they must ask Anusha's father this afternoon if he had any idea where it was from. Even the thought of facing Mrs Palmer was better than spending any more time in this house.

The three of them climbed into the front of the van, Zaki in the middle. 'I suppose you'll want the usual rubbish,' said their father, selecting Radio 1. Michael leant across in front of Zaki and turned the radio off.

'Oh, for heaven's sake, ease up, will you, Michael!' snapped their father. But Michael maintained his stony silence as they reversed out of the drive and headed into town.

'Is it OK if I go to a friend's place after school?' Zaki asked. He had the logbook in his rucksack. They could look at it at Anusha's house.

'Sure. Are you going to Craig's?'

'No – someone you don't know.'

'A new friend – good – what's his name?'

'Anusha,' said Zaki. 'And it's a girl.' Zaki glanced at his brother, expecting some quip, but there was no reaction.

'Fine,' his father said. 'Will you be home for tea?'

'Probably.'

'Well, call me if you're going to be late.'

Feeling that the atmosphere in the van had lightened, Zaki decided to try to penetrate his brother's brooding silence. 'I spoke to Mum last night,' he said brightly. Michael turned slowly to look at him, and that's when Zaki saw the terrible darkness behind his brother's eyes and he shivered, even though it was hot in the van's crowded cab.

'What did she say?' Michael asked.

'Just what she's been doing, and that,' said Zaki.

'Nothing else?'

'No.' Zaki waited for his brother to say more. 'Why?'

A sudden sense of dread, a fear of something he didn't know that he should know, gripped Zaki.

'So she didn't say she wasn't coming home?'

The words circled around Zaki's head but his mind refused to let them enter.

'What?' Zaki said.

'Michael!' growled his father.

'She's not coming home,' Michael repeated.

His father braked hard and swung the van to the side of the road. There was an angry blast from the horn of the car behind as its driver, taken by surprise, had to swerve to pass them.

'Michael, it's not as simple as that,' he heard his father say, but Michael's words had broken through and were now imbedded deep inside Zaki like a barbed hook in the gut of a fish.

'It seems pretty simple to me,' said Michael.

'Michael . . . listen – your mother and I need some time – that's all. Nothing's settled, nothing's definite.'

'You're splitting up! Admit it. Just admit it! Don't you think we deserve to know?'

'Dad, is this true?' Zaki managed to force the words out, willing his father to deny it.

Michael opened the passenger door and got out. Slamming the door shut, he set off down the road on foot. His father lowered his head to rest it on the steering wheel as though utterly exhausted, then, taking a deep breath, straightened and sat back.

'Zaki, I'm really sorry,' he said. 'We should have talked to you.'

Zaki didn't think he was crying, his body was quite still, but the tears were pouring down his face, dripping off his chin into his lap. He picked up his rucksack from the floor by his feet, opened the van door and followed after his brother. His father made no move to stop him, but remained sitting in the parked van.

Michael was walking fast. At first Zaki wanted to run and catch him up, but it was as though the earth's gravity had suddenly doubled, dragging him down, making his limbs heavy, and it was all he could do to keep walking. The gap between Zaki and Michael steadily grew wider and wider until eventually Michael was no longer in sight.

When Zaki reached the intersection at the bottom of the hill he should have continued around to the right towards school but he felt an overpowering urge to be alone, and he turned left instead, taking the road that led out of town. He walked past the local moorings. The tide was out and the little motorboats and day-sailors were sitting on the mud, leaning at drunken angles while gulls and ducks searched the silt around them for anything edible. He continued on past the waterside apartments and pubs and then up a small rise, away from the harbour through the scatter of suburban houses on the outskirts of Kingsbridge. He hadn't meant to skip school; the thought that that was what he was doing hardly entered his head. It took all his concentration to walk steady and upright in a world that had been knocked off kilter. Surrounded by the familiar, he felt totally lost.

After walking for a further quarter of an hour, Zaki reached the top of the rise and the road began to drop back down to the water. The downward slope kept Zaki moving forward, but when he came to the long, low stone bridge with its many arches that carries the road across a branch of the estuary he hesitated. Should he continue on across the bridge? Where was he going, anyway?

To the right of the road a short flight of steps led down to a large old landing stage, evidence of the days when fast fruit schooners traded between Salcombe, the Bahamas, the Mediterranean and the Azores. Now, local people used the stage to store dinghies and yacht tenders. Zaki and Michael had sometimes come here to fish. Being early on a weekday, there were few people about. Zaki descended the steps and sat on the big rough-cut stone blocks that formed the edge of the landing stage and stared out across the water. A woman walking a small dog came up the slipway from the water's edge. The dog trotted around sniffing busily at tufts of grass and weeds. The woman paused near Zaki. 'Shouldn't you be in school?' she asked. Zaki ignored her. The woman waited, but when Zaki continued to stare into space she tut-tutted, then called her dog and climbed the steps up to the road.

A hole was opening up in Zaki's stomach, a hopeless, aching emptiness. He had a desperate longing to be anywhere in time except in this moment.

A herring gull alighted a few metres from where Zaki sat. It folded it wings, shaking the feathers to settle them into place. Zaki felt a rising irritation at this new invasion of his solitude, but when he turned to look at the bird his attention was trapped by the glitter of the gull's eye. He began to gather together some part of himself – something that wasn't part of his body. He detached this inner self until he was free from physical sensation, and then, riding on a breath, he fled from his body into the body of the gull; fled the aching emptiness and the desperate feeling of loss. Escaped, for a time at least, from his brother's words.

He stretched his wings, bent his legs slightly for the take-off spring, then launched himself into space. As he climbed upward, wing beat by wing beat, he saw his human self still sitting on the stone edge of the landing stage. He flew fast down the estuary, drawn by the emptiness of the open sea and the desire to be lost among the endless rolling waves.

He passed over lines of boats moored bow to stern, then over the clusters of larger craft on swinging moorings all turning together like compass needles to face the incoming tide. Soon he was flying past the wind-carved, rocky outcrops of Bolt Head and when other gulls called from the cliffs his own gull's voice cried back, a cry that came from another time, from the time before speech, a cry of pure loneliness. He flew on. 'Out to sea, out to sea,' beat his wings, keeping on until the land dropped away from sight behind him. He allowed his gull-nature to take over and lost himself in the thrilling pleasure of flying; gliding just above the water, dipping one wing so the tip brushed the surface, wheeling round then sliding down, down into the deep, green hollows between waves, there to swoop up, up again over the crest of the advancing swell. He had no past or future, just the exhilarating sensation of flying.

He had no sense of time passing, but eventually the solitude of the ocean that had drawn him out to sea drove him back to the shore. Loneliness swept him like the flood tide back up the estuary to the landing stage where he had left his human self.

Circling, he looked down and was shocked to see that, rather than sitting lifelessly staring, his body was standing, moving, gesturing, talking. It had an independent life, an independent will. While his will was guiding the body of the gull, some other force was inhabiting his body, directing it, animating it. What? Who? Panic gripped him. Could his life somehow continue without him? He wanted desperately to be reunited with his human self, but he was shut out. No longer needed.

Now he saw that there was someone else on the landing stage, a girl. It was Anusha and she was shouting. He flew lower to hear what she was saying.

'What's wrong with you? What's wrong with you?' she was screaming.

She was keeping her distance, slightly crouched as if ready to run. As he watched, the two figures moved around each other like fighters in a boxing ring.

He heard his own voice say, 'Come here. I'm not going to hurt you,' and Anusha say, 'No, stay away from me!'

What had happened? What was going on? What had he done to her? He felt guilt, horror; like a sleepwalker who wakes to find he has committed some awful crime in his sleep. This was worse, because he was condemned to watch himself menacing his friend with no power to stop what was happening. He was certain also that Anusha could not possibly know that his human body was not under his control.

Then he saw Anusha stumble, tripping on the uneven stonework, and he saw his body bending, heaving up a jagged rock with both hands, pausing for a split second to balance the rock, then rushing at Anusha with a triumphant yell. He dived, shrieking, beating his wings in the face of Anusha's attacker, driving him back, forcing him to drop the stone. He was fighting against himself, but in that nightmare moment all he knew was that he must give Anusha a chance to escape. Eye to eye with his own body, Zaki saw evil looking out, and that evil thing directed the body to seize a piece of broken plank and lash at him, slashing the air so that he was forced to fly out of reach. But he must keep the attacker's attention, not let him go after Anusha. He dived again, aiming for the face, again the plank lashed out, but the bird swerved clear and attacked again and again, forcing a retreat. Back they went towards the edge of the landing stage until Zaki saw a look of horror cross his own face as his body stepped back into empty air and toppled slowly, then fell on to the rocks and shingle below.

Three beats of his powerful wings and Zaki the bird was looking down at his inert body lying stretched out below, one leg in the water, the right arm flung out to the side. Dead or alive? He searched for signs of life. Had he killed the body, or the thing in it? Could one die without killing the other? If his body was dead, what then? What did that mean for him? A short life as a seagull, is that all he had to look forward to? Panic gripped him once more, then all his senses lurched and he seemed to be sliding, falling, plunging through total darkness. The world steadied and he was left with a dizzy nausea, like the feeling at the end of a rollercoaster ride. He slowly sat up, then rolled to one side and vomited. He wiped his mouth with the back of his hand.

His hand! His mouth! He was back in his own body! He examined his hands, touched his legs, felt his face. There was a stinging cut on his cheek where the seagull's beak had found flesh. His head ached. He felt the back of his head. There was no blood, but a lump was starting to rise where his head had struck a stone. He pulled his wet leg out of the water, then tried making small movements. He was bruised and sore, but nothing seemed to be broken. He looked up. Anusha was standing at the edge of the landing stage, looking down. She took a quick step back.

'It's all right. It's me. I mean . . . it's really me,' he said.

Warily, Anusha returned to the edge.

'It wasn't me. Whatever happened, it wasn't me.' He knew he wasn't making much sense but how could he explain? 'I was in the seagull. Something else took over my body. I know it's not possible, but that's what happened. You have to believe me.'

'Stay there,' she called, her voice cold and hard. 'I'll get help.' And she disappeared from view.

'No! Wait! Don't go. Please.'

Zaki waited, hoping she had heard him. She reappeared and cautiously looked down. Zaki felt a wave

144

of relief; somehow he had to make her understand that he hadn't been responsible for his body attacking her.

'I'm not coming down there,' she said flatly.

'Please, Anusha, it's OK now – really – I'm not going to do anything.'

'You just tried to kill me with a great big rock!'

'No – no I didn't.'

'You bloody did! If it hadn't been for that seagull, I'd be dead!'

'I – was – the – seagull! That was me!'

It was hopeless. How could you explain something as crazy as this? But she'd seen the hawk in the classroom, knew that he had made that appear.

'Look,' he struggled to make it sound logical, 'it was like the hawk, only this time I left my body.' He watched her face, watched doubt and distrust losing their grip. 'It really wasn't me that attacked you.'

She took a big breath, lifting her shoulders then dropping them as she huffed the breath out.

'Well, you do sound more like you.'

'Where did the gull go?' asked Zaki.

'I don't know – I didn't see. When you fell over the edge it seemed to hang in mid-air and then it was off.'

'That's when it happened. That's when I went back. I thought I'd killed my own body and I was going to be stuck as a seagull for the rest of my life, and the next I knew, I was back in my body.'

Zaki got shakily to his feet.

'Wait,' called Anusha, 'I'll come and help you.'

Zaki sat back down on a large, flat stone; he still felt

very giddy. Anusha came down the slipway to join him. She stopped a few feet away. Zaki raised his head and tried to smile. Would she trust him?

'You look really rubbish,' she said.

'I feel rubbish.'

'What about your shoulder?'

He hadn't thought about his shoulder, which, in itself, was odd since the fall should have made it worse. He tried it now. There was no pain. In fact he could even lift his arm above his head, something he had been unable to do that morning when he was dressing. He prodded his collarbone. Nothing. It was as though he'd never fractured it.

'It's fixed.'

'How fixed?'

'I don't know how, but it seems to be fixed. It's gone and mended itself.'

'I don't think bones can grow that quickly.'

'This one has. Look.' He waved his arm wildly.

'OK, OK. No need to go crazy. I don't suppose you could have lifted that rock you wanted to brain me with if it had still been broken.'

'I was the seagull, remember?'

'I know, I know – it's just that this swapping bodies stuff is a little difficult to get my head round.'

'How do you think it feels when it's your body?'

Anusha looked thoughtful. 'If you were the seagull, then who was in your body?'

'I don't know.'

She studied him carefully, as you might study a dog

that sometimes bites.

Zaki stopped trying to smile and looked down at his feet.

Anusha swung her rucksack off her shoulder and came and sat beside him on the stone. Now it was Zaki's turn to be puzzled.

'Why are you here?' he asked.

'Because I've decided to help you get cleaned up instead of reporting you for attempted murder!' She took a water bottle and some tissues from her rucksack.

'What I meant was, why aren't you at school? How did you know where I was?'

'Simple – I followed you. Let me see your face.'

'Ow!'

'Don't make a fuss. It's not deep.' She washed the cut on his cheek.

'Followed me from where?'

'The high street. I was on my way to school. I saw you get out of the van. At first I thought I'd catch you up, but then you went the wrong way and I wondered what you were going to do. I brought my dad's camcorder, like I said I would, and I thought if I filmed you and something interesting happened, then we'd have it on tape. I thought it was better if you didn't know I was there. You never looked round so it wasn't difficult.'

She gave Zaki the water bottle so that he could rinse the sick taste out of his mouth.

'When did you start recording?'

'It was hard to do it while I was walking along and trying to keep out of sight, so I waited until you sat down over there and I hid amongst that stack of dinghies.'

'So you've got everything! Me and the gull – all of that?'

'Well, yes, but – it was just an ordinary seagull. It didn't suddenly appear or anything.'

'What about the fight?'

'No, I'd dropped the camera by then. It was the camera that started it. After the seagull flew off the first time I waited and waited – I must have stayed hidden for over an hour, but as nothing really much was happening I stopped hiding and came across to talk to you. You seemed a bit confused, like you didn't quite know who I was.'

'What did I say?'

'Not much. You were in a very strange mood. You called me "maid". I thought that was a bit odd.'

'My grandad calls girls maid. It's proper West Country.'

'Then I showed you the camcorder. I played back what I had recorded and you went mad – said I was trying to steal your secrets – called me a witch!'

'A witch! Wow!'

'I said I didn't come here to be insulted and that I was going. I got halfway to the steps and you grabbed me, tried to get the camcorder off me. We fought – I got away but you kept coming after me and I couldn't get to the steps. I dropped the camera just before you picked up that big rock.'

'I saw the rest.'

'Hmm.' Anusha looked thoughtfully at Zaki.

'What?'

'When you say you were the seagull,' she asked slowly, 'what do you mean, exactly?'

'Well . . . I was sitting up there and the seagull landed next to me. It looked at me and I looked at it and then – whoosh! – I was looking out of its eyes and feeling what it was feeling. I was the seagull! Except I could still think like me. I could choose where to go and what to do. So I flew out to sea.'

'Why out to sea?'

'I wanted to be by myself.'

'But your body stayed here?'

'That's where it gets really weird.' Zaki tried to bring his mind to focus on the problem of how his body could have continued to act once he had left it. And Zaki? Who was Zaki if he wasn't his body? His mind shied away, searching for distractions. There was something very nasty lurking at the bottom of this question and his mind didn't want to look at it.

The tide had crept in and the water was now lapping near their feet. Zaki watched the little ripples covering and uncovering the shingle. As he watched, a small, spiral shell clambered through the pebbles. He knew what it was. He reached down and picked it up.

'Look,' he said, holding up the shell with its occupant for Anusha to see. 'It's a hermit crab. That's not his shell, but he's taken it over and he'll fight anything to keep it.' As Zaki spoke, the tiny crab's legs and pincers appeared from the shell's mouth and the little claw opened and closed as the crab attempted to attack Zaki's finger.

Anusha laughed. 'It's very brave! Can I hold it?' Zaki passed her the shell. 'Hello little crab,' she said, holding it centimetres from her nose.

'I'm like that shell. There's something else inside my body,' said Zaki. 'I think something crawled in while I was in that cave. I'm sharing my body with something evil.' He looked at the crab in Anusha's hand. 'I wonder if that crab ate the creature that made the shell.'

Anusha carefully placed the crab back in the water. 'Off you go, little crab. I'm not sure I like you any more,' she said quietly.

Zaki looked at her. 'I think whatever it is that got into me is getting stronger; maybe not strong enough to push me out yet, but you saw what it could be like – and it's doing home improvements – it fixed my shoulder. How do you fight against something that's inside you?'

Anusha shook her head, then she sat up slightly. 'The voice – the one you told me about yesterday. The one that called the girl's name . . .'

A wave of dread flooded through Zaki's body. He nodded . Yes, Anusha was right; that thing that had called out the girl's name and the evil thing that had looked out of his eyes – it was one and the same. It had crept into him when he was in the cave; he had brought it into the open. He was like the carrier of a plague, of a deadly virus – and he knew now what it wanted.

'It's using me but it's after the girl. That's why she doesn't want me to go near her. I've put her in danger – maybe others. You saw it just now; it tried to kill you!'

'But why? What is it?' Anusha searched his face.

150

'I don't know.' Zaki's head hurt; he felt confused; he didn't know what was going on.

Anusha got to her feet. 'Come on. We're going to get wet if we stay here much longer. Anyway, I'm hungry. Have you got anything to eat?'

'No.'

'I have. You can share mine; you look like you need it.'

They climbed back up to the top of the landing stage and returned to the spot where Zaki had originally been sitting. Anusha laid out the contents of her lunch box between them and Zaki added the water bottle from his own rucksack and a snack bar that he found in his pocket and now broke it in half.

Zaki's mind returned to the awful conversation that morning in the van. He pictured his mother among a group of strangers, laughing happily. He picked up a pebble and threw it as far out into the water as he could. Then he threw another and another, each with more force and anger.

'Why did you come here?' Anusha asked softly. 'Is something going on?'

Zaki flung another pebble across the water.

'I don't mean all this, but . . . You don't have tell me if you don't want to, but, if something's wrong . . . you know, something else . . .' She left the sentence unfinished.

'What makes you think there's something wrong?' Zaki asked defensively. It was none of her business.

Anusha looked away. She fiddled with the snack-bar wrapper. 'Just then you looked like you wanted to cry.'

Zaki bit his lip. He stood up and wandered to the back of the landing stage. Did telling people things make them more likely to happen? If he told Anusha that his parents were splitting up, would that mean that they would split up? When his throat stopped hurting, he went and sat down again.

'My mum's been away a long time,' he said. 'I don't think she's going to come back.' There – it was out. It was real. He'd given it life. He couldn't stop it happening.

They sat in silence, looking out across the estuary. Grey cloud was spreading from the south-west and the water had lost its sparkle, turning dark and uninviting. The breeze was picking up, ruffling the surface, the cold gusts sending cat's paws racing, like shadows, towards them.

Anusha shivered. 'It's getting chilly. What do you want to do?'

'I don't know. I don't much want to go home.'

'Why don't you come back to my place for a bit? We can have a look at the tape from the camcorder. Maybe we'll be able to see something if we watch it on a big screen.'

'Would that be OK with your parents?'

'They won't mind. And you could dry off; you're still half-soaked.'

School would be out in an hour and Zaki had no desire to meet any of his classmates; he set a brisk pace on the walk back into town, hoping to get indoors before the surging mass of school uniforms flooded up the high street. Much of the time, passing traffic forced them to walk in single file, so there was little chance for further conversation, which left plenty of space for one question to nag at Zaki's mind – when the unknown thing had control of his body, why hadn't it tried to use the bracelet? Had Anusha disturbed it before it had a chance?

Zaki could feel the weight of the bracelet in his pocket. Anusha had suggested that her father might know where it was from. Should he show it to him, if he got the chance?

CHAPTER 14

They were seated around the dinner table, Zaki, Anusha and her parents. At first Zaki had felt uncomfortable, not sure how he should behave, watching the others for clues. The food had been placed in the middle of the table and Mr Dalal had said, 'Help yourself! Help yourself! No need to wait for an invitation in this house.' But Zaki thought there might be a special order in which he should help himself from the different dishes and he was worried about taking too much. In the end Mrs Dalal had come to his rescue, spooning a large helping of rice on to his plate and then samples from the other bowls with the instruction to 'See what you like and help yourself to more'.

It had been a long time since Zaki had taken part in a family meal. At home, since his mother left, they seldom ate together and, if they did, it was usually in front of the television. The novelty of all eating together added to Zaki's discomfort, but the Dalals made sure he was included in the easy chatter and Zaki soon found that he was enjoying himself.

On arrival at Anusha's place, Zaki had been sent

upstairs to take a shower while his clothes were rinsed and tumble-dried, then Mrs Dalal had inspected his injuries and applied ointment to the cut on his cheek. Quite what Anusha had said to her while he was showering he never discovered, but there were no awkward questions during the meal and no one mentioned their absence from school.

The white walls of the room in which they ate were decorated with pieces of brightly coloured, printed fabric – Indian, Zaki supposed, but he didn't really know. He thought of the bare walls of the living room at home. Nobody could see the point of putting up pictures when they all knew they would soon be moving on again.

There were shelves with a great many books and CDs. Woven rugs were scattered on the wooden floor.

A curious, grotesque mask hung on the wall directly opposite Zaki's place at the table. Its gaping mouth was full of large, discoloured teeth, and curved fangs protruded from the corners. The eyes were bulbous and the forehead was crowned with a coiled cobra that appeared ready to strike. The skin was painted yellow and the lips a garish red.

Zaki couldn't help noticing the large number of drums, musical instruments and instrument cases around the room and when Mr Dalal saw Zaki's eyes wandering from one instrument to another he struck his forehead in mock horror crying, 'Ah, how rude! We should have introduced you to the rest of the family.'

'Sandeep! Don't tease him,' scolded Mrs Dalal.

'Who's teasing? All the instruments have names, don't they?'

'Just ignore him, Zaki,' said Mrs Dalal. 'Poor Sandeep is a musician, so he can't help being mad, and he's also a mathematician, so he's doubly crazy.' She was passing behind her husband's chair as she spoke and she put her arms around his shoulders and gave him a playful hug.

'That's why she loves me,' said Mr Dalal, looking very pleased with himself.

'Go and fetch the ice cream. Make yourself useful,' said Mrs Dalal.

'Do you know that we Indians are the greatest mathematicians in the world?' asked Mr Dalal as he prepared to leave the room. 'It's true! We invented everything, even zero. Without us, you'd still be counting on your fingers.'

'Out!' shouted Mrs Dalal, shaking a large serving spoon at him while she cleared plates from the table.

Mr Dalal danced out of the room while his wife shook her head despairingly.

'I met him in Vienna,' she said, as though that explained his antics.

'Were you on holiday?' asked Zaki.

'No, I was studying the cello; Sandeep was studying mathematics and teaching classical Indian music. I went to one of his classes – thought it would make a change from Mozart. After that I seemed to keep bumping into him and every time we met he complained about being hungry – Sandeep's a vegetarian and Austrian food's all meat. One day, he said if I could find the ingredients he would teach me to cook an Indian meal. And that's how

156

we got to know each other – food and music.'

'Music is the food of love,' sang Mr Dalal, returning with the ice cream. 'It was your good karma that guided you to your wonderful husband.'

Mrs Dalal stuck her tongue out at him and carried the plates to the kitchen.

'What's karma?' asked Zaki.

'It means you cause what happens to you,' said Anusha. 'If you do good things, then good things will happen to you.'

'More or less,' said Mr Dalal. 'It's a bit more complicated than that.'

'So if bad things are happening, then you must have done something wrong,' said Zaki, and the empty, hopeless feeling started to grow inside him again.

A quick look passed between father and daughter.

'What's happening now can be to do with something in a previous life, and you can be affected by other people's karma, and some people believe in the karma of places, even countries – collective karma if you like,' said Mr Dalal.

'Is it like you're being punished?' asked Zaki.

'No, no, no.' Mr Dalal waved his hands. 'Karma should not be confused with rewards and punishments. This is not the way to think about karma. No, no. Karma is more like a natural force – like gravity. Listen – if I park my car on a hill and forget to put on the handbrake, what will happen?'

'It will roll down the hill.'

'Yes, and most likely smash into something at the

bottom. But was the car trying to punish me?'

'Not really.'

'No, of course not. The car was just doing what it had to do because of gravity and no handbrake. Now, I might feel as though I was being punished for being stupid, but the car wasn't punishing me, God wasn't punishing me, it was simply cause and effect – physics. You see? Karma is more like that.'

Zaki nodded. 'Do you think we really do have other lives?' he asked.

'This is getting very serious,' remarked Mrs Dalal, who was leaning in the kitchen doorway listening to their conversation.

'Yes, but very interesting!' said Mr Dalal with enthusiasm.

'Wouldn't we remember being alive before if – you know – we had been here before?'

'Can you remember being a baby?' asked Mr Dalal.

Zaki shook his head.

'But you wouldn't deny that you were a baby! Can you remember having a very vivid dream?'

Zaki nodded. He'd had rather a lot of those recently.

'But while you were having that dream you were actually lying in your bed and not flying through the air, or whatever it was you remember doing in your dream. True?'

'Well, yes I suppose.'

'So what we do or don't remember is not a very good guide to what has actually taken place. Just because you don't remember being here before doesn't mean you weren't here. Does it?'

'But, Dad,' Anusha interrupted, 'our bodies weren't here before. How could we be here before our bodies were even born!?'

'It depends whether or not we're just bodies and it depends what we mean by "before". Time, to a mathematician, is a very interesting thing.'

'Speaking of time,' said Mrs Dalal, 'I think it's time Zaki called his father.'

Zaki felt instantly miserable. He hadn't spoken to his father since stepping out of the van that morning. *Now*, Zaki thought, *I'll be in trouble for skipping school.* Well, it wasn't his fault everything was such a mess!

'I told my dad I might come here,' he said, rather weakly.

Zaki saw a look pass between Anusha and her mother. Mrs Dalal smiled. 'Would you prefer me to call him?'

Zaki could think of nothing he would like more.

'Would you like to stay over? We've got a spare room?' asked Mrs Dalal.

He felt a great surge of relief. 'Would that be OK?'

'Tell me your number and I'll see what I can do,' said Mrs Dalal.

Zaki told her the number and she left the room.

'Now, where were we?' asked Mr Dalal, clapping his hands together. 'The problems of life and time – yes? The question of who we really are and where we really are. What is life? What is real?' His eyes sparkled as he looked from Zaki to his daughter. He was obviously enjoying himself.

'Well, are you going to tell us?' Anusha demanded.

'Me?!' cried Mr Dalal, throwing up his hands. 'What makes you think I know?'

'You're older. You've lived longer.'

'Ah! Only in this life,' said Mr Dalal with a sly chuckle.

'What's the point of having other lives if you can't remember them?' asked Zaki.

'Does there have to be a point?'

'Well . . .' began Zaki.

'We'd like there to be a point. We all want a reason for being here, but that suggests there is somebody out there who thought it all up – an inventor God with a big master plan. Perhaps there is, perhaps there isn't. Personally, I like to invent my own life. I don't want life to be a test that I can get right or wrong. Do you think, when we die, God gives us marks out of ten? "Dear, dear, deary-me! Sorry, Mr Dalal – nought out of ten for you. You completely missed the point of your life."'

The cut on Zaki's cheek began to itch and prickle. He rubbed it with the tips of his fingers. His present life was complicated enough; he didn't want to contemplate the possibility of others.

'If we're not just bodies, what else are we?' asked Anusha.

Zaki looked expectantly at Anusha's father, hoping for a clear answer. Hoping for some explanation for today's events. How was it that he had been able to slip out of his body? After all, he'd always thought he was his body. He hoped Mr Dalal would talk about souls or spirits.

Mr Dalal thought for a minute. 'You'd agree, wouldn't

you, that a dead body is not the same as a living one?'

'Of course,' said Anusha.

'Doesn't that answer your question?'

'That's the trouble with Dad,' Anusha said to Zaki, 'he can never give you a straight answer!'

'Sometimes, when I'm sailing our boat, I forget about everything,' said Zaki slowly. There was something here, he was sure, but it kept slipping out of his reach.

Mr Dalal leant forward. 'Go on.'

Zaki hesitated, searching for the right words. 'It just feels right – right to be there – right to be doing what I'm doing. I think that's when I'm really me. I don't think that particular me has got anything to do with being in this particular body.'

'I would say you've found your true identity,' said Mr Dalal with a big smile.

Mrs Dalal came back into the room and sat down next to Zaki. 'Your dad says that's fine and I told him I'd make sure you found your way home tomorrow.' This time it was Mrs Dalal who shot a meaningful glance at her daughter, who pulled a face. It seemed to Zaki that there was always a second conversation going on in this family, a conversation of the eyes in which unspoken under-standings flashed backwards and forward.

'Thank you,' said Zaki. It felt good to be looked after.

'What have I missed?' asked Mrs Dalal.

'Dad's been going on,' said Anusha.

'Sandeep, you're not boring our visitor, are you?'

'Not even minutely,' declared Mr Dalal, quite unabashed.

161

Zaki felt for the bracelet in his pocket. He eased it out and laid it on the dining table. Mr Dalal's expression became suddenly serious. He looked from the bracelet to Zaki and raised one eyebrow.

'Anusha said you might know where it's from,' said Zaki.

'I thought it looked Indian,' added Anusha.

'May I take a closer look?' asked Mr Dalal.

'Yes, but I don't think it's a good idea to handle it too much,' said Zaki.

Without enquiring why that should be, Mr Dalal took a table napkin and, with it, picked up the bracelet as though he were handling an ancient relic in a museum.

'Probably Sri Lankan, rather than Indian,' he said. 'This metal is quite unusual. It's bronze, you see, but not the common bronze alloy; this is a high-tin bronze. Look at the colour. Look where it has become a little polished. You see? It's quite pale; that's the effect of plenty of tin. High-tin bronze was developed in Sri Lanka for making bells. The tin makes the bronze brittle, but it gives the bells a special clear tone. Whoever made this was probably a bell maker, maybe from Kandy in the hill country. This type of bronze is made in very, very few places.' He turned the bracelet so that he could examine the rim. 'Ah ha! This bracelet was made for a musician.'

Mrs Dalal leant close to her husband. 'How can you be so sure?'

'Look at the inscriptions, my dear.'

'Oh yes,' said Mrs Dalal.

'What are they?' asked Zaki. 'I thought they were

some kind of writing.'

'More like musical notation, I would say,' replied Mr Dalal. 'I think they are drumming patterns. The Indian word is *theka*. But these are not from northern India. They look a little different, perhaps because they are Sinhalese, or perhaps because this bracelet is quite old.'

'Why write music on a bracelet?' Zaki asked.

'Probably decoration. In India we learn to play drums by chanting the rhythms, not by reading music. Ah ha! But you need a demonstration!' Mr Dalal sprung up from the table and rubbed his hands together, delighted with the opportunity to perform. 'I will show you.'

'You might ask our guest if he wants a demonstration!' protested Mrs Dalal.

'Of course he wants a demonstration,' declared her husband, selecting a long, double-ended drum from the collection in the corner of the room and slinging it around his waist.

'No stopping him now!' Anusha laughed.

'You must excuse me, I am really a tabla player but, since I think the bracelet is from Sri Lanka, I am going to play the *yak bera*. It's the drum they use to accompany the Devil Dances.'

Mr Dalal began to chant and as he chanted his hands flicked and slapped and tapped the tightly stretched skins on the ends of the long drum, echoing back the rhythms and tones of the chanted syllables: 'Dhin-dhin,' he chanted. 'D-hin-d-hin,' sang the drum. 'Dha-ge-ti-ra-ki-ta, ta-na, ka-ta, dha-ge, ti-ra-ki-ta . . .' Faster flew the hands, faster and faster; driving the rhythm into ever more complex configurations, drawing out deep bass notes over which exploded cascades of high, staccato beats that he struck from the very edges of the skins. To Zaki it seemed as if a whole band of drummers had entered the room; it was impossible that one person could produce the intricate crossings of rhythms and tones.

Quietly, Mrs Dalal rose and opened one of the larger instrument cases. She lifted out her cello and her bow and tightened the bowstring. Soon, the cello's sonorous voice joined the cavorting dance of the drum, filling the whole room with its resonance. Sitting a few feet away, it seemed to Zaki that the cello's strings were within his body and that every note, every change of pitch and rhythm, vibrated through every living cell.

Now a third voice joined the other two and Zaki turned to see that Anusha had her violin. The fiddle's bow rocked and sawed across the strings, sending a flurry of notes to skip lightly around the cello's measured steps. Then the cello swept its counter melody between and around the fiddle and drum. Zaki was flying again, but not as a seagull, not as a hawk. The music lifted and carried him. Occasionally, he would become aware of the musicians, see the looks that passed between them, and he understood how this family had developed its word-less method of communication.

Looking up, Zaki's eyes fell again on the grotesque mask that hung on the wall. Now all the light seemed to drain from the rest of the room and the colours of the mask to glow with greater intensity in the surrounding gloom. As Zaki watched, the eyes of the mask bulged, swelling out from their sockets like boils about to burst. The protruding teeth twisted into a ghastly grin, the nostrils flared and a snake wormed its way out of one ear and proceeded, tongue flicking, to coil itself around the hanging head. The cacophony of voices that Zaki had first heard in the cave, and then again in *Curlew*'s cabin, burst in, drowning out the music; a press of faces, some painted, all streaked and shining with sweat, crowded in around the grinning mask. Zaki's nose, mouth and lungs filled with the choking smell of wood smoke. Then the awful voice that had first growled the name 'Rhiannon' two nights before on the dark street spoke again: 'No! You will not drive me out. Time for you to die!'

Zaki would have screamed if someone else hadn't screamed first. The sudden, shrill cry broke the spell and all was bright and normal in the room, except that Anusha was pointing excitedly at the bracelet on the table and shouting, 'Look, everyone! Look!'

The etched inscriptions on the rim of the bracelet, instead of being dark lines and curls, now shone as if lit from within, shone with the intensity of liquid metal in a crucible, shone like the white heat of a furnace. And they were moving, transforming as though being written and rewritten by an invisible hand.

Zaki, instinctively, reached for the bracelet but dropped it with a cry of pain as its heat seared the skin of his hand.

As Zaki and Anusha watched, the markings on the bracelet darkened and stood still.

Anusha's mother, having laid her cello in its case, came to see what had so excited her daughter. 'What happened?'

'The bracelet! Didn't you see? The writing was moving!'

'And it's burning hot!' added Zaki, nursing his hand.

Mr Dalal leant between his wife and Anusha to touch the bracelet. 'Warm. I wouldn't say hot.'

'But, Dad! Look at the writing!'

Once more, Mr Dalal used the napkin to lift the bracelet.

'Hmm. That is odd.'

'What is?' asked Zaki.

'The inscriptions – they don't look quite the same.'

'I told you, they were moving! And they were shining!'

'But that's not possible,' said Mrs Dalal.

'No, but – they do look a little different.'

'You've not remembered them right, surely.'

Mr Dalal scratched his right earlobe thoughtfully. 'Where did this come from?'

Zaki and Anusha glanced furtively at each other. 'It was Zaki's grandmother's,' lied Anusha.

'Was?'

'She's dead,' Zaki explained.

'Oh, I'm sorry.' Mr Dalal passed the bracelet to Zaki. 'You should take great care of it. It's certainly most unusual. It may even be quite valuable.'

Zaki returned it to his pocket. It was no longer even warm but the glare of the fiery inscriptions seemed burnt into his retina so that their bright traces danced in his vision and swam in a sea of red each time he closed his eyes.

'Bedtime, I think,' said Mrs Dalal, with a yawn.

Zaki stood up, then realised he didn't know where he was going to sleep, and waited, rather awkwardly, for someone to show him to his room.

'Come on,' said Mrs Dalal. 'I'll show you where everything is.'

'That mask,' asked Zaki as he followed Mrs Dalal upstairs, 'where's it from?'

'That's Riri Yakka the Demon of Blood,' said Mrs Dalal, rather dramatically. 'It goes with the drum Sandeep was playing. They both came from Sri Lanka. They're used in the Devil Dances.'

'Devil Dances? What are they?'

'Ceremonies for driving out demons.' She opened the door to the spare bedroom. 'Here you are. Sleep well. And I hope that mask doesn't give you nightmares!'

CHAPTER 15

Lying in a strange bed in a strange room, Zaki thought he had only just closed his eyes when he was woken by a soft tap on his door. He sat up quickly and wondered, for a moment, where he was. The door swung slowly open. In the darkness, he could just make out a figure in the doorway.

'Are you awake?' It was Anusha.

'Yes,' Zaki whispered back. 'What are you doing?'

'There's something you have to see. Come on,' said Anusha, and disappeared.

Zaki struggled into some clothes and stumbled, half awake, into the corridor.

'Follow me,' said Anusha.

She led him to the back of the house and out through the back door, which she held open and then closed carefully behind him. The concrete paving slabs were cold and wet under Zaki's bare feet and it was very dark in the back yard.

'This way,' hissed Anusha.

Zaki followed her shadowy form to another door at the end of a short path. They stepped inside the building.

Little lights and dials glowed in the darkness. There were banks of knobs and sliders on a sloping, black desk, and one end of the room was closed off by a glass partition behind which were microphones on stands.

'Wow!' said Zaki. 'You've got a recording studio. My brother would love this!'

'My mum and dad do music for films and stuff,' said Anusha.

'Do you . . . ?'

'Play on the soundtracks? Sometimes, when they need an extra violin. I had to sing once. But look at this.'

She sat at a keyboard to the side of the mixing desk. Her fingers clicked expertly over the keys and a large video screen flashed into life.

'You can sit there if you want,' she said, indicating an office-type chair beside hers. Zaki perched on the chair and stared up at the screen.

'I've downloaded the camcorder recording. You can see a lot more on this big screen than you could on the camcorder's screen.'

Anusha clicked the mouse and an image appeared on the screen. Zaki saw himself, back to the camera, sitting on the edge of the landing stage. It was the recording Anusha had made that morning.

'Wait, I'll fast-forward it; nothing happens for a bit except for that stupid woman with the dog.'

The image jiggled and there was a scrabble of sound from the surrounding speakers. The woman and her dog appeared and seemed to scamper about like comic figures in a silent movie, then the picture steadied and the sound returned to the soft sighing of the wind. A gull flew in from the left side of the image and settled on the landing stage not far from the seated Zaki.

'Can you stop it there?' asked Zaki.

Anusha froze the image just after the figure of Zaki turned to look at the gull.

'Yeah. Now can you zoom in?'

The image got larger in a series of jerky steps until the head of the gull, with its bright yellow eye, filled the screen.

'OK. Go on, and watch the eye,' said Zaki, knowing instinctively that the eye was what they should be looking at.

Anusha unfroze the image; the eye blinked but still retained the gull's characteristic glassy stare. The eye blinked again and it was as though a shadow passed across its surface, like the wind-ruffled shadows that race over the water on a sunny day. When the shadow had gone, the eye appeared to have gained added depth, reminding Zaki of peering down into deep water on a still morning. Although the eye was the eye of a gull, it no longer appeared to be the spirit of a gull that looked out through it.

'Did you see?'

Anusha nodded. 'It changed. It stopped looking like a gull's eye. It was you, wasn't it. You were looking out of the eye.'

'Yeah, it was me. I know it's weird, but . . .'

Anusha gave another little nod; he didn't have to go on; he didn't have to explain. She had seen it and she believed him.

The eye still filled the screen.

'Can you zoom out?' asked Zaki.

Several clicks of the mouse and Zaki's seated figure came back into frame. There he was, sitting beside the gull, except . . . the gull was now him and the thing that looked like him – was what? Something, somebody else.

'Shall I run it on?'

'Yeah – please.'

Anusha allowed the action to resume; the gull took off and flew out of frame, the camera remaining on the seated figure. Obviously, Anusha had been quite unaware of the significance of the gull while she was filming.

'Can we run it back?'

'There's something more important you need to see.' Anusha's fingers click the keys and the image jumped forward. 'I kept the camera running as I walked towards you.'

Zaki heard Anusha's voice on the soundtrack call his name. He saw the figure's head and shoulders turn and the eyes looked straight into the camera. Anusha froze the image once more and zoomed in on the face – his face – but not his face. Not his face because the eyes were not his eyes.

A chill of fear ran up Zaki's spine. A cornered wolf might look like that just before it leapt for your throat – treacherous, vicious, cruel, waiting to attack.

Anusha allowed the recording to run on in slow motion. The wolfish eyes shifted uneasily and then the head turned away as though trying to hide the face from the viewer. A few moments later the screen went black.

'That's all I have. Do you want to see anything again?'

'No thanks,' said Zaki.

Anusha was busy for a few minutes shutting down the equipment, then she swivelled her chair to face him.

'I'm sorry if I didn't believe you straight away – about being the gull and about it not being you that attacked me – but it's all so strange. Where do you think that thing – the thing that took over your body – where do you think it is now? Maybe it died when you – when it – when your body fell over the edge. Maybe it's gone – maybe you've killed it. Do you think?'

Zaki tilted his head. 'Is the cut on my cheek still there?'

Anusha leant forward. The only light in the room was the glow from the dials and the little LEDs.

'It's kind of hard to tell. It's very dark in here.'

Zaki ran his fingertips across the smooth skin. 'It's gone – feel.'

Anusha felt along his cheekbone then sat back. Zaki could sense she was frightened.

'So that means . . . ?'

'That the thing is still there; it's still inside my body. How else could that cut have healed up so quickly? And it spoke again.'

'When?'

'Tonight, when you were all playing that music and the bracelet was going crazy.'

'What did it say?'

'It said, "Time for you to die."'

'Die! What did it mean? Aren't you frightened?'

'Of course I'm frightened!'

'There must be someone we could talk to – someone who could help.'

'And what do we tell them? That I'm possessed? That I'm in danger of turning into the beast from hell? Do you seriously think anyone would believe us? No – I've got to sort this out.'

'You mean, we've got to sort this out.'

'You don't have to.'

'I know,' said Anusha firmly, 'but I'm here, aren't I.'

They sat in the semi-darkness, wrapped in their own thoughts, each waiting for the other to say something.

Eventually, Anusha broke the silence. 'The bracelet . . . and the music . . .' she said slowly.

'And the mask,' added Zaki.

'What? Our mask?'

'On the wall – it came alive.'

'Perhaps you *are* possessed.'

'Your mum said the masks were used to get rid of demons.'

'That's right, the shaman wears the mask and becomes a demon, then, through the music, he can drive out the demon that's in the person they're trying to cure.'

'Perhaps that started to happen tonight. Perhaps my demon felt threatened. Perhaps that's why he spoke. Listen, I want you to find out everything you can about these Devil Dances. Ask your mum and dad; see if they've got any books or pictures, or anything.'

'OK, but . . .'

'I know; it's completely unreal.'

'I'll get everything I can.'

'Do you suppose I could borrow the mask?'

'Yeah, I'm sure you could. I'll say we need it for school – for Mrs Palmer.'

'Yeah, good. What about music? I think the music's important.'

'Don't ask me to play the drums, I'm useless!'

'Pity. And we can hardly ask your dad.'

'How about a recording?'

'A recording – hey! Yeah – it might work!'

'Drums on soundtracks . . .' Anusha thought for a minute. 'Yes . . . I think . . . Yes! I'm certain! "Varanasi" – he used that drum on "Varanasi".'

Anusha pulled open a filing drawer and flipped through the rows of filed CDs and DVDs. She pulled out a CD and held it out for Zaki. 'Here. This just has the drum track on it.'

'Fantastic.' Zaki took the proffered CD.

'Now what?'

'We need to know what we're doing. We need to read the logbook. It might tell us all sorts of stuff we need to know.'

'Tomorrow's Saturday. We've got all day.'

'Well, not quite all day. I need to take the dinghy back to *Morveren*. Remember?'

'We'll take the logbook with us! Read it on your boat. Then no one can disturb us.'

'Brilliant! And there are charts on the boat if we need them.'

Zaki felt better now that they had a plan of action. He had to admit that it wasn't a very clear plan but at least they were going to do something, not just wait for things to happen.

Anusha locked up the recording studio and they crept back into the house. Back in his unfamiliar bed, creatures with eyes of fire pursued Zaki through his dreams so that he woke feeling more tired than when he had gone to sleep.

CHAPTER 16

Zaki lay in bed wondering whether or not he should get up. He couldn't hear any sounds of people moving about. What time did the Dalals have breakfast? Did they have breakfast? He should have asked Anusha. He decided to get up anyway, dressed, and made his way to the kitchen, where he found Mr Dalal seated at the kitchen table, working on something on his laptop computer.

'Sorry,' said Zaki, when Mr Dalal looked up, 'didn't mean to disturb you.'

'Not at all, not at all,' said Mr Dalal. 'I am only doing some stupid emails and I am only doing that because I have nobody to talk to. Did you sleep well?'

'Quite well,' Zaki lied.

'Good, because there were some people creeping around the house last night, and I thought they might have woken you. Cup of tea?'

'Um – thank you,' said Zaki, embarrassed that their midnight comings and goings had not gone unnoticed.

While Mr Dalal was busy making a fresh pot of tea, Zaki looked around the room. Every available surface seemed to support a little line of carved elephants. Some lines were arranged in ascending height; in other lines all the elephants were more or less the same size but were carved out of different materials. The majority were made from wood, but some were fashioned from coloured stone. They marched across the tops of cupboards, shared shelves with the crockery, and one very large stone elephant served as a doorstop.

'The elephants belong to my wife,' said Mr Dalal. 'She bought one when I first took her to India. My family decided she must love elephants and now they send her one every time they find a new one, which in India can be very, very often.'

Mr Dalal poured mugs of tea and pulled a chair out for Zaki at the table.

'I was thinking about something you said last night, about not being just bodies,' Zaki said.

'Body and mind?'

'Yes. Do you think it might be possible for our minds to – I don't know – to get changed somehow?'

'I change my mind all the time. Ask my dear wife.'

'I didn't mean like that.'

'No, of course you didn't. Excuse me – I was only teasing.'

'What I meant was . . . can something happen so that your mind can exist without your body?'

'Some say there is really only one mind, that exists everywhere, and that each of our minds is a little bit of it.'

Zaki shook his head, 'I don't understand.'

'Imagine a big, big window that has been painted completely black. Now, I scratch a hole in the paint on the left side and you scratch a hole in the paint on the right side. When we look through the holes, we can both see the same view but we see it from slightly different angles. The holes are our minds, what we are looking at is the one mind. Does that help?'

'A little,' said Zaki.

'When we talk about mind like this, we are not talking about brain.' Mr Dalal wagged his finger.

'Could my mind work in somebody else's body?'

This time it was Mr Dalal's turn to shake his head in puzzlement. 'That is a truly wonderful question . . . and, if you ever find the answer, you must tell me what it is.' The next to arrive in the kitchen was Anusha's mother. She regarded the two at the table, heads together, like a pair of conspirators.

'Sandeep, has that poor boy had any breakfast?'

'Certainly! Cup of tea, and yogic wisdom.'

'Oh, honestly! You could at least have given him some cereal. And where is Anusha?'

'Sleeping, I expect. Perhaps I should wake her.'

'Perhaps you should. Now, Zaki, what would you like? Cereal, toast, eggs?'

'Toast would be fine, thanks.'

Mr Dalal left to wake Anusha while his wife bustled around the kitchen making toast, and setting out plates, bowls and cereals on the kitchen table.

Zaki went back to examining the carved elephants. He noticed one that looked rather odd and he got up from the table to take a closer look. The little elephant had been given a place of honour. It was seated in a niche in the wall. Unlike the other elephants, it was brightly painted. Now Zaki saw that it had the head of an elephant but the body of a human, except that the body had four arms. One of the four hands held a noose, one held a sort of stick, the third was held up, palm forward, the fourth held a broken tusk. There was a snake around the creature's waist and a mouse at its feet.

'That's Ganesha,' said Anusha.

Zaki turned to find her standing behind him. Her hair was still wet from the shower.

'Why does he look like that?'

'Well, there are two different stories, but anyway he lost his head when he was a baby and his father, Shiva, who is a god of course, gave him an elephant's head. The really important thing is that he's the remover of obstacles.'

'The remover of obstacles,' Zaki repeated.

'What are all those things he's holding?'

'That's a goad, a stick to prod you forward, and that's the noose he uses to catch all the difficulties that are in your way. The snake is energy. He's got big ears so that he can listen to you, and his elephant head is full of wisdom, it's like the soul, and his human body denotes earthly existence. I've forgotten about the tusk. Mum? Why does Ganesha have a broken tusk?'

'He used it as a pen to write the Mahabharata.'

'Oh yes – that's this huge big poem about all the gods and heroes and so on.'

'And the mouse shows that he's humble because he's

the destroyer of pride and selfishness,' added Mrs Dalal.

For the next quarter of an hour they concentrated on eating. Mr Dalal didn't rejoin them. Maybe he had gone to the recording studio, Zaki thought. He obviously knew they had been down there last night. Did he mind? Was he checking to see what they had been up to? Anusha didn't seem at all concerned. Well, different families had different rules, he supposed.

'The remover of obstacles' – the words kept repeating in Zaki's head. He could really do with one of those right now! Michael used to be his remover of obstacles. The one who went first: the first to climb a cliff, the first at the secondary school. He went ahead and came back and told Zaki what it was like, that it was safe. But now the obstacles had grown bigger and not even Michael could remove them.

He looked up from his plate and found Mrs Dalal smiling at him.

'Mum,' Anusha asked, as they tidied away the breakfast things, 'can Zaki borrow the mask from the living room?'

'There seems to be a lot of interest in that mask all of a sudden,' her mother remarked.

'We're doing myths and stuff with Mrs Palmer and Zaki's got to do a project.'

'Well, yes, take it, by all means. But you might need to give it a bit of a dust.'

Anusha wrapped the mask carefully in an old tea towel and it joined the logbook and the borrowed CD in Zaki's rucksack. Then they made themselves a picnic lunch to take with them to the boat.

CHAPTER 17

It was the sort of September day that seems to have borrowed its weather from mid-July; there was no wind to speak of and the sun shone out of a clear blue sky. Sitting beside Anusha, while the bus wound its way through the lanes to Salcombe, Zaki felt rather self-conscious in his school clothes on a Saturday, and, despite the sunshine streaming in through the bus window, he kept his jacket zipped up over his pale blue school sweatshirt. He could feel the slight weight of the bracelet in his jacket pocket.

'What if *Curlew* is still anchored near your boat?' asked Anusha as they walked from the bus to the boat shed. Zaki had been wondering the same thing, but they needn't have worried.

'She's long gone,' Grandad told them.

'Up the estuary, or out to sea?' asked Zaki.

'Out to sea. Only one person aboard, far as I could tell.'

Zaki fetched *Morveren*'s cabin key from the nail by the door, lifejackets for himself and Anusha and the oars for the dinghy. Grandad offered to tow the dinghy out with the launch, but Zaki replied that Anusha could do with the rowing practice.

'That shoulder of yours all right for rowin'?'

'Seems to be fine,' Zaki replied nonchalantly.

Grandad raised a quizzical eyebrow but let it go at that.

'If you intend leavin' the dinghy on *Morveren*, fly the mermaid when you want fetchin'.' 'The mermaid' was a large square flag with a mermaid on it. 'Flying the mermaid' was the family's way of letting those ashore know that they were wanted onboard. During holidays, when the mermaid was run up the mast, it was the signal that lunch was ready and that Zaki and Michael should stop whatever they were doing and get back to the boat. Zaki's mum had made the flag. This summer it hadn't been flown.

They had the tide with them until they were level with the harbour office, but as soon as they headed out across the estuary the ebb swept them sideways and they had to pull hard at their oars to make the moorings by the opposite shore. However, Zaki's newly healed shoulder allowed him to use both arms to row and he and Anusha were a well-balanced pair, matching stroke for stroke, so they were soon aboard *Morveren* with the dinghy tied to the yacht's stern.

It was the first time Anusha had seen inside *Morveren*'s cabin. Every detail that was so familiar to Zaki was new to her. She was amazed at how many things had been dovetailed into such a small space. Eventually, when

Anusha had made a thorough inspection of every nook and cranny and Zaki had satisfactorily answered all her questions, they settled themselves at the saloon table and opened the logbook.

The first entry was dated 15th October 1907 and gave details of a day's oyster dredging in the Carrick Roads including notes on the size and quantity of oysters harvested. Similar entries continued throughout the autumn and winter months – mostly oyster-dredging but some days the boat had been used for fishing. There was no mention of crew, so the skipper must have worked alone.

Occasionally, in the margin beside an entry, there was a drawing of a dolphin. Around a third of the way through the book the short log entries stopped. Zaki flicked forward through the remaining pages. They were all filled with the same neat, sloping handwriting. It appeared to be one long entry.

'What's this all about?' Anusha wondered.

'Only one way to find out,' Zaki replied, turning back to the page where the entry began.

Heads together, their elbows on the table, they settled down to read.

CHAPTER 18

1st March 1908

Oh Una – where are you? If only I could talk to you. If only I could ask your forgiveness for what I have done. But I did it to stay near you – you must know that – or as near to you as I can be. No – no, perhaps it is you who should ask me for forgiveness! After all, it was you who deserted me.

Yes, I went back. Yes, I took some of the more valuable pieces that I had hidden. And yes, yes! I know they are for ever stained with blood – the blood of other innocent people. It would have been so much easier to have died along with our parents the night of the wreck. You saved us. You see? It was you! You really are to blame! I don't mean that. You know I don't mean that. But why save me and then leave me on my own, trapped in this life? It was cruel of you, Una, so cruel.

I know you are sometimes not far away. That is why I bought this boat. And some days you come to play. It is you? You and your friends?

Yes, Una, I went back and I took a few valuables. And I know I swore I would not, but how else could I get the money for the boat? Now I have blood on my hands.

And I have nightmares. I should never have gone back to that cursed rock. I dream every night that I am him again and I am on that beach, killing, killing, killing. I think I will go mad. There is no one I can talk to. I am becoming confused. Even during the day I sometimes wonder who I am. Is it possible I once had a normal life – was a young girl with loving parents and a sister? Una, what shall I do?

Yes, Una, you are right. How sensible of you. You always were the clever one. I must set it all down. I must start from the beginning. Get it clear in my poor, confused head. That is the thing to do. I will imagine I am telling a stranger, somebody kind and patient who listens and asks no questions, somebody – and this is important – somebody who is capable of believing the unbelievable.

Dear Stranger (may I call you that?) – how should I start? Shall I tell you who I am? Yes, since we have not met before, I should introduce myself. My name is Rhiannon Davies. I have a twin sister named Una. We were born in June under the twin sign of Gemini and were so alike that even our parents had difficulty telling us one from the other. (Our parents! Oh, Una, I'm beginning to forget what they looked like!)

I'm sorry – let me continue. Our father was the Reverend Bryn Davies, our mother Gwyneth Davies.

Our father believed that God wished him to be a missionary, to preach the Word in those dark corners of the world where it had not been heard. And it was this belief that propelled our little family of four in the spring of 1851, with our few possessions and a great many Bibles, from the Welsh Valleys to a tropical paradise, where there were already a good

185

many gods and where my father was amazed to discover that his own god had been known since the time of St Thomas, although considered to be no greater than any of the others.

We arrived in Ceylon, or Serendip as the ancients called it, soon after Una and I had celebrated our ninth birthday, and we remained there for a little over five years. While our father and mother were engaged in 'civilising the natives' and 'steering them away from their dark superstitions', the natives were engaged in steering us, their children, towards those very same dark beliefs and practices. Our chief instructor in this was the local Edura (or 'idolatrous witch doctor' as our father called him), a kindly old man who, when not driving out demons, cast bronze statues of gods and goddesses and of all the local saints, and made bells and cymbals for ritual dances.

It is the belief, in those parts, that there exists a host of different demons and that every illness and misfortune is caused by a particular one of them. It is the Edura's duty to determine which demon is the cause of each affliction and then, through the terrifying Yakum Natim or Devil Dances, in the disguise of that very demon, to persuade it to leave the body of the sufferer.

Every day, as soon as our mother had finished giving us our morning lessons, my sister and I would scamper off to the Edura's. There we would squat in the heat and semi-darkness, watching him work and listening, wide-eyed, to his tales of the Yakka, or demons, and the many tricks and ruses he had used to overcome them. All around us, on the walls, lit by the red, flickering glare from the hearth, hung the masks of the Yakka, their faces twisted and distorted in cruel reflection of the diseases they caused: Naga Sanni Yakka, bringer of night-

mares; *Kori Sanni Yakka, the paralyser; Amuku Sanni Yakka, green-faced inflictor of stomach ills; Dala Sanni Yakka, causer of whooping cough; Riri Yakka, the fearsome blood demon; Kola Sanni Yakka, leader of the devils, and all the rest of his ghastly retinue.*

The Edura worked stripped to the waist, his old skin, like creased leather, moving over the protruding bones of his arms and ribs as he shaped an image in wax or fanned the coals to a white heat to melt metals for casting. From time to time he would pause and point a finger at one of the masks, cackling as he recounted the ways in which he had outwitted this or that demon.

Best of all was to watch as the Edura cast a new god or goddess; the hot, smoking wax pouring out; the molten metal pouring like liquid fire from the crucible into the mould and then the miracle of the moment when the lithe, beautiful, dancing body of the god broke from its clay shell. What chance had my father's dry sermons and crucified God against this astonishing marriage of heaven and hell?

Some days when we went to the Edura's hut we would find him beneath his favourite tree, legs crossed, face serene, deep in meditation. We would settle ourselves on either side of him, copy his pose and see which of us could sit for the longest. Una always won. I would begin to yawn, then to fidget, and soon I would run off to find something else to do.

Who knows how long we would have remained in Ceylon had we not fallen ill? Always doing everything together, Una and I succumbed to fever on the same day. My mother nursed, my father prayed, but our condition rapidly worsened. Our bodies seemed on fire one moment and frozen the next; one moment the sweat poured from us, soaking the bed sheets, the next we were seized by such shivering that our teeth rattled in our heads. We could eat nothing and soon we sank into delirium. Our father, fearing the worst, set out on the three-day overland journey to the coast in the hope of finding a doctor, but each day he was away we grew weaker until finally, in desperation, our mother turned to the Edura. The old man came and stood at our bedside. He bent low over each of us and smelt our breaths, then nodded; he knew this devil well – one of the worst, Riri Yakka, Demon of Blood. This devil drove a hard bargain; the price would be high. My mother cried that she would give anything, anything if our lives could be spared. The Edura said he would do his best. We must be brought that night to the clearing behind his hut; he would go and make the necessary preparations.

When darkness fell, we were carried out and laid in the clearing. Flaming torches were lit and the drumming began; slow at first, a single drum with a beat like a pounding heart. Then the rhythm quickened, other drums joined and the circle of drummers closed in around us, hands and sticks beating faster, whipping the air until it throbbed with a pulse that deafened our ears and convulsed our bodies.

Suddenly there was silence and the circle broke. There stood the Edura, his back to us, his face hidden. The old man's body was transformed: bronze and silver bracelets encircled his arms and legs; muscles swelled where the skin had once sagged; his back was straight as a rod of iron; from our position on the ground, he seemed twice his previous height. Then, quick as a cat, as all the drums roared into life, he spun round and leapt

188

towards us, his face hideously disfigured by the Yakka mask. As we watched, terrified, the mask was no longer a thing carved in wood, but alive and moving, a devil incarnate. The Edura had become the Yakka and he was about to devour us!

Shaking and screaming, we clung to each other on the ground as the monster descended. Saliva poured from its jaws. Its eyes flashed and flamed. Clawed hands plunged through our flesh and tore dark, smoking forms from each of our bodies. We lay twitching in the dirt, emptied like gutted fish, as the drums pounded and the battle of the demons raged above us in the resin-filled, smoky torchlight. Then it was over. The demons fled. The drummers vanished. All was silent except for the sputtering of the dying torches.

We sat up and looked at each other. The fever had gone. The warm night air enfolded us. The smoke cleared and the stars glittered. A little breeze sprang up and rattled the palm fronds. And then our mother was helping us to our feet, supporting us, guiding us home and repeating over and over, 'Thank God, thank God, thank God, thank God,' as the tears streamed down her face.

Of course, after that, my father's mission could not continue – the local gods and demons had triumphed. All knew that the missionary's wife had begged the help of the Edura. All could see that the Edura had succeeded where my father had failed. What could my father do but pack up his family and return to Wales?

In the days before we left, my sister and I were forbidden to visit the Edura, but we could think of doing nothing else; it was as if an invisible cord tugged at something deep within us, drawing us towards his hut. We fidgeted through our morning

189

lessons, sulked on the veranda in the sweltering heat of the afternoons or plucked peevishly at the luxuriant plants that grew in the garden. But when we were certain no one was observing us we scuttled to that forbidden place. Furtively, we crept to the rear of the building, where a hole in the thatched wall afforded us a view of the Edura bent over his crucible, into which he was dropping small fragments of copper and other metals. He turned and lifted something small, wrapped in a piece of cloth, from the low table by the wall. He carefully unwrapped the little parcel and lifted up a fine silver chain from which dangled the simple silver cross that always hung around our mother's neck. We both gasped and then, fearful that he would detect us, held our breaths. What was he doing with our mother's precious cross? Had he stolen it? Had she given it to him? If she had, what could this possibly mean? Gently, he lowered the cross and then the chain into the molten metal in the crucible. We pressed our faces closer to the hole, eager to see what would happen next, but we were suddenly seized from behind by two strong hands that dragged us from the wall. We found ourselves, in the next instant, confronting our father, whose face was purple with rage.

We were only to see the Edura one more time and that was on the day that we departed for the coast. Our father had gone ahead and we were preparing to follow with our mother on the ox cart with all our possessions. As the cart began to move, the Edura emerged from the shadows and pressed something into our mother's hands with an instruction that I could not overhear. She quickly hid whatever he had given her in a bag that she kept with her for the rest of the journey.

Five days later we boarded the barque Persephone and set

sail for England. As the palm-fringed shores dropped away, I felt as Eve must have felt when the angel of the Lord drove her from the garden of Eden; I was losing my paradise, but I was not to know that this ill-omened ship was carrying us into Hell!

For us children, the passage home was long, the monotony of the many weeks at sea only broken occasionally by the sight of dolphins that came to leap and play about our ship. Some sixth sense seemed to tell my sister, Una, when the dolphins were coming and she would hurry us all on deck to watch them.

The weather was, on the whole, fair and, although we encountered large seas when rounding the Cape of Good Hope, there were no serious storms until we had crossed the Bay of Biscay. Then, as we approached the English coast, the skies darkened, the seas rose and the ship was struck by a sudden and violent squall. Our first sight of England was just before nightfall when a headland, that the ship's master took to be Lizard Point, was briefly visible through the driving rain. As the sun set, the storm increased in ferocity. Now each black wave that rushed upon our ship was crowned with a crest of foaming white and towered like a toppling mountain above the deck. Each wave seemed certain to overwhelm us. The motion of the ship grew ever more extreme and the sound of the storm rose to a deafening crescendo.

Now the waves swept across the decks. The longboat was carried away into the blackness of the night together with the unfortunate crewmen who bravely threw themselves in its path in a desperate attempt to save it. With a terrible splintering crash a hatch cover was breached and a dark, freezing torrent cascaded into the cabin where we two girls clung to our mother,

191

believing that every moment would be our last. All hands above ran to man the pumps while our father exalted us to fall to our knees and pray to the Lord for our deliverance. It was clear to all that if we could not reach shelter soon the ship would surely founder.

A shout went up, 'Lights! Lights ashore! Lights off the port bow!'

'God be praised!' my father cried. 'Salvation is at hand!'

Despite the ever-present danger of being washed overboard, all who were not too sick to stand clambered on deck. Only those who have been in such mortal peril could understand the comfort that we gained from those glimmers of light. To know that safety, warmth and comfort were within our reach; surely these lights were lit to guide poor mariners home!

''Tis Plymouth,' the boatswain yelled, ''Tis Plymouth! I know the lights!' And all believed him because that is what we all wished to believe – safe harbour and an easy entrance.

How cruelly we were deceived! Too late we heard the roar of breakers on the rocks. Too late we saw the plumes of spray that burst against the cliffs and leapt a hundred feet into the air. Too late the master saw the trap that had been set. In a panic he ordered the ship about and four seamen threw themselves upon the wheel, but she would not come round. The seas drove us on; the wind drove us on; the sails were blown to rags and tatters but still we were driven on. Then a great black wave rolled out of the night, lifted the ship like it were a toy, rushed with it on its shoulders and flung it down on the waiting reef. The ship's back was broken; the mainmast snapped and crashed with its yardarms and tangled rigging to the deck; many were flung into the sea.

Our family, clinging to each other and to the stern rail, managed to keep from sliding from the sloping deck. But each breaking wave pounded the shattered hull of the doomed ship, driving her ever further across the jagged reef, tearing fresh holes in her belly.

The ship lifted for the last time, struggled to right herself like a dying animal, then, with an awful groan, fell back upon the rocks. Our father ordered us to remain where we were and went to find the master, but our mother, seizing us by the arms, dragged us back down the companionway. Below deck it was so dark we could see almost nothing and everything was awash. Spouts of water exploded through splintered holes in the hull. Wading knee-deep in the icy water, we at last gained our cabin, where our frenzied mother searched frantically among the floating debris until she found her holdall. From it she took two bracelets, which she thrust on to our arms. Then she fell to her knees in the water and hugged us to her. 'These will protect you. Whatever happens, my darlings, don't take them off. Do you understand?' We nodded. We were children. She was our mother. She must know best.

'Father will be looking for us,' she said. She took my hand and I took my sister's and we plunged back through the flooded hull and out into the mayhem of the night.

As we reached the deck, we looked up to see a curving wall of water that seemed to hang above our heads, blotting out the sky. With a roar, the wave collapsed, engulfing us. Rolling and struggling, we were carried over the side of the ship and dragged down by the powerful current. I felt my mother's grip on my arm and then it was slipping, slipping. Desperately, I tried to entwine my fingers in hers but the current prised us *apart. I stretched out, reaching for her hand, but she was gone!*

It was Una who managed to get her arm over a piece of floating wreckage and dragged us both on to it. All around us was the turmoil of broken water and the howling of the wind. We screamed and screamed for help and for our mother, but no answer came. At last, exhausted, we could only cling to each other and to the wreckage.

In this nightmare, I imagined, or thought I imagined, that we were suddenly propelled through the water. I thought there were creatures surrounding us, their dark, smooth backs visible when they broke the surface and blew spume into the air. Had I not been half drowned, I would have been afraid, but the creatures did not attack us and I found myself thinking that I must tell Mother about them when I woke up. But it was my sister who was shaking me and begging me to let go of the wreckage and drag myself up the beach that we had somehow reached. Bewildered, I did as I was told.

We lay in the wet sand, just beyond the reach of the waves. How long we lay there I do not know. It was the sound of voices that roused us, and when we sat up, we saw that there were lights coming along the beach. A rescue party! Our hearts lifted and as they drew nearer we were about to call out when a dreadful sight choked the cries in our throats. They paused by the water's edge and, while some held up the lanterns, others dragged a poor seaman from the water. The sailor tried to raise himself from the sand but, as he did so, one of the party, a giant of a man whose face was disfigured by a great, white scar, drew a long knife and plunged it into the sailor's body. What kind of people were these? Returning to our homeland, had we fallen among savages? Supporting each other, we stumbled across the beach and hid behind some boulders at the foot of a small cliff. From here we watched the awful proceedings on the beach. Following the advance party came horses drawing carts. On to one of these the bodies of the drowned were loaded. If any still showed signs of life, they were swiftly dispatched. A second cart was loaded with anything of value that washed ashore. A third cart carried a boat that was launched in the sheltered water, where the rocks of the reef provided protection from the breaking waves, and rowed out to the stricken ship. Clearly, the intention was to plunder the wreck before she broke up in the storm.

Sickened and terrified we huddled in our hiding place but it was clear that if we remained where we were we would eventually be discovered. Fear gave us new strength and when the wreckers moved further away we fled into the trees behind the beach. Finding a rough path that led up the steep hillside we decided to follow it, hoping that it might lead us to a place of safety. As we climbed the hill we saw the two beacons still burning that had lured our ship on to the rocks; the first on the pinnacle of a great, black rock, the second on the headland behind the rock, and so arranged to give the appearance of a harbour's leading lights.

The sound of a horse's hooves on the rocky path sent us darting into the gorse and bracken. As we lay peering through the undergrowth, we were surprised to see that the rider, judging by his manner of dress, was a gentleman. I was about to hail him when my sister pulled me firmly back down. 'How do we know that he isn't one of them?' I heard her ask but her lips did not appear to move, and it occurred to me that neither of us had spoken since we had hidden on the beach but we had somehow managed to converse.

We lay still until the rider had passed.

Further on, we came to a settlement of roughly built hovels, some of undressed stone, the rest made from driftwood, broken spars, timbers and canvas scavenged from wrecks. Dogs barked as we approached. These were obviously the habitations of the wreckers, so we made a wide detour through the surrounding woodland and rejoined the track further on. The track now became no more than a footpath that wound its way out on to a headland. Should we continue? It led, no doubt, to a lookout at the cliff-edge.

Far out along the headland a lone cottage perched above the sea. A light in one of the windows drew us to it. At what point I fainted I can't say. Did I reach the cottage, or was I carried? I awoke to find that we lay on a bed of straw in a simple room. An old woman dressed in black sat by the smouldering fire.

And so began our life in the Orme Valley. Of the wreck of the Persephone we were the only survivors. Our poor parents and most of the ship's company were drowned. Had old Mrs Ball not taken us in, we would certainly have met the same fate as the other unfortunates who reached the shore alive, only to die at the hands of that murderous gang. By hiding us at first and then declaring us to be the children of distant cousins, who had come to care for her in her old age, Mrs Ball ensured our survival. The old lady enjoyed a unique position in the local community, having been the childhood nurse of the landowner Robert Stapleton, the 'gentleman' whom we had seen riding down to the shore, no doubt to oversee the plundering of the Persephone. Moreover, she was the midwife and known to be skilled in the use of medicinal herbs.

With the help of these herbs, our physical injuries healed soon enough. But what could heal our hearts? Our parents had been taken from us and we now must live among those who lured them to their deaths. Una, who had shown such strength on the night of the storm, lapsed into a state of melancholy from which nothing but the sight of dolphins would rouse her. She spent every day on the rocks below the cliffs watching for them, learning to call for them so that they would come to her.

I knew what she was doing and I knew I was losing her. Una and I had been together from the moment we were conceived. We were born within minutes of each other, spent every day of our lives together, learnt to walk together and run together. Our very first words had been to each other, and now I was losing her, losing her to the sea and to the dolphins. For we had learnt now the power of the bracelets and Una was using these powers to become one with the creatures of the sea.

I do not know what ancient sorcery the Edura employed when he cast those bracelets, what demonic powers he called up and trapped within their sacred alloy. It seemed to us that he had breathed life itself into those metal bands. They often felt as though they pulsed upon our wrists and became inflamed like living things. When Una and I wore the bracelets we could hear every thought in the other's head, and we could slide from our own bodies into each other's and into the bodies of birds and animals. Even when we removed the bracelets, some of their powers remained with us, as though we had absorbed a little of the potency instilled in them. At first, we had little control over those powers and our waking lives became like dreams, but gradually we became adept at manipulating them so that we could inhabit our own bodies when we wished to and move into others whenever we chose. Then we discovered we could create phantasms, creatures that seemed completely real but owed their existence to our imaginations. These phantasms would only exist for as long as we held their images in our minds; as soon as we ceased thinking about them they vanished. We could see through their eyes, hear with their ears, feel what they touched. Una had little interest in creating them, preferring instead to flee her own body as often as she could to share the bodies of dolphins, but I spent many hours perfecting a phantom grey cat that I could send wherever I wished in order that I could spy on our murderous neighbours.

Dear stranger, you may be wondering why did we not use the powers of the bracelets to leave the Orme immediately and find our way back to Wales. Una had lost all interest in human society. From the night our parents died, she turned her back on the land and looked only to the sea. Even I, her twin sister, received little more than the odd word, and I now had to invade her mind to discover what she was thinking. More and more often when I attempted to contact her I would find that she had left her body to be with the dolphins. I began to fear that one day she would not return or that her body, left so long without her spirit, would die.

And what of me? Of course, I would never leave without my sister, but I had my own reason for staying – I wanted revenge.

I took to helping Mrs Ball on her missions of mercy. She was often called on to treat illnesses with her herbal remedies, to set broken bones, to stitch up wounds and, occasionally, to deliver babies. The old woman's sight was failing, so she welcomed my assistance, as did her patients. Soon I, and my grey cat, were as accepted as the old woman herself. She taught me how to prepare potions and salves, which plants healed and which were poisonous. I helped tend her herb garden and she sent me along the cliff paths and into the woods to gather berries, leaves, roots and the bark of certain trees. I was biding my time, waiting for my opportunity and getting to know my enemies, chief among whom were Mr Maunder and the Honourable Robert Stapleton.

Maunder was that scar-faced brute we had seen going about his murderous work on the night of our shipwreck. He was six foot three in his sea boots, with a chest like a barrel of herrings, his thick grey beard streaked with yellow stains from the tobacco he constantly chewed. Maunder was a smuggler and wrecker who could take another's life as easily as snuff out a candle. All were afraid of him, even Stapleton.

The Honourable Robert Stapleton was as thin as Maunder was broad and as subtle as Maunder was brutal. His soft, fleshy mouth seemed too big and loose for his sharp, bony face. His skin had the grey pallor of an invalid, for he was a creature of the night, addicted to drink and gambling.

Stapleton, no longer able to support his evil habits on the income from his estate, lived like a leech on Maunder's smuggling and wrecking, allowing Maunder and his gang to remain on his land and pass themselves off as his estate workers to avoid the attentions of the excise men. Maunder, for his part, cheated Stapleton whenever he could by hiding the most valuable items of plunder.

Which was the parasite and which the host? It was hard to tell. Each needed, hated and distrusted the other.

These men had robbed me of all I loved. They had murdered

my parents and driven my sister's spirit to hide among the creatures of the sea. To wreak my revenge I had to discover their weaknesses, find some way of gaining a hold over one or other of them. Maunder, I surmised, might survive without Stapleton, but Stapleton would not survive long without Maunder. Maunder, then, would be my target. Bring him down and I could destroy both of them. Easily said but, despite the extraordinary powers given me by the bracelet, I was still a child, and these were vicious, powerful men with a gang of cut-throats that would do whatever their leaders bid them. I had seen them at work on the night of our shipwreck and I knew the bodies of their victims fed the crops in Stapleton's fields.

It was over a year before my chance came. Fights were common in that place. Petty jealousies and rivalries fuelled by the strong liquor their smuggling brought in would erupt into violent clashes and we were often called upon to treat the wounded. This particular night I was helping Mrs Ball to her bed when there came a thunderous hammering on the door. When I opened it I found the one they called Crab standing outside, a pinch-faced ruffian with a twisted hip that made him walk in an odd sideways fashion.

'Come quick as you can. It's the Captain,' he shouted as soon as the door was open, then turned and hurried off into the night with his strange shuffle and skip. The Captain was their name for Maunder.

'Not the first time someone's tried to kill 'im,' Mrs Ball muttered as we gathered together all we might need. 'With luck, we'll be too late to save 'im.'

One half of me agreed with the old woman's sentiment, the

other half feared I would be cheated of my revenge.

Maunder's house, although it was the largest in the settlement, was cold and dark and it stank. Entering it was more like entering an animal's cave than entering a human dwelling. We found Maunder lying on a filthy bed with Crab holding a glass of rum to his lips. Maunder's normally dark face was pale, almost as pale as the white scar that ran down from under his left eye, through both his full lips and made a parting in his beard.

'What took 'ee so long?' he managed to grunt. Maunder's right breast was a mass of blood.

'I'll need light,' Mrs Ball said calmly. Crab did not move. He clearly took no orders from women.

'Fetch a light, you scabby cur!' snarled Maunder. Crab leapt from the room and returned with a lighted lantern.

'Stabbed or shot?' enquired Mrs Ball.

'Shot,' Maunder muttered. 'The dog fired on me before I could finish him. But we'll throw him off Devil's Rock in the mornin'.' He laughed an ugly laugh, then coughed blood into his beard. Mrs Ball probed the wound and shook her head. 'It's in too deep.'

'Dig it out,' commanded Maunder.

'No, Mr Maunder, I will not. My hands are not as steady as they were. One slip and I fear I will kill you. You need a surgeon.'

'Fetch my pistol, Crab.'

Crab did as he was told.

'Hold it to the girl's head. If the old woman's hand slips, shoot the girl.'

And so the operation began, Crab gripping me tightly

201

around the shoulders, his breath stinking of rum, the gun pressed to my head, Maunder groaning and cursing, beads of sweat on his forehead, Mrs Ball bent over him in the dim light of the lantern.

At last, Mrs Ball straightened. She threw a desperate glance in my direction. I could see how her hands were shaking. My whole body began to tremble uncontrollably as the cold sweat ran down inside my clothing. Crab was smiling a nasty smile. I was sure I was about to die.

The flickering light, my cold, shaking body, the rush of fear, reminded me of the night of the Devil Dances. I remembered the Edura – his old body transformed, powerful, the hideous mask on his face, standing over me as I lay with Una on the ground. I closed my eyes and thought I would faint but instead I seemed to slide, merge with the Edura's image. I was the shaman and he was Riri Yakka, the Demon of Blood. I felt my body swelling, my face transforming; I was becoming the demon.

I heard a cry. Looking down, I saw Crab cringing away from me, the gun in his hand. He fired, but the shot bounced harmlessly from my body. Mrs Ball stood, her mouth open, shaking her head in bewildered disbelief. In the low room, I had to bow my head to avoid bumping it on the ceiling as I stepped towards Maunder. My impulse was to use my mighty devil's body to crush the life out of him, but instead my hand plunged into his chest, plucked out the bullet and then gently closed up the flesh. The Edura's bracelet had given me the power to cure but not to kill.

In a flash, it was over and I was myself again. For a moment there was absolute silence, then Maunder began to roar, Mrs Ball screamed and Crab gibbered and whimpered nonsense in the corner. Quickly, I took Mrs Ball's arm and drew her out of the house. When the uproar inside had subsided, I instructed her to re-enter Maunder's house with me and to behave as if nothing out of the ordinary had happened. I knew that both men had taken a good deal of rum before we arrived and I hoped that they might put the apparition they had just seen down to the effects of the drink.

We cleaned the blood from Maunder's chest and I made a great play of dressing the wound, although there was now not even a scratch on his body. I knew this sleight of hand would not hide the truth for long and that Maunder, when sober, would come demanding an explanation for the 'miracle' cure, but I needed time to think. I was sure I could use the events of the night to my advantage but I needed to work out how.

It was almost morning by the time we returned to Mrs Ball's cottage. Una was waiting. As soon as Una saw us safely home she wanted to leave, to go down to her place on the rocks by the water's edge. I forced her to remain with us while I told Mrs Ball about our lives in Ceylon, about the Edura and his gift of the bracelets. I even showed Mrs Ball how I could make the grey cat appear and disappear. Mrs Ball listened and watched without asking any questions. Perhaps, being a midwife and a healer, she already knew a good deal about that mysterious thing we call life. Had she and the Edura ever met they would, no doubt, have sat down together and discussed the efficaciousness of different charms and herbal cures. When I had finished my story she called us to sit by her on the settle. She put an arm around each of us like an old mother hen who spreads her wings over her chicks. 'I have done what I can to

203

protect you,' she said, 'but you have shown your hand. These are terrible wicked men. Take care, my dears, take care.'

I did not need Mrs Ball to warn me of the danger we were in but it touched my heart to know that there was still one person in the world who cared for our safety.

Midday brought Maunder to the door with Crab trailing at his heels. 'I've come for the witch,' were his words when Mrs Ball opened the door to him.

'Leave the girl be,' Mrs Ball pleaded, but he pushed past her with a growl and an oath.

'Here I am,' I said, as steadily as I could, holding my ground as the giant advanced, menacingly across the room.

'How do you explain this, witch?' he demanded, opening his shirt and thrusting a chest covered with matted hair into my face. 'Where's the wound?'

'It appears to have healed,' I replied, coolly, taking a step back.

'Witchcraft! That's what this be – witchcraft!'

'Witchcraft, aye, witchcraft,' echoed Crab, sidling around Maunder.

'Shut yer hatch,' snapped Maunder and Crab hopped quickly back behind his master.

Maunder placed a huge, rough hand on the back of my neck. 'What you did last night – I want to know what you did last night – and I want to know how you did it.' He tightened his grip on my neck and I felt that with one twist and he could snap my spine like a twig.

My mind was racing. For a start, I didn't know how I had summoned the demon, it had just happened. Secondly, I had no desire to reveal the secret of the bracelets. In addition, I had learnt one very important thing the night before and that was that the bracelets had the power to mend but not to destroy. They could not be used as weapons.

'I will reveal the secret of my powers,' I said, grandly, 'but to you and to you alone. If the secret were to fall into the wrong hands, it could be used against you.'

A sly smile spread across the brute's face. 'Crab, get out!'

'No,' I said, 'I can't show you now. I need to make some preparations and I need to be certain that we will not be disturbed.'

Maunder's face darkened with suspicion but I stared him out. 'All right, I'll give 'ee till tonight. Meet me on the beach.' He released the hold on my neck and marched out of the house. Crab scuttled after him but paused before leaving. 'You'll see what we do to witches,' he sneered before disappearing.

So, I was a witch, was I? Then I would make a witch's brew. As soon as Maunder and Crab were out of sight, I took up Mrs Ball's basket and set out to collect those leaves and berries I knew to contain deadly poisons. If I could not use the bracelet to rid the world of Maunder, then I would use the secrets Mrs Ball had taught me. As I gathered my ingredients I began to plot how I might persuade Maunder to swallow my medicine. The skull of a sheep, complete with curling horns, lying by the cliff path gave me an idea. Maunder was already half convinced that I was a witch. I might not be able to call up a demon any time I wished, but I could create phantasms: birds, animals, serpents, anything I was capable of imagining I could bring to fleeting life. With a bit of stagecraft and imagination I would become the witch he imagined me to be.

Returning to the cottage, I set my evil brew over the fire while I prepared the properties for my performance. The sheep's horns would be my drinking vessels, its skull and leg bone would be my drum, and Mrs Ball's cooking pot would be my cauldron. I mixed wood ash with fat and made a grey paste with which I painted my face in a ghostly mask. With a finger dipped in charcoal I drew black rings around my eyes. I rubbed red earth into my hair and plaited small bones into the ends of the matted tresses. I chewed berries until my mouth turned blue. My clothes were already worn to rags; it took little effort to convert them into a witch-like costume of shreds and tatters.

Mrs Ball's screamed with horror when she caught sight of me, but I wonder whether this ruse would work on Maunder?

As the sun began to set, I hid my disguise beneath a hooded cloak borrowed from Mrs Ball, placed the sheep's bones and horns in a bag, took up my cauldron and stepped out to keep my rendezvous. The brave old lady offered to accompany me, but I begged her instead to look after my sister. As I made my way down the hill into the darkness of the valley, I wondered if I should have told Una of my plan.

Approaching the beach, I saw a cluster of shadowy figures out on the pale sand, some holding lanterns. Drawing nearer, I saw others held unlit torches made from timbers dipped in pitch. To my dismay, Maunder had brought a group of his vile henchmen with him. 'Who are these people and why are they here?' I demanded with as bold a voice as I could muster.

'Some friends o' mine.' Maunder replied. And I recognised Crab's evil snigger from amongst the gathering.

'I said we were to be alone!'

'Follow me,' was all the answer I received.

I was now very much afraid that my masquerade was all for nothing and felt like a silly little girl who dresses up to play-act for the amusement of adults.

The tide was out and Maunder led us across the estuary's sandy floor. My steps faltered as the realisation struck me; we were headed for Devil's Rock! Was I, like that poor unfortunate who attempted to shoot Maunder, to be thrown to my death from the rock's black summit? Two of the party were carrying spades. Maybe they intended to bury me in Stapleton's field. I chased these morbid thoughts from my mind. No – Maunder wanted to know the secret of my powers. He was not about to kill me before he had gained what he wanted to know.

Reaching the opposite side of the empty estuary, we stopped by a low, seaweed-covered cliff. Half a waning moon peered through the branches of the trees on the hill above and the long ribbons of kelp that hung from the rocks glistened in its thin light. All this would be below water at high tide.

'Wait here,' Maunder ordered his followers. 'You, come with me.'

'Where are we going?' I tried to sound forceful but my voice shook.

'Ye'll see.'

I began to follow Maunder around a boulder that sat like a ball in front of the cliff.

'I'll need a fire,' I said, stopping, 'to brew the potion that will give you my powers.'

Maunder retraced his steps and stood glaring down at me. Then he turned to his men. 'Light two of the torches.'

A taper, lighted from a lantern, was held to each torch until it burst into spluttering flame.

'Give one to me and one to the girl.'

'Tell your men to leave,' I said imperiously.

'I don't follow your bidding. You'll do as I say. Last night you did change yourself to a fiend from hell. Heaven knows what dark powers you may possess. These men will wait until we both come out. If you should come out without me, they have orders to kill you.' And again I heard Crab's demonic giggle.

Now I saw how stupid I had been. A rogue like Maunder does not survive without being cunning. I was a fool to think he could be tricked so easily. Even if I could persuade him to take the poison I had prepared, I would not escape with my life.

Maunder led the way into the low mouth of a cave behind the boulder, the shadows twisting and leaping in the light from our flaming torches. Once inside, I saw we were in a passage, partly the work of nature, partly hewn by human hands. Soon rough steps climbed upwards and then we entered a chamber with a soft sandy floor. Around the walls were piled sea chests, boxes and oak casks that I assumed contained liquor. Here was Maunder's treasure trove – that part of the plunder that he hid from Stapleton.

Maunder threw back the lid of one of the chests, revealing silver tableware, ornaments, jewellery, and candlesticks, all jumbled together.

'Do right by me, maid, and a share of what you see could be yours.' He slammed the lid shut. 'Cross me and I'll slit yer throat!' He unsheathed his knife and ran his thumb menacingly across its sharp edge. In the confines of the cave, the man seemed huge, taking up all the space, breathing all the air, his monstrous shadow dancing across the rough walls and ceiling behind him. How could I possibly prevail against him? What

208

hope had my puny plan? I was in despair. All was lost. I was too young, too weak, too small. Why was there no one to help me? I felt again my mother's hand slipping from my grasp. I closed my eyes and saw her gentle, smiling face. Then anger and hatred boiled up inside me. Here was the man who wrecked our boat and caused her to drown. Here was the man who killed both my parents and drove my sister mad with grief. He, Maunder, had done this. He must pay for what he had done!

'Lay your torch on the floor!' I commanded.

Maunder looked surprised, but slowly did as he was bid.

'Sit against the wall.'

I laid my torch by his and placed the pot between them. The smoke began to fill the air, lit eerily by the flickering flames. I tipped the bones and horns from my sack on to the sand then threw off my hood and cloak, revealing, for the first time, my painted face and witch's hair. I snatched up the skull and leg bone and began to walk slowly around the fire, tapping the bones and chanting the numbers one to ten in Singhalese, hoping that to Maunder it sounded like a mystical incantation. Time to create some phantasms; I would start with a snake.

In my mind, I pictured a huge, writhing python. As soon as I had all the details clear in my head, the serpent appeared sliding across the cave floor. I sent it slithering towards Maunder, who cried out and struck at it with his knife, but I turned it into a hundred crawling spiders that swarmed across his legs. Then the spiders became a cloud of bats that rose up and flapped their leathery wings around his head, forcing him to crouch, striking out in all directions. Next I pictured a snarling tiger that pinned Maunder to the wall. Its roars

209

echoed about the chamber, to which I added my screams as I leapt through the smoke in a frenzied dance.

Seizing one of the sheep's horns from the floor, I scooped up a lethal dose of poison from the pot, intending to thrust it into Maunder's hand – then froze. If he drank it and died, my fate would also be sealed. Crab and his companions were waiting like hungry wolves just outside the cave. A mad, desperate scheme presented itself. I put the brimming horn to my lips, threw back my head and swallowed the bitter contents in one gulp. As the first agonising spasms gripped my stomach I concentrated on filling the cave with as many beating wings, writhing bodies, snarling mouths and flashing eyes as I could hold in my head at one time. I needed Maunder to be utterly terrified. But I needed to work fast. The poison was already in my blood. My heart would cease to beat in less than a minute.

I let my spirit slip from my body into Maunder's. What I found there was a mind half crazed with fear and a spirit that was crushed and cowering. I must drive his spirit out. I went to work in his mind, raising up the image of the Demon of Blood, Riri Yakka. I knew that if Maunder's spirit left his body it would go straight to the nearest living thing – and that living thing was my poisoned body. As the demon's image filled his deranged mind I felt the flood of fear cascading through every cell of his being – then he was gone. I had become Maunder and he me – he was trapped in my dying body like a doomed mariner in a sinking ship. I watched as my own body writhed in its death throes on the sand, a hand gripping at its heart, black mucus oozing from its nose and mouth. Seconds crept by – and then it lay still.

Maunder's spirit did not return to Maunder's body. I had it

to myself. But oh, the abomination of that loathsome mind! All his past crimes, debauchery, desires and cravings were there. A mind corrupted by greed and addicted to cruelty. To live in that body was to live in a cesspit of depravity. Surely it would have been better to choose a clean and honest death? But I had to think of Una. My spirit had to lock the door on Maunder's thoughts and memories and tune his mind to my purposes.

I lifted the body that had been mine and laid it on a low stone shelf by the cave wall. I must have the bracelet. I attempted to slip it off the lifeless arm. But it would not move! It was as though it were welded to the flesh. I tugged and twisted but I could not free it. Should I cut it loose and mutilate what had so recently been me? No, my spirit recoiled; I could not bear to do it.

I had betrayed the power of the bracelet and now it would not be mine. I had killed, even if the body I had killed was my own. Had the bracelet the power to resurrect as well as cure? Might my body return to life and Maunder's spirit with it? I must seal the cave. With what? How? Even with the strength of Maunder's powerful body, I could not do it alone. But I was Maunder! His gang would obey me! I need only give the order.

I blundered through the blinding smoke to the cave-mouth. As I emerged, the faces of the waiting men, half lit by their lanterns, turned expectantly. My instinct was to flee but I reminded myself that who they saw was Maunder. 'I have killed the witch!' The shock of hearing Maunder's voice speak my words momentarily confused me.

'Do we bury 'er, Cap'n?' asked Crab.

'No! We must seal the cave.'

'What of our booty?' asked another.

'Aye!' the others chorused.'

'You wouldn't be tryin' to double-cross us, would 'e, Cap'n?' wheedled Crab. 'Yer wouldn't be thinkin' of keepin' our share to yourself? The girl is dead?'

'You have my word she's dead,' I said firmly. But I saw my mistake. They would never close up the cave with the treasure inside. 'We will empty the cave and divide everything between us.' No sooner were the words out of my mouth than there was a stampede for the cave. 'Don't touch the girl, or anything she's wearing!' I shouted.

Fighting broke out almost immediately, but I drew Maunder's pistol and forced them to make a pile of the chests and casks on the sand. When the cave was empty, I ordered the rest of the torches lit and then set them to work shovelling the sand from under the boulder on the side of the cave-mouth. While this was being done, a runner was sent to bring ropes, timbers and as many extra hands as he could muster. When all was ready, I assembled my crew around the boulder – some to push, some to pull, others to lever it into place – and the great stone was rolled into the mouth of the cave, where it fitted with remarkably few gaps. Those spaces that remained were filled with smaller stones until I was satisfied that no creature could enter or exit.

'Crab,' I said, 'see that the booty is fairy divided.' I knew the mayhem this would unleash, and I was not disappointed. As I strode off into the darkness, the sounds of shots, cries, curses and the clash of steel echoed about the valley.

The business of sealing the cave had occupied me so fully that I had had no time to consider my own predicament. I was alive *but, to the rest of the world, I was Maunder. I was desperate to see Una but without the bracelet I could not give her warning of my transformation. I took the path out along the headland towards Mrs Ball's cottage but when I drew near I chose a vantage point where I could observe the house and still remain hidden among the gorse and rocks.*

As I expected, Una's thin figure appeared as soon as the sun was up and struck off down the rough track to the shore. I waited a few minutes and then made my way down to the cottage. The door stood open as Una had left it (as Una now always left it). The cottage was empty. I had hoped to find Mrs Ball – to explain to her the situation and ask her to speak to Una. But the old lady must have waited for me to return and, when I did not, gone to make enquiries. I pondered what I should do. I was concerned that, having rid themselves of one witch, Maunder's pack would decide to rid themselves of the witch's sister. Perhaps I could watch over Una without showing myself to her.

I knew where Una would be and, keeping out of sight, I climbed down to a ledge from which I could observe her. She sat motionless on the flat rock like the statues of Buddha I had seen in Ceylon, legs crossed, hands resting in her lap, the palms open, gazing out to sea. There she remained throughout the day, never moving while I waited and watched. I longed to go to her, to put my arms around her and hold her. She was all that I had left to love. My sole reason for being alive. But I knew I must not. Her poor disturbed mind would never grasp what had happened to me. If she caught sight of Maunder, she would believe I was dead.

It grew dark and still she sat there. I could bear it no longer.

I left the ledge and crept down close to her, keeping behind rocks, then whispered as softly as I could, 'Una – it's me – Rhiannon.'

I waited. There was no response. I whispered again – louder this time. But no – not even the slightest movement.

At last I went up to her and laid my hand gently on her arm. To my horror it was cold. Not the coldness of one who has sat too long in the wind, but the coldness of death. I held my hand by her nose and mouth – was there a faint breath? I laid my ear to her chest, praying for a heartbeat – but I heard nothing. Her eyes were open, unblinking. Her spirit had stayed away too long. If not already dead, her body would die very soon.

Being Maunder, I had no trouble lifting her. I carried her up the track to the cottage. Stepping through the doorway, Una's body limp in my arms, I came upon Mrs Ball.

'Murderer!' she screamed. 'Wicked, evil monster! Wasn't it enough for you to murder Rhiannon that you must murder her sister as well? Poor simple creature, what harm could she do you?'

Seeing what she saw, what else could she believe? I tried to stammer an explanation but she rushed past me, only pausing on the threshold to shout, 'You will hang for this!'

I laid Una on her bed. Kneeling on the floor beside her I let my head rest on her still body and my hand toyed with the bracelet around her thin, cold wrist. Let them hang me. What did I care? I had no desire to live as Maunder and with Una gone there was nothing to tie me to this world. I comforted myself with the thought that Una was where she loved to be, swimming in the body of a dolphin. A great tiredness weighed *me down and sleep soon released my spirit to travel where it wished. I was with Una. We were dolphins together, leaping and playing, sending pearls of spray glittering high into the sunlight.*

Daylight woke me. As the fog of sleep cleared I had a vague sense that something dreadful had happened or was about to happen. I half raised myself and saw Maunder's huge body slumped on the floor beside the bed. A swirl of confused thoughts filled my head. I was back in my own body! But my body was dead and sealed in the cave. I should be Maunder – but now Maunder appeared dead! My body felt familiar, yet unfamiliar, lighter, yet still a perfect match for my spirit. On my wrist was the bracelet – but it was loose now – I could slide it on and off. Gradually my careering mind slowed and steadied. I was Una – and I was Rhiannon. My stricken spirit and her dying body had been drawn to each other, had merged and become one. Perhaps, we always were one. Born of the same cell, we became two halves of the same self. I let the realisation take hold, then closed my eyes and searched for her spirit. Like an entity of pure joy I found her revelling in the intoxicating freedom of her life in the ocean. At once I was certain of two things: that she would never come back and, nevertheless, I would always wait for her. I wept. And when I had finished, I dried my eyes and swore I would never weep again.

Maunder's body was dead – stone dead. It took me an hour to drag it outside and down to Mrs Ball's herb garden. It took a further four hours to dig a hole big enough to bury it behind

215

the sage bush. That done, I returned to the cottage to await Mrs Ball's return.

Mrs Ball did not return for two days and when she did it was with the excise men of the Plymouth garrison. She was astonished to find Una (as she believed me to be) recovered. I told her and the men of the garrison that Maunder had left me for dead and was probably miles away by now. A search was mounted but, of course, he was never found. Maunder's followers were rounded up and marched to Plymouth, where many were hanged when the Honourable Robert Stapleton, seeing which way the wind was blowing, informed against them. The rest were transported to Australia.

Once they had gone, I searched the abandoned hovels for the plunder from the cave. Not for myself, I wanted no part of their booty, but I did not want it to fall into Stapleton's hands. I took everything of value to the one place I thought he would never look, the top of Devil's Rock, where wind and weather had carved out a deep crevasse. It took three nights to haul it all up there but there was no one to disturb me. And when I was satisfied I would find no more, I filled the remainder of the hole with loose stones and built a cairn on top.

One piece I did keep, a locket my father had given to my mother the Christmas before our departure from Wales. The two miniatures it contained were much damaged by salt water but I could still make out my dear parents' faces. It is all I have to remind me that I once had love and happiness.

Drinking and gambling soon reduced Stapleton to penury and the estate was sold to cover his debts. The new owners had no enthusiasm for farming the fields around the Orme and so we were allowed to remain in the old cottage where I cared for

Mrs Ball until she passed away.

After the old woman died, I could not bear to remain alone in the cottage. I left and took work where I could get it in the great houses of Devon and Cornwall. Ten years passed, then twenty and thirty but, as the years went by, I found I grew no older. Others grew up, had children, raised families, aged and passed on, but year after year my sixteen-year-old face stared back at me from every mirror. At first I thought it a blessing to always have my youth, but I soon learnt it was a curse. If I remained in one place for any great length of time, people would begin to remark on my enduring youthfulness, then the whispering would start and I would be forced to move on.

I understood now that when Una left her body to live with the dolphins and I took Maunder's body and then her body for my own, we had violated the great universal law that says you cannot move from one life to another without first dying. We had broken the cycle of birth and death. I was trapped in a body that would never change, that could not change until it was reunited with Una's spirit. Only then could we both be freed. So I returned to the Orme, to the cottage – certain that Una's spirit was still out there somewhere in the great ocean. But how to find her? I became obsessed by the idea of having my own boat – with a boat I could search for my sister, and I could earn a livelihood. My obsession finally drove me to climb the rock and do what I swore I would never do – I took some of Maunder's treasure and sold it.

Now I have my boat and I work the oyster beds in the season, and I fish, and I call the dolphins, and I search the sea for my sister's spirit.

* * *

Dear stranger, that is my story. Pray for me. Pray that one day I may be free. Pray that one day my sister will remember me and return.

Oh, Una, wherever you are, when you do return, you will find me here, waiting.

CHAPTER 19

Zaki looked at Anusha to see if she had finished reading. Anusha nodded and Zaki closed the book. Neither spoke but when their eyes met, Anusha let out a long breath. Zaki climbed up on deck and stood looking at the familiar scene – a few dinghies out sailing, the South Sands ferry busily making its way down the inlet, the harbourmaster's launch going about its business. How could everything appear so normal? Anusha emerged from the steps and stood beside him.

'It's Maunder. That's what got into me in the cave.'

'But how could he still be there? It was over a hundred years ago! And she killed him.'

'No. She poisoned her own body thinking Maunder's spirit would die with it. The bracelet held his spirit until I put it on, then it passed into me. I let it out. I released it from the cave. I'm like a carrier. It's like I've got a disease but I don't know the cure.'

'What about the girl – Rhiannon – maybe she knows what to do?'

'I think she's as puzzled as we are. She's been watching me ever since we got back from the Orme.'

'The cat?'

'Yes.'

'So she knew we were on her boat!'

'She knew we got on but she must have thought we'd left before she cast off.'

'Perhaps she meant us to find the book.'

'Perhaps. But I wasn't supposed to take the bracelet. I wish I could talk to her but I know she doesn't want me anywhere near her. And you can't blame her. What if Maunder suddenly took control of my body and I went for her?'

'Well, you can't talk to her – but I can.'

Zaki looked at Anusha. She was right! There was no reason why Anusha and Rhiannon shouldn't meet. Was there?

'What about some lunch?' Anusha asked suddenly. 'I'm starving!'

'Food. Good idea.'

They ate on deck in the autumn sunshine. Despite everything, it was good to be on the boat on such a beautiful day. Anusha asked questions about the rigging, about how everything worked, and Zaki answered them, happy for the chance to show off his knowledge.

'What about a sailing lesson?' Anusha asked as they tidied away the picnic.

'What? Now?'

'Why not?'

Yes – why not, thought Zaki. A nice little breeze had set in – perfect for a beginner. 'OK. We'll have to rig the dinghy.'

Zaki pulled the dinghy up alongside *Morveren* and climbed down into it. Soon, the dinghy was rigged and they cast off from *Morveren*.

'Where are we going?'

'Frogmore Creek?'

'Sounds good to me. I like frogs.'

Any girl who likes frogs has got to be all right, thought Zaki and grinned at Anusha.

'What?'

'Nothing.'

They had the wind behind them at first and then on the beam as they rounded Snapes Point and headed up towards Kingsbridge. After the point, they entered the part of the estuary known as The Bag, where the shore-line on each side falls away, creating a wide but well protected anchorage. The many yachts and launches on their swinging moorings provided Zaki and Anusha with an obstacle course through which to sail.

Zaki taught Anusha how to adjust the sails to suit the wind. During their lesson, the wind picked up and Zaki showed Anusha how to tuck her toes under the foot strap and lean out to keep the boat upright.

'Ever fallen out?' asked Anusha, as they both threw their weight back, leaning out as far as they could to balance a fresh gust.

'Not yet!' laughed Zaki.

'Hey, yeah! I could learn to like this!' shouted Anusha as the dinghy took off, skimming across the water in a flurry of spray.

'Look there!' Anusha pointed to something behind them.

Zaki saw the distinctive cotton sails and black hull of *Curlew* as she rounded the point and entered The Bag.

'Do you think she's following us?'

Zaki shook his head. 'But let's keep out of sight and see where she goes.' He looked around for a suitable hiding place and spotted the high sides of *Queen of the Dart*. 'Over there – we'll tuck ourselves in behind my grandad's boat. Get your head down, I'm going to gybe.'

'What?'

'Head down!'

Anusha ducked just as the boom whizzed over her head. 'Does it have to do that?'

''Fraid so. Now, get ready to drop the sails. Those two ropes on the mast – let them go when we're alongside.'

Hidden from view, they waited until they saw *Curlew*'s sails pass by on the other side, then Zaki eased the dinghy forward so that they could peep around the bow of the motorboat. *Curlew* turned into Frogmore Creek, dropped her sails and let go of the anchor.

'Can I borrow your dinghy?'

'What do you mean?'

'I mean, I want to go and talk to her.' Anusha's voice was determined.

'But . . .'

'Don't worry. I can row that far.' The determination in her voice had a nervous edge.

'I don't know . . .'

'This is your grandad's motorboat, right? So you can wait here. Look, it's the perfect opportunity.'

She was right, and yet . . .

'Listen! I'm going – so get out of the boat!'

Reluctantly, Zaki climbed on to *Queen of the Dart*.

Anusha slotted the rowlocks into place, drifted for a moment while she arranged her oars and then began to row towards the mouth of the creek. At first, her progress was a little erratic and her path far from straight, but she kept at it and the distance between the dinghy and *Curlew* gradually closed.

Watching from the deck of the motorboat, Zaki saw Rhiannon reach down and take hold of the dinghy as Anusha came alongside. Anusha scrambled on to *Curlew* and she and Rhiannon stood facing each other in the cockpit. Zaki did not need to hear what was being said to know that Anusha was not being made to feel welcome. Rhiannon's arms were folded and her head tipped slightly back. It looked as if she would order Anusha off her boat at any moment. But Anusha was doing all the talking; she was gesturing with her hands – explaining, perhaps even pleading. Then Zaki saw her lean slightly towards Rhiannon and place her hand on the stiffly folded arms. They stood frozen, neither saying anything, looking into each other's faces, until Rhiannon let her arms fall to her sides and indicated that they should sit down.

Round one to Anusha, Zaki thought.

Now they sat, their two heads close together. Anusha was still the more animated of the two, obviously asking lots of questions. At first, Rhiannon hardly looked at her and seemed to say little in reply. Then something Anusha asked made Rhiannon sit up and turn towards her. Now it was Anusha who hung her head and listened. Zaki was too far away to read the expression on Anusha's face.

At last, they both stood up. Anusha asked one last question and Rhiannon shook her head.

They looked over towards him and he wondered if he should wave but decided against it. Rhiannon held the dinghy while Anusha stepped into it. She waited on deck until Anusha had pushed off and begun rowing back across to *Queen of the Dart*, then went below into *Curlew's* cabin.

Soon the dinghy was alongside and Anusha climbed up beside Zaki. She brushed away the hair that the wind had blown across her face. 'Do you want to talk here, or do you want to get back?' Zaki could tell by her expression that the news wasn't good.

'Can she help us?' he asked.

'No,' said Anusha simply.

'What about Maunder? What does he want?'

'He wants to live.'

'And that means . . .'

Anusha hesitated, took a deep breath and said, 'She says you can keep the bracelet. That it might help you in some way.'

Zaki could hear that Anusha was trying to offer him some hope. 'But Maunder?' he persisted.

'He will try to take over your body.'

'And if he does?'

'And if he does, then he will try to kill her. She thinks he wants revenge for what she did to him.'

'Can she be killed? What about the bracelet? Doesn't that protect her in some way?'

224

'The bracelets let you move from one body to another. Some part of you, like your soul, can even hide in the bracelet. That was where Maunder was when you put the bracelet on in the cave.'

'And what about me?' Zaki asked. 'What happens to me if Maunder does take over my body? Do I become a sort of ghost like her sister and live with the dolphins?'

'She doesn't know. But that's not going to happen, Zaki! We're going to think of something!'

Why, thought Zaki bitterly, *why did I have to put the bracelet on? Why didn't I leave it alone?*

Anusha waited for him to say something. When he remained silent, she said quietly, 'There's something else.'

'What?'

'She says you have to stay awake.'

'All the time?'

'Yes.'

'That's not possible.'

'I know. But every time you go to sleep it gives Maunder a chance to draw strength from your body. He was weak when you put the bracelet on, hardly a human spirit, but he's strong now. She says, when we sleep our spirits wander. One night Maunder may be strong enough to shut you out.'

Zaki could feel the fear taking hold of him. 'What else did she say?'

'She thinks Maunder will win.'

'Over my dead body!'

'Maybe not a good choice of phrase?'

'Yeah, thanks. Maybe not.'

Zaki looked across the water to where *Curlew* swung at anchor. He felt the now familiar weight of the bracelet in his pocket. The bracelet had let Maunder in – could it be used to get him out?

'I'm sorry,' Anusha said.

'For what?'

'I thought she might know a way out of this.'

'It's not your fault,' said Zaki but, of course, he had hoped for the same thing.

'Come on – we'd better get back. Grandad'll be wondering where we've got to.'

They climbed down into the dinghy, hoisted the sails and cast off.

'What was she like?' Zaki asked, after they had sailed for some time in silence.

'A bit scary!'

'How?'

'She looks so young – but her eyes – it's like she's looking at things all the time that you can't see.'

By the time they had sailed back to *Morveren*, Anusha had tacking down to a fine art.

'Fancy crewing for me next time I'm racing?' Zaki asked.

'Yeah, any time!' said Anusha with enthusiasm.

Once they had the dinghy stowed on *Morveren*'s deck, they hoisted 'the mermaid' and it wasn't long before Grandad's old launch was put-putting towards them with Jenna standing in the bows, her tail wagging.

Back ashore, Grandad sent them across the road to the cottage while he finished up in the boat shed.

'Give the ol' dog 'er dinner. I'll be over directly.'

Zaki fed Jenna while Anusha had a look around.

'Zaki! You have to look at this!' she called from the small front room. When Zaki joined her he found she was examining the framed black and white photograph that always sat on top of Grandad's television.

'Who's this?'

'My great-grandfather. Why?'

'Look at what's behind him.'

The photograph had obviously been taken on the slipway behind the Luxtons' boat shed. A stocky old gentleman in a cap and a waistcoat, his shirtsleeves rolled up to the elbows, stood with his thumbs tucked into his grubby trouser pockets. The picture was grainy and faded.

Anusha passed the photograph to Zaki.

'Look at the boat.'

Behind Zaki's great-grandfather was a boat that was being built or repaired. Of course Zaki had seen the picture heaps of times, but he took it across to the window to examine it in better light.

'Do you see?'

Then, Zaki saw what Anusha had seen and it made the hair on the back of his neck creep – it was something he'd never noticed before, but then, why would he? It would never have meant anything to him before. The lettering on the boat's bow said *Curlew*.

'Your great-grandad built *Curlew*!'

'No,' corrected Zaki, 'rebuilt. Look, don't you see? They're putting a cabin on her. She was an open fishing boat and they're converting her to the way she is now.'

'What's so very interestin'?' They turned to find Grandad standing in the doorway.

'This boat . . .' Zaki began.

'What of it?'

'Do you remember who the owner was?'

'I wasn't much more than a boy when that was taken.'

'But do you remember the owner?'

'P'rhaps.'

'Grandad, it could be important.'

'Matter of fact, I do 'cause it was unusual.'

'How?' asked Zaki.

'Why?' asked Anusha.

Grandad looked from one to the other.

''Cause it was a young woman. Unusual in them days.'

'What was her name?' demanded Zaki.

'Her name? No, I can't recall her name.'

'Please try,' begged Zaki.

'Was it Rhiannon?' asked Anusha.

'Why's it so important?'

'It's important because I think we've met her!'

'No, boy. She'd be dead by now. Or if she isn't, she'd be an old woman.'

'She's on this boat anchored up Frogmore Creek!'

Grandad took the photograph from Zaki, ran his hand gently over the frame, then carefully returned it to its place on top of the television.

'Same boat p'rhaps – different owner.'

228

'It was a fishing boat – right? An open boat, and your dad put a cabin on her.'

'Oyster boat from Falmouth. Now, I've listened to enough nonsense. Time I was takin' you two home.' It was clear that for Grandad the subject was closed. Zaki wondered why he was so reluctant to talk about it. Had the girl talked to Grandad all those years ago? Told him her story? No, she wouldn't have; she kept herself to herself. But perhaps he had sensed there was something strange about her.

'What are you going to do about not sleeping? How are you going to stay awake?' asked Anusha as they followed Grandad out to the car.

'I don't know. I suppose I'll just stay awake as long as I can.'

'Maybe you should have sort of catnaps – don't go to sleep for too long.'

'Once I'm asleep I tend to stay asleep.'

'I could telephone you. Wake you up every half-hour.'

'You'll probably get my dad or Michael.'

'Have you got an alarm?'

'Yeah – I've got an alarm.'

'If you want to talk to someone, just call me. I'll have my mobile in my room. Doesn't matter what time it is.'

They'd reached the old Volvo. Its doors creaked and complained as they opened them, and they needed to be slammed shut. Then they were off back to Kingsbridge.

CHAPTER 20

Zaki went straight upstairs to his room. He took the mask out of his rucksack and looked around for somewhere to hang it. Like all the rooms in the house, except Michael's, the walls were bare. Michael had ignored their father's fretting about the fresh plaster and covered his walls in posters.

There was a solitary picture hook on which hung a mirror. Zaki took down the mirror and leant it against the wall. He hung up the mask and sat on his bed for a moment looking at it.

The sound of Michael's guitar came through the adjoining wall. The guitar stopped. After a pause there was the sound of a computer-generated drumbeat and the guitar began again over the top of the rhythm.

Zaki left his room and opened Michael's door.

'What you doing?' He tried to sound cheery. It was the first time they had spoken since the moment Michael slammed the van door.

'What's it look like?'

'Can I use the computer later?

'What for?'

'I want to look up some stuff – that's all.'

'I'm going out later – so you can do what you like.'

Zaki hung in the doorway, hoping Michael would say something else. But he didn't.

'Is there anything to eat?'

'There's some pizza in the kitchen.'

'You want any?'

'I've had some.'

Zaki thought about asking whether their father had been home but decided not to. He waited a while longer but Michael remained hunched over his guitar, so he closed the door and went down to the kitchen. He found the cold remains of the pizza and put them in the microwave to warm up. When it was ready, he took his meal through to the front room to eat it in front of the television. He flicked through the channels until he came to a nature programme. On the screen, a wasp was injecting her eggs into the soft, yielding body of a caterpillar.

'You found something to eat, then?'

Zaki looked up to find his father looking in from the corridor.

'Mm – yes – thanks,' he mumbled with his mouth full.

'Good.' His father continued on to the kitchen.

The wasp eggs hatched and the wasp larvae grew and swelled in the caterpillar's body.

Zaki heard his brother's bedroom door slam shut and the sound of his footsteps on the stairs.

'Michael,' his father called from the kitchen, 'where are you going?'

There was no reply but Zaki heard the rattle of the front-door latch. His father hurried past the open living-room door.

'Michael! I asked you a question! Michael!'

The garden gate opened and closed and, after a long pause, the front door clicked shut and his father returned, more slowly, to the kitchen.

The pizza seemed to stick in Zaki's throat. He picked up the remote and turned off the television. He sat staring at the dead screen. This was awful. Someone needed to do something. He got to his feet and carried his plate into the kitchen, where he found his father, hands deep in his overall pockets, standing in the middle of the room doing nothing. He waited for his father to move. To say something. To look at him or smile. But his father remained as he had found him.

'Don't you think you ought to talk to Mum?'

Now his father did turn – slowly until their eyes met. His father shrugged and looked away. Zaki gripped his empty plate more tightly. He had a sudden urge to smash it on the kitchen floor but he resisted and placed it carefully on the kitchen table.

'I just thought . . . she might know what to do.'

'Maybe.' His father picked up the plate without looking at him and put it in the dishwasher.

Zaki felt his stomach tighten with anger. Why was his father behaving like this? He wanted to hit him! Instead, he left the kitchen and went to his room.

He sat on his bed. Inside him, something was growing, hidden from the outside world.

He lay back on his bed. No! He mustn't go to sleep. He got up and went to his brother's room. Of course it was empty. He couldn't talk to his father. He couldn't talk to Michael.

He returned to his room and sat on the bed.

Then he remembered the slip of paper in his drawer with his mother's number in Switzerland written on it. He retrieved it. He returned to the bed and sat staring at the number. Why shouldn't he call her? Something made him hesitate. What was the problem? The problem was that he believed what Michael had said – that she wasn't coming home. But he didn't want to hear her say that that was true.

He forced himself to his feet. Somebody had to face what was happening to his family. He went out on to the landing, where there was a telephone extension. Was his father still in the kitchen? He listened. The television was on again in the living room. He picked up the telephone and dialled the number. As soon as he heard his mother pick up the telephone at the other end of the line he said, 'Mum?'

'Zaki?'

'Mum,' he said, keeping his voice down so that his father wouldn't overhear.

'What is it?'

'Mum, we need you.'

'Zaki . . . it's a bit difficult.'

'No. We need you.'

'Zaki . . .'

'We need you here.'

He put down the telephone before she could say anything else. Would she call back? Ask to speak to his father? He waited by the telephone. Nothing happened. He went back to his room and closed the door.

There was the mask on the wall. It was just a mask. Something carved out of wood and painted. Something someone had made. How could it help him? He took the bracelet out of his pocket and put it on the table beside the bed. It didn't look very special. Yes, but what about all that weird stuff he could do? Make birds appear and disappear. Was he going mad? Had he imagined the whole thing? He decided to try an experiment.

He thought about the pet guinea pig he had had when he was younger. It was white with brown spots. He thought carefully about where the spots were positioned, pictured its bright little eyes and quivering whiskers, the little bit of pink on its nose, the sound its feet made on a polished floor. He let it take shape in his mind while staring at a dirty sock on the floor beside his bed. The sock developed a bright little eye and then the sock was gone and the guinea pig popped into existence around the eye. His concentration wavered and the guinea pig went back to being a sock. This obviously takes a bit of practice, he thought.

Each time he brought the guinea pig into being he held it there a little longer until, eventually, he was able to reserve a piece of his mind for the guinea pig while thinking about something else entirely.

He let the guinea pig run around the bedroom while he took a clean pair of socks from his drawer. He thought

234

of two more guinea pigs. Two perfect clones of the first guinea pig scuttled about the floor, around his feet and under the bed. He wiped them all from his mind; three guinea pigs disappeared and were replaced by three socks. So what did that prove? That when something appeared, something else disappeared. The flapping plastic bag turned into the first seagull, the poster turned into the hawk, the socks into the guinea pigs.

All very interesting, but turning socks into guinea pigs wasn't going to help him against Maunder! The logbook was still in his rucksack. Maybe he'd missed something. Maybe something she had written could help him. What did she say about the Devil Dances?

Zaki sat on his bed, the book open against his knees. He reread everything Rhiannon had written about the Devil Dances, about her transformation into the demon in Maunder's house and about the events in the cave. He rested his head back against the wall and closed his eyes, trying to picture everything she had described. Did he fall asleep? He felt another face pressing against the inside of his, as though his face were a mask worn by somebody else. He felt his features stretching and distorting as the face inside pushed outwards. Then his mind filled with memories that weren't his own. He saw Devil's Rock, black against the sky. A wrecked ship lay on the reef beneath; bodies floated in the water, carts were being loaded by the light of flaming torches.

Zaki sat up quickly. He looked for the mirror on the wall but saw the mask, then remembered he had put the mirror on the floor. He picked it up and examined his face. Did he imagine it, or did he see a white scar running down from under his left eye, through his lips to his chin? Yes – it was faint, but it was there, like a pale puckered line. Maunder!

He mustn't wait any longer. He had to act. He found the CD of drum music that Anusha had given him. But he needed something to play it on. He went to Michael's room and fetched the laptop and his brother's headphones. Back in his own room, he set the computer up on the table beside his bed, put the CD in and put the headphones on. Then he put on the bracelet. The mask was on the wall in front of him. He was ready. Could he drive Maunder back into the bracelet?

The drum music began to play. Through the headphones it sounded as if the drum was in the middle of Zaki's head. A second drum joined the first, then a third and a fourth. Mr Dalal had obviously laid one track over another. The rhythms crossed and recrossed but every now and then the drums would beat together in unison and the rhythm throbbed like a great heart echoing the beating of Zaki's own. Zaki kept his eyes fixed on the mask. Slowly, the mask's features came to life: the sightless eyeholes became eyes that fixed their penetrating gaze on him; the mouth widened in a terrible grin; the hair became alive with snakes. From the head grew a body, its belly smeared with blood. From the shoulders sprouted four arms that ended in four clawed hands. One hand gripped a rooster, on another perched a parrot; the third held a sword and from the fourth hung a human head. As the demon advanced towards him, Zaki saw that it was mounted on an enormous boar. Zaki wanted to turn and run, but he knew he must face the demon – speak to it, make it obey him.

'Wait! Who are you?' he demanded.

'I am Riri Yakka – Demon of Blood. My home is the graveyards. I hunt the dead. Why have you called me?'

Zaki swallowed back his revulsion. He must make the demon serve him.

'I have someone for you to hunt. Follow me!'

Now Zaki turned, or in his mind he turned, and he saw in front of him a tunnel, like the entrance to a deep cave. He plunged into the cave-mouth. The tunnel beyond the entrance was lit by a red glow that he realised was coming from the demon behind him. Zaki quickly set off down the passage.

Ahead of him the passage divided. What was this? A maze? A labyrinth? How would he choose which way to go? He decided that where he could continue straight ahead he would always go straight ahead, otherwise he would always choose left. That way, to find his way out of the labyrinth, he need only reverse the rule.

The passage twisted and turned, divided and divided again, but Zaki stuck to his rule and the demon followed close on his heels. Another division and Zaki chose left. A dead end! But he mustn't turn round. Zaki began to walk backwards. Now, as he got closer, he could feel the heat of the demon's body and smell its sulphurous smell, but he didn't look – he mustn't look. The heat became unbearable and the smell suffocating – then he felt the heat diminish and saw the red glow receding. The demon was moving back. When he reached the turning, Zaki turned right. From now on he would have to count the turns and remember the pattern. On they went, deeper into the maze. There were more false turns but Zaki forced himself to remember the number of lefts between each right. He repeated over and over in his head, 'Three lefts, right – two lefts, right – five lefts, right – two lefts, right.'

Then, up ahead, the darkness seemed darker, as though a denser black crouched in the centre of the blackness. They had reached the centre of the maze. Maunder could retreat no further. The demon gave a warning growl and Zaki flung himself to the side of the passage as, with a deafening roar, the blood-streaked demon, sword held high, charged past. The hunt was on! With a howl of fear, the black shape hurled itself past the charging demon and raced back down the passage. The mounted demon turned and galloped in pursuit. The demon's roars and Maunder's cries echoed through the labyrinth, the hooves of the demon's mount thundering through the tunnels. When the red glow from the demon faded, Zaki was left in total darkness to feel his way slowly back. If he clung to the left wall, he could miss a turning to the right. If he followed the right wall, he could miss a turning on the left.

Unable to see the turnings, Zaki soon knew he was lost. He listened, hoping the roars of the demon would give him a clue, but all he could hear was a steady beating as though the maze itself had a gigantic heart.

Suddenly, the maze dissolved as a circle of excruciating

pain seared his left wrist. He was back in his room. The beat of the drums still pounded in his head. He tore off the headphones. The bracelet was burning his wrist. He struggled to pull the burning bronze band from his arm. As he tossed the scorching bracelet on to the bedside table, he saw that the engravings were shining and dancing. He dived from his room into the bathroom, twisted on the cold tap and thrust his blistering wrist under the flow of water. As he looked up, he saw his face in the bathroom mirror. The white scar had gone. He examined his reflection more closely and saw only himself.

He had done it! He was certain he had done it. He had driven Maunder back into the bracelet.

When the pain had subsided a little, he wrapped his arm in a towel and returned to his room. He didn't want to touch the bracelet, but he was too tired to think what to do with it. He turned off the light and lay on his bed. In a few minutes, he was asleep.

CHAPTER 21

When Zaki woke, the first thing he noticed was the pain from his burnt wrist, then that the laptop was gone from the bedside table. Michael must have come back in the night and taken it. On the table, beside where the laptop had been, there was a circular scorch mark. No wonder the bracelet had burnt his wrist.

The bracelet! With a jolt of panic, Zaki was fully awake. The bracelet! Where was it? Had Michael knocked it on to the floor? He searched under the table, under the bed, the whole room. There was no sign of it. Michael must have taken it. Picked it up, perhaps, to see what it was. What if he put it on?

Zaki flung himself out of the door and raced the few feet to Michael's room. No Michael. There was the usual mess, but his brother wasn't there. Frantically, he began to search the room. Where in all this clutter had Michael put the bracelet? It must be here! Please, God, let it be here! He searched every surface, threw the jumbled bedclothes off the bed, ferreted through the boxes of CDs, sifted through the piles of discarded clothes, shook out every garment and went through every pocket.

When he had finished, he went back and did it all again. The bracelet was not in the room. Michael must have it with him.

Fingers of ice gripped Zaki's heart. Maunder's spirit was thriving now. Like some monstrous larva that devours its living host, it would overpower whoever next wore the bracelet.

What was the time? Just after seven – very early for Michael to be up and about on a Sunday. Maybe he never went to bed. As he left Michael's room, Zaki almost collided with his father. His father looked him up and down.

'Zaki, did you sleep in those clothes?'

Zaki realised that he was still in his uniform from Friday.

'Zaki, go and have a shower and put something clean on, right now! Honestly! I don't know what's go into you two!'

'Dad, have you seen Michael?'

'No I haven't. Isn't he in his room?'

'Dad, he's gone. I think we should look for him.' Zaki headed for the stairs.

'Zaki! Come back here and get in the shower, now!'

'Dad, it's important!'

'Get in the shower! Do what you're told! Your brother may be a teenager but you're not. Don't you start acting up!'

'But, Dad, you don't understand . . .'

'No I don't. Now go and wash.'

What should he do? Disobey his father? Make a run

for it? No – maybe he should keep him happy. Perhaps then he'd help him look for Michael.

He turned and went to the bathroom but as he opened the door his father called after him, 'Zaki – your shoulder – shouldn't you be wearing your sling?'

'No, it's fine. Seems to be better.'

'Zaki, are you sure . . . ?'

'It's fine!'

Zaki shut the door behind him. He didn't want a long discussion with his father about his shoulder and he didn't want him to see his burnt wrist.

He washed quickly and put on clean clothes, making sure his sweatshirt sleeve covered the livid red burn. He found his father in the kitchen, eating breakfast.

'I'm going to look for Michael.'

'Eat some breakfast before you go anywhere.'

'Dad, I think Michael might be in trouble.'

'He is. He's in trouble with me. You can tell him that if you find him! Where did he go to last night?'

'I don't know.'

Zaki's father shook his head, then, in a gentler voice, said, 'Come on, sit down and eat something.'

Zaki poured himself cereal and milk and ate it standing up.

'Dad,' he said through a mouthful of cereal, 'won't you help me look for him?'

'No I will not – I've got better things to do.'

Zaki finished his mouthful.

'Right. I'm going.'

He put down his bowl and bolted for the door.

'Aren't you going to have anything else?'

'No!' Grabbing his jacket from the hooks by the front door, Zaki was out and in the street before his father could mention homework or any other thing that might delay him.

Where to start? Was Michael acting like Michael, or was Michael acting like Maunder?

He was acting like Maunder. If he had been acting like Michael, he would still be in bed. Where would Maunder go? What would he do? He was from another time. What would be familiar to him? The harbour. He'd make for the harbour. That seemed the most likely . . . The girl! Rhiannon! He'd try to find Rhiannon!

Zaki's route to the harbour took him close to Anusha's place. He decided to make a short detour. He was going to need help.

It was Mrs Dalal who opened the door and she ushered him in with a big friendly smile.

'We're all having breakfast. Come and join us.' Then she called, 'Anusha! It's Zaki!'

Anusha looked up, in surprise, from her breakfast, but Mr Dalal jumped to his feet as Zaki entered the kitchen, as though Zaki were an honoured guest.

'Zaki! What brings you out so early? Take a seat! Take a seat! What will you have? Tea? Coffee? Some toast?'

'Thanks, Mr Dalal, but I've already had breakfast.'

'My! What a very early bird you are!'

'I was wondering if Anusha could help me.'

All looked at Anusha.

'What's happened?' she asked, her eyes searching

Zaki's face.

'We have to find Michael. It's quite urgent.'

'Michael?' asked Mrs Dalal.

'My brother.'

'I'll just get my trainers.' Anusha was gone and back in a matter of seconds.

'Is something wrong?' enquired Mrs Dalal, looking concerned.

'He's supposed to be helping my grandad in Salcombe, but he hasn't turned up,' Zaki lied.

'Is there anything we can do to help?' asked Mr Dalal.

'You couldn't give us a lift to Salcombe, could you? He's probably there, but he's met up with some mates, or something.' Grandad's launch, Zaki thought. They could borrow Grandad's launch.

'No problem. Do you want to go now?'

'Yes please.'

They bundled into Mr Dalal's car and fifteen minutes later he dropped them off by the boat shed.

'If you need a lift back, just call me.'

As soon as her father had driven off, Anusha seized Zaki by the arm. 'What's happened? What's going on? Why are we looking for Michael?'

As briefly as he could, Zaki told her about the mask, the bracelet and Maunder, and the fact that the bracelet was gone when he woke up. 'We need to find Michael and we need to warn Rhiannon. I thought we'd take Grandad's launch and see if *Curlew* is still in Frogmore Creek.'

The boat shed was locked and Grandad's car was

missing from its parking place.

'He's gone somewhere. Probably taken Jenna up to Bolt Head for a walk.'

'So, what do we do?'

'He never locks the back. Dad keeps telling him he ought to.'

They squeezed down the narrow passage between the boat shed and the shed next door and let themselves in. Zaki got the lifejackets and helped himself to Grandad's bunch of boat keys. He scrawled *Taken the launch, Zaki* on a scrap of paper and left it on the workbench.

The old launch's engine kicked over twice then juddered into life. They cast off and headed out through the moorings, setting the small craft rocking as the launch's wake fanned out behind them. There was a stiff southerly breeze blowing up the estuary from the sea and Zaki wished he'd put some more clothes on. He looked at Anusha sitting in Jenna's favourite spot in the bow. He was impressed by the way she hopped in and out of boats as if she'd been doing it all her life. Should he have brought her? Should he have got her mixed up in all this?

They swung round Snapes Point and into The Bag. Ahead, the mudbanks were already appearing as the ebbing tide drained the shallow upper reaches of the estuary. As they passed *Queen of the Dart*, Frogmore Creek opened up to starboard. There was no sign of *Curlew*.

'She's gone!' shouted Anusha over the throb of the engine.

Zaki turned into the mouth of the creek, just to make

245

sure she hadn't moved the boat. The bottom was mud and weed here and no good for anchoring, she might have moved upstream. He continued round the next bend but there was no sign of her. Any further up would be too shallow for *Curlew*.

'What now?' asked Anusha, coming astern so that they could talk more easily.

Zaki put the engine into neutral and let the launch drift downstream on the tide. Now the engine was quieter, Zaki could hear the calls of the waders feeding on the mudbanks, the oystercatchers' high, whistling cry and the haunting liquid song of the curlews. Some said these birds held the souls of the drowned. Is that why Rhiannon had chosen their name for her boat?

'I don't know,' said Zaki. 'If Rhiannon was wearing her bracelet, she might have known what happened. Perhaps she's trying to get away before Maunder catches up with her.'

'What if he did catch up with her?'

'You mean Michael . . . Maunder is on *Curlew*?' It hadn't occurred to him. But it was possible, of course it was possible. It wasn't difficult to steal a boat. He could have taken a dinghy from Kingsbridge and come down on the tide.

Anusha nodded. 'Can you still make phantom creatures without the bracelet?'

'I think so. I could last night.'

'Could you use one to look for *Curlew*; see who's on board?'

'I can try. You take the helm.'

246

'What do I do?'

'Push the tiller the opposite way from the way you want the boat to go. You'll soon get the hang of it.'

They changed places and Anusha eased the boat ahead, slowly at first, while she got used to steering. Zaki sat in the bows and gathered his thoughts. He would use the hawk; its exceptional power of sight was what he needed. He recalled the moment in the classroom when it alighted on his arm; its piercing yellow eyes, the hooked beak, the mottled feathers, the way it swivelled its head to look over its shoulder. He held his right arm out level and thought only of the bird . . . nothing happened. How stupid! He'd tried to create it out of thin air! He looked around for a suitable object to transform and found a coil of rope in the bottom of the boat. He stood, cleared his mind once more and thought of the bird, then flung the rope as high into the air as he could. The coil spun end over end, seemed to hang, suspended, go out of focus, blurred, developed an eye, and then the hawk was wheeling and soaring above him.

He sat, closed his eyes, and imagined the world from the hawk's point of view. Immediately, he was seeing through the hawk's eyes. The horizon swung up and down in a dizzying see-sawing motion as the hawk's flight dipped left and right. He saw himself and Anusha in the launch far below. He thought the hawk down the estuary and out to sea and let the strengthening head wind lift it higher and higher until it rose above the rocky pinnacles of Bolt Head. He turned the bird's head, scanning the coast east and west.

There she was! Reaching fast under full sail, half a mile to sea of the Ham Stone, heading west. The angle of the sail prevented him from seeing how many people were on the boat. He sent the bird after her. *Curlew* leapt and bucked in the short, steep waves that the southerly wind had already whipped up off the headland. Now he could see the cockpit. Now he could see how many were aboard. He let out a groan. Only one person was visible but that person was Michael – at least it appeared to be Michael from the back, but when he saw the scarred face he knew it wasn't really his brother who was steering the boat. Where was Rhiannon? Had he killed her?

Zaki brought the hawk back across the headland. He held up his arm and made the hawk alight on it, then released it from his mind and the coil of rope dropped back into the boat.

'I still can't really believe you can do that,' said Anusha.

'I could only see Maunder.'

'Where's Rhiannon?'

'In the cabin, perhaps. Let's hope so. They're heading down the coast.'

'Can we catch them?'

'Not in this.'

'Where are they going?'

'My guess is they're heading for the Orme.'

'What if we took *Morveren*?'

Zaki didn't answer. He looked at Anusha and she looked steadily back at him, waiting for his reply. Take *Morveren*. *Morveren* was a bigger boat than *Curlew*, but

248

heavier. She had a motor and *Curlew* didn't. They might overtake her.

'You take the launch back. I'll take *Morveren*.'

'Oh no! You said next time you raced you wanted me to crew. Well, this is a race and I'm crewing.' She altered course, swinging the launch towards *Morveren*'s mooring.

'Anusha, it's looking rough out there.'

'What are trying to say? You think because I'm a girl I'm going to get in the way?'

'No, it's just . . . Hey! Not so fast!'

The launch was pointed straight at *Morveren* and in another minute would hit her at full speed. Zaki leapt for the controls, swung the engine into reverse to take off speed and pushed the tiller over. He held his breath. The launch slowed and came to rest alongside the yacht.

'You could have told me to do that!'

'Yeah – right,' said Zaki and remembered he needed to breathe.

Anusha scrambled out of the launch and stood looking down from the yacht's deck.

'Just tell me what I need to do.'

'You can start by getting the sail-cover off the main.'

Anusha set to work while Zaki made the launch fast to *Morveren*'s mooring then he too climbed aboard. There was a set of keys to the yacht on Grandad's bunch of boat keys. While he opened up the cabin, Zaki kept thinking, *This is not a good idea, this is not a good idea*. He thought about what his father would say, what his Grandad would say. Anusha didn't know anything about the sea. He should tell her that they weren't going; that they couldn't

249

do it. But what about Michael? What would happen to Michael if they did nothing? *It's my fault*, thought Zaki. *It's my fault. If I hadn't gone into the cave – if I hadn't picked up the bracelet* . . .

'What now?' Anusha's shout brought him back to the job at hand.

'We'll put the sails up when we're under way. Better put some oilies on.' He dived into the cabin and returned with two sets of wet-weather gear. Once they were dressed, Zaki started the engine and sent Anusha forward to cast off.

'Can you take her, please,' he asked as Anusha returned. 'I want to get a forecast.' He pointed out the port and starboard channel marks off Black Rock and the Wolf Rock buoy then handed over the helm and went below to the radio. They'd missed the Brixham coast-guard's forecast, so he selected channel 12 and called the harbour office. They shouldn't be too busy at this time of year, he reasoned, and anyway, everyone knew *Morveren*.

'Salcombe Harbour, Salcombe Harbour, Salcombe Harbour, this is *Morveren, Morveren, Morveren* – over.'

'*Morveren* – Salcombe Harbour. Over.'

'Can I have a forecast? Over.'

He got a pad and pen ready and jotted down the details as they were read out.

Wind south veering south-west 5 to 6,
increasing 7 to gale 8 later.
Weather fair – rain later.
Visibility good.
Sea moderate to rough.

'Over.'

'Thank you, Salcombe Harbour, out.'

He retuned the radio to listen out on channel 16 and went up on deck. As *Morveren* came out from behind the shelter of Black Rock, she lifted her bow to the first of the swells. They needed to get the mainsail up before they reached the rough water over the bar, and they'd need to sail fast to have any hope of catching *Curlew*. Having hoisted the mainsail, he took over the helm. They were heading dead into the wind. They'd be better off motoring until they rounded the point and turned west.

'Better clip on. If you go over the side, you'll stay attached to the boat.' Zaki clipped his own lifeline on and showed Anusha how to attach hers. He studied her face to see how she was coping with the sudden violent pitching of the boat as they entered the steep chop over the bar.

'How are you feeling?'

'Fine,' Anusha replied, a little too earnestly.

When they were clear of the Little Mew Stone, Zaki eased the mainsail and turned away from the wind. *Morveren* heeled and picked up speed as the sail filled. Now they were no longer butting straight into the swell and they had the wind in the sail to steady them, the motion of the boat was much more comfortable. He knew the passage to the Orme off by heart and set a course that would take them straight across Bigbury Bay. 'Time to set the foresail,' Zaki said. 'You let this line out while I winch in the sheet. OK! Slowly now!'

Morveren pushed up a foaming white wave and powered through the swell. Zaki cut the motor – they'd go just as fast without it – and for a moment he allowed himself to enjoy the familiar thrill of boat, wind and water.

But this was no pleasure trip. Zaki scanned the sea ahead for *Curlew*. The waves were capped with white horses – she'd be hard to spot and she'd had a good head start. Would she still be in sight?

'There!' shouted Anusha.

Zaki looked to where she was pointing. At first, he could only see the white crests of waves and then he saw the unmistakable shape of a sail on the far side of the bay.

'There's a pair of binoculars in the chart table. Could you fetch them up please?'

'It's her all right,' Anusha said, once she'd got the binoculars focused. 'But what's she doing?'

'Let me see.'

Anusha passed the binoculars to Zaki.

'Could you take the helm?'

'What do I do?'

'Just follow *Curlew*, but stay up wind of her.'

'I wish you'd speak English!'

'I mean that way. A bit out to sea.'

Zaki trained the binoculars on the distant sail. 'She's hove-to.'

'And what does that mean?!'

'It means she's not going anywhere. It's a way of stopping when you're under sail.'

'Why would Maunder do that? Does he know we're

252

following him?'

'No – I don't think so.' Zaki tried to keep the binoculars steady but it wasn't easy with *Morveren* pounding along at full tilt. He lost *Curlew* and found her again. 'The wind's too strong for him. He's reefing.'

'He's what?'

'Making the sails smaller. We should catch up a bit,' Zaki said, as he and Anusha changed places again.

'What are we going to do if we do catch them up?'

Zaki had been wondering the same thing. He didn't have a plan. He just hoped he could do something – anything, to help Michael fight against Maunder. Drive him out like he had driven him out. There had to be a way.

'I don't know.'

'We'll think of something.'

'Yeah – we have to catch them first.'

As the morning wore on, the wind gradually but relentlessly veered from south to south-west and grew in strength until *Morveren*, leaning at a crazy angle, was driving through the mounting seas. As the wind veered, it freshened. Now streaks of white spray were being blown off the tops of the waves.

The fresher conditions favoured *Morveren*, as she was the bigger boat. They were definitely gaining on *Curlew* now, but Zaki knew that if the wind got any stronger they wouldn't be able to control *Morveren*. They had to reduce sail. He was reluctant to throw away the ground they had made up but the darkening cloud-bank he could see building to the west told him that worse weather was on the way.

'I'm going to reef the mainsail.' Zaki had to shout to make himself heard over the roar of the wind. Do you think you can manage the helm?'

'I think so. But you'd better tell me what to point at.'

'You see that far headland? Keep that to starboard.'

'That's the right, isn't it.'

'Yes.'

'I'll do my best.'

With Anusha on the helm, Zaki got to work. Just as he was returning from the side deck, the boat slid down the back of a wave, dug her nose into the next one and sent a torrent of green water flying across her deck, most of which seemed to go down Zaki's neck.

'Oi!'

'Sorry!'

He rejoined Anusha in the comparative shelter of the cockpit.

'Didn't mean to soak you,' Anusha said.

'Try to take the waves at more of an angle – you'll keep us drier.'

'I'll try. How much further?'

'Can you see *Curlew*?'

'Yes.'

'Follow the shoreline along to her left. Do you see that tall rock?'

'Got it.'

'That's Devil's Rock. The entrance is beside the rock.'

'So they're almost there?'

'Yeah – but I can't believe he's going to take her in this weather. It's madness. They don't even have an engine!'

'Looks like he's going to try.'

'What could be so important?'

'The treasure? What if he's made Rhiannon tell him what she did with it?'

'My God!'

'What?'

'He's not going to try to get into the bay. He's aiming for the rock! Half tide – the sand bar will still be uncovered – he's going to beach her at the foot of the rock. He's a wrecker – he doesn't care what happens to the boat.'

'What about Rhiannon? Will he leave her on board?

'If she is on board.'

They watched as the distance between *Curlew* and Devil's Rock gradually diminished.

Anusha suddenly gave a shout, 'That's it! Don't you see? It's part of his plan.'

'What is?'

'The boat's wrecked – Rhiannon's body's onboard – it looks like an accident. Nobody looks any further. And the only one he thinks knows about the treasure is out of the way.'

The grim logic was convincing, but Rhiannon would not be the only victim. If Maunder escaped, Michael was lost.

The two boats were now no more than a quarter of a mile apart but there was no way *Morveren* would catch *Curlew* before she began her suicidal run through the gap in the outer reef.

Zaki knew what he must do, and he knew he should have done it long ago.

'Keep her on this heading. I'm going to put out a mayday.'

He dropped down into the cabin, took a deep breath, picked up the microphone and began the message that every sailor practises but hopes he will never need to send:

'Mayday – Mayday – Mayday. This is yacht *Morveren* – yacht *Morveren* – yacht *Morveren* – Mayday . . .'

CHAPTER 22

Zaki put out the distress call three times, giving their position and situation. He paused between each call, as he had been taught to do, and listened for a response. None came. This area had always been bad for reception. He was beginning the fourth call when *Morveren* was knocked down. The cabin turned on its side and Zaki found himself, together with every other moveable object, flying through the air. He landed heavily, still clutching the microphone, its lead, torn from the radio, dangling from his hand. He threw the now useless microphone aside and scrambled across to the companionway as *Morveren* shook herself, like a punch-drunk fighter, and struggled upright.

Emerging on deck, he saw the helm was deserted. Where was Anusha? With relief, he saw her lying against the guardrail.

'You all right?'

'Think so.'

'What happened?'

'Big wave. I couldn't hold her.'

Zaki helped Anusha back into the cockpit. The foresail

had been ripped in two by the weight of wind and water. Zaki freed the sheet and let the sail fly. The freed ropes whipped back and forward across the deck like wounded snakes. He started the engine and got the boat head-to-wind.

'We need to get that sail in.'

It took both of them on the furling line and all their strength, but with the sail furled and the engine running, *Morveren* was under control and they could pay attention to other things. The clouds to the west had darkened from grey to near black. A vivid orange streak of dying sunlight ran along the horizon as though the edge of the sky had cracked, allowing a glimpse of heaven beyond, its eerie yellow light catching the streaming crests of the breaking waves.

'Look!'

Zaki turned. *Curlew*, all sails set, was riding a wave through the opening in the reef. The black mass of Devil's Rock towered above the little boat and it seemed certain that she would be dashed to pieces at the Devil's feet. At the last possible moment, *Curlew* broached, the wave ran from under her, and she slewed sideways up the bank of the half-exposed sandbar beside the great rock. As the wave retreated, a figure leapt from the boat and ran to gain the safety of the rocks before the next wave could overwhelm him.

Now, as they watched, wave after wave pounded the stranded boat. With the rising tide, each successive wave reached higher up the bar.

Zaki brought *Morveren* as close to the outer reef as

he dared.

'Pass me the binoculars.'

What he saw made him sick to his core. The hatches were lashed shut. Wordlessly, he passed the binoculars to Anusha.

As she lowered the glasses, she looked in desperation at Zaki. 'What do we do? We've got to get her out.'

It was impossible. To follow *Curlew* would be to suffer the same fate, or worse. Zaki watched, helplessly, as the swells surged through the reef and burst against the glistening side of Devil's Rock.

As he watched, he noticed that in every new set of waves there were one or two that, driven by the south-westerly wind, ran in at an angle. Instead of crashing against the rock, they were deflected and ran along the sandbar. He looked at Anusha. It would be terribly risky.

Before he could say anything, she said, 'If you think we can do it, we have to do it.'

Zaki found he was shaking. He was very cold, they hadn't eaten all day and he was frightened.

'What do we do?' Anusha bit her lower lip.

Zaki tried to stop the shaking. 'Watch the waves . . . There! You see? Watch this one. It doesn't run straight in. We have to catch one of those. But if we get it wrong . . .'

'I know. You don't have to explain.'

Zaki turned *Morveren* away from the reef and began a circle that would take them to the point just west of the opening, where he reckoned they should begin their run in. They needed to be moving at speed when they caught

259

the wave. If they slid off it, the next one would catch them from the side. Every time *Morveren* climbed to the crest of a wave, Zaki studied the waves in the distance, trying to see which were running at an angle. As he completed the circle, Zaki slipped the engine into neutral and let the mainsail out as far as it would go. With just the reefed sail to drive them they were moving forward – but not quite as fast as the waves. The white crests of the waves behind them seemed to advance in regimented rows.

'When I shout, give her full throttle, then hang on tight.'

Anusha nodded and moved to be by the engine controls.

In the distance a wave reared above the others as though lifting itself up so Zaki could see it. It was skewed out of line and bearing down on them at great speed.

'Now!' Zaki screamed.

Anusha gunned the engine and Zaki heaved hard on the mainsail, filling it with wind. *Morveren* quickly gathered pace, each passing wave adding to her speed until the chosen wave was beneath them and they were careering on its hissing crest towards the reef.

Where was the gap? With so much spray and surf and the angle of their approach it was hard to see the break in the rocks. There! Yes, there! Zaki willed *Morveren* to stay on course. His hands stopped shaking. He, the boat, the gap in the reef – that was all that existed.

They were through!

'Keep down!' Zaki shouted as he heaved the helm over

and the boom flew wildly across the deck. He hauled the sail in so that it would force *Morveren*'s stern round and keep them from being driven on to the bar. To starboard, angry waves threw themselves at The Orphans, tearing themselves apart in their desperation to break through and devour the yacht.

He looked up at the cliffs ahead. There was the cottage – Rhiannon's cottage. The last time he had seen it, it was just a landmark, just an abandoned ruin.

'When we're round the sandbar, I'd like you to take her. I'll get the sail down.'

'How are we going to get to *Curlew*?'

'The dinghy. Look – you see? That side of the bar – it's sheltered. We can land there, but it's too shallow for *Morveren*.

When the sail was down, Zaki unlashed the dinghy while Anusha steered them into Dragon Pool. He had been so preoccupied with getting them this far in safety, that he hadn't spared a thought for Maunder – not Michael – he couldn't think of him as Michael. Now, he searched the rock for movement. Daylight was fading, and the rock was silhouetted against the grey sky. A small figure was climbing towards the summit.

'He's almost there,' Anusha said, as she too looked up.

They anchored close to the entrance of the pool, launched the dinghy and rowed back as fast as they could. As soon as they rounded the small headland that divided Dragon Pool from the outer bay the wind struck them. The air was full of salt spray from the waves that pounded on the other side of the sandbar and the roar of wind and waves made speech almost impossible. Their progress slowed to a crawl and their arms ached from the strain of battling against the wind. Eventually, the dinghy's bow grated on sand and they jumped out to pull the boat clear of the water. The biggest breakers were now sweeping right across the bar and threatening to wash the dinghy back into the bay.

'Stay here and hang on to the boat,' Zaki yelled.

He staggered up the low bank against the gale. The spray stung his eyes, forcing him to bow his head and pull his hood down over his face. *Curlew*'s mast was broken, her boom and gaff torn away, but her hull was still intact. She lay on her side, her deck towards Zaki, waves exploding over her. Zaki huddled in the shelter of the hull as he fished the clasp knife from his jacket pocket. His stiff, cold fingers refused to work and he had to resort to using his teeth to open the blade. He hacked through the ropes tying down the forehatch and prised it open.

'Rhiannon!' he screamed. There was no reply. He clambered, headfirst, through the hatch. Inside it was almost pitch-black. The waves half lifted the hull and slammed it back down against the sand. Zaki was terrified *Curlew* would roll onto her deck and they would both be trapped.

'Rhiannon!' he screamed again. This time he heard a groan. He felt his way back into the saloon, where he found her, a crumpled ball in the corner of the cabin.

'Rhiannon, we have to get out.' He crouched to help her up. He could just make out her face; something wet and dark glistened on her forehead – blood. She'd hit her head or been hit on the head.

'Come on!' He felt panic rising. Slowly, she unfolded herself.

'I've got the forehatch open, but we've got to hurry.'

She crawled after him into the bow and allowed herself to be helped out on to the sand. There was no time to lose; most of the sandbar was underwater and Zaki could see that Anusha was struggling to keep the dinghy from being washed away by every wave.

Together, they got Rhiannon into the stern of the dinghy.

'Do you think you can get her back to *Morveren*? You'll have the wind with you.'

'What are you going to do? You can't stay here!'

'I'm going for Michael.'

'How? What will you do?' Shock and concern filled her voice.

'Rhiannon.' Zaki lifted the girl's limp arm. 'Rhiannon, I need your bracelet.'

She seemed to understand. She let him slide the bracelet over her hand.

'I'll hold the dinghy. You get in.'

Anusha climbed in and took her place at the oars.

'There's a portable VHF radio by the chart table. Keep calling Mayday, maybe someone will hear you.' He pushed the dinghy off before Anusha had a chance to say anything more and then waded through the dark rising water to the foot of Devil's Rock.

CHAPTER 23

As he began to climb, it occurred to Zaki that, in all the years they had been coming to the Orme, he and Michael had never attempted to scale the rock. Had they been told not to? He couldn't remember it ever being discussed. Perhaps it just lay outside their private world of Dragon Pool. It wasn't particularly difficult but in the twilight it was hard to scout out the best route and on several occasions Zaki found he had reached an impasse or an overhang and had to climb back down and search for another way up. His bulky wet-weather clothing got in the way and snagged on the protruding roots and branches of the stunted gorse bushes that grew out of the cracks and crevasses. He considered taking it off, but his clothes underneath were wet through and the waterproofs gave some protection from the biting wind.

When he reached the summit, he was careful to keep low. The top of the rock was like a miniature plateau, dipping slightly to the middle. There were some larger gorse bushes and a few weathered boulders but otherwise it was quite bare.

He wanted to know what Maunder was doing but he didn't want to be seen, so he crept forward using the bushes and boulders for cover. In the near-darkness, with the howl of the wind drowning out all sound of his movement, he was able to get within a few metres of Maunder and remain undetected.

Maunder was removing the stones that covered his hoard. He was bent over, throwing the stones aside as fast as he could, without looking up, without stopping – like a dog, thought Zaki, digging for a bone. What did he intend to do with it all when he uncovered it? Would it still be of any value?

Zaki strained his eyes to see if Maunder was still wearing the bracelet. Yes – good. He could find out what Maunder was thinking. Zaki took the other bracelet out of his pocket and slipped it on to his own arm. He was careful to keep his own mind quiet. He listened – there was nothing. There were no thoughts. Maunder was acting out of some base instinct – the desire to reclaim what he felt to be his. He was like a beast that will fight to the death to defend its territory. After so many years in the cave, his spirit was less than human. Lying on the wet ground in his wet clothes with nothing but a gorse bush between him and Maunder, Zaki shuddered. But this creature was not just Maunder, it was also Michael – Michael, who had taught Zaki to row, to build dams, to ride dragons. This was his big brother, his remover of obstacles. He had to reach Michael – wake him – bring him back. The bracelets connected them. He must think things that Michael, and not Maunder, would understand.

Two boys astride a dragon. The smaller one behind – the bigger one holding the reins. The smaller boy has his arms around his brother; his head is turned to the side and rests against his big brother's warm back. They are flying high, so high that, although the earth is already in darkness, they are still in the light. The dragon has huge golden wings that shimmer and flash as they beat up and down, catching the last rays of the setting sun. The dragon's body, legs and tail are jewelled with sparkling, green scales. Flames leap from the dragon's mouth. Now they are plunging down, down – the boys waving and whooping with excitement.

Zaki saw all this in his mind. But when he looked up, he saw that Maunder was looking up – staring in astonishment because in the sky there was a great, fire-breathing dragon with two boys on its back.

In the glow from the dragon's fiery breath Zaki could see that Maunder's face was changing, softening – the terrible white scar fading to nothing. And it was no longer Maunder but Michael who stood there, face upturned, watching their dragon. The bracelet on Michael's wrist lit up; the engravings flashed and danced.

Zaki sprang to his feet, ripped the bracelet from his brother's arm and hurled it with all his strength over the cliff. He watched it fall, still shining, spinning around and around, until it was swallowed by the dark heaving waters below. When he looked back, the dragon had gone.

Michael's legs slowly bent, folding under him, until he was sitting on the pile of stones. He hunched his shoulders, wrapped his arms around himself and began to shiver. Zaki took a step towards him but stopped when he heard the roar of powerful engines out to sea. An elongated circle of bright light swept across the water and seemed to bounce along the reef. The beam halted when it found the wrecked yacht on the bar.

The noise of the engines came closer, the unmistakable throaty growl of a lifeboat. Now the light was searching the water and rocks near the wreck, probing the darkness. A second finger of light shot out from the boat and slid up the rock. Zaki raised his arms and waved wildly. He glanced over his shoulder and saw that Michael was also standing. The light stopped short of the summit and slid back down.

'They haven't seen us. We've got to get down. They won't look for us up here.' Michael look dazed and confused. Zaki took him by the arm. 'Come on – follow me. I know the way.'

Climbing down in the darkness was more difficult than climbing up and Michael needed constant prompting and guidance. Several times Zaki missed his footing and almost fell but halfway down the searchlights found them and the rest of the climb was easier.

As soon as they reached the bottom, an inflatable rescue boat darted through the reef and around the rock to meet them. There, strong arms helped them aboard and they were whisked swiftly out to the waiting lifeboat.

'Are there any others?' asked the lifeboat's coxswain as soon as they were inside. Zaki explained about the two aboard *Morveren* and the crew of the rescue boat was dispatched to fetch them. Zaki wanted to go with them but the coxswain wouldn't hear of it.

'Did you get our Mayday?' Zaki asked.

'They picked it up in Plymouth. That's where the inshore rescue boat came from. But it was your grandad who knew where to find you. He called us out. Seems he guessed you'd be here. Though heaven knows why anyone would try to get into the Orme in this weather. Good thing you fired that flare, though.'

Flare? There was no flare. The dragon. Zaki looked at Michael – *their* dragon. No way of explaining that to their rescuers.

As soon as Anusha and Rhiannon were safely on the lifeboat, exhaustion took its toll. And afterwards Zaki's memory of the trip back to Salcombe seemed a disordered jumble of noises and pictures: Michael, silent and dazed, wrapped in a silver survival blanket; Rhiannon with her head bandaged; Anusha, her face so pale, asleep in a lifeboatman's arms; people asking questions that seemed to float in the air around him without finding answers; sudden, unexpected rushes of emotion – gratitude, guilt, elation. He remembered Anusha hugging him and one or other or maybe both of them crying. He remembered taking off the bracelet that was still on his wrist and giving it back to Rhiannon, and he remembered her saying, 'I suppose that makes us even,' and then suddenly smiling, and he had never thought she would have such a warm smile. And he remembered wishing and wishing Michael would say something, anything, to prove to him that he was bringing back the real Michael, the whole Michael and not just an empty shell.

CHAPTER 24

O f the faces in the small crowd that waited as they were helped off the lifeboat, his mother's was the only one Zaki really saw. That face was still there many hours later when he opened his eyes after the deepest sleep of his life.

Several weeks went by during which no one in Zaki's family seemed to say very much about anything in particular, as though a need for quiet had settled on them all. Although they said very little to each other, they sought out each other's company and if all four of them were at home at the same time they would usually be found in the same room. Zaki's father gave up working late and meals were eaten together at the kitchen table. During this time, the house itself began to change. Small additions at first: a painting on the wall here, a blind for a window there. Then carpets were laid and shelves were built for books that had been in boxes since the last time the family moved. Zaki made a close study of his parents' behaviour. They asked each other's opinions about home improvements and discussed the usual domestic arrangements, but when they spoke it was with a slightly strained politeness that Zaki found unsettling.

The way the story of the wreck of *Curlew* was reported in the local paper was that 'Three brave young people from Kingsbridge rescued a lone sailor when her yacht was wrecked on the notorious Devil's Rock.' And that ,'Zaki Luxton, in a feat of quite remarkable seamanship, steered his family's yacht through a maze of reefs in a south-westerly gale to effect the rescue.' Grandad was generally considered to have been the source of the story.

During a spell of calm weather, *Curlew* was refloated and towed back behind *Morveren* to Grandad's slipway. Her black hull was deeply scarred and her rigging gone but Grandad set to work rebuilding her.

Zaki never saw Rhiannon at the boat shed, but when he asked his grandfather why he was repairing the boat he said, 'Because she asked me to.'

Zaki and Anusha often wondered where Rhiannon went during the weeks when her boat was out of the water. Zaki thought she was probably at the old cottage but they decided she wouldn't want them to go looking for her.

Then, on a raw, cold November morning, Grandad collected Zaki, Michael and Anusha and drove them to Salcombe to see *Curlew* launched. And Rhiannon was there to meet them.

At high tide, *Curlew* slid back into the water and lay rocking gently, her new varnish gleaming in the pale sunlight. Rhiannon stepped aboard, raised the sails and cast off. Zaki, Michael, Anusha and Grandad followed *Curlew* down the harbour in Grandad's launch, stopping only when they reached the harbour mouth. As they watched, *Curlew*'s sails were lit up by the low winter sun, shone for a moment, and then faded as she vanished like a ghost ship into the morning mist.

Anusha became a frequent visitor to the Luxtons' house and one day when she, Michael and Zaki returned home after school, they found Grandad's car parked outside and something very like a party going on, laughter erupting from the kitchen.

'You're just in time for the celebrations!' Zaki's mother called as they came in.

'Why? What's happened?' asked Michael.

'I've just sold the *Queen of the Dart*, that's what's 'appened, boy! And I've sold 'er for an awful lot of money!' boasted Grandad.

'You never!' said Michael.

'I 'ave. And guess what we're going to do with all that money?'

Michael shrugged. 'No idea, Grandad.'

'We're going to build another boat.'

'What sort of boat?' asked Zaki.

'Do you remember this one?' asked their father. And Zaki saw that the old plans were once more spread out on the kitchen table.

'Do you want to sail round the world?' asked their mum.

Zaki and Michael looked at each other.

'Not if I have to share a cabin with him!' said Michael.

'Who'd want to share a smelly cabin with you?' mocked Zaki in return.

'Just have to go without you, then,' their mother laughed.

'Can I come?' asked Anusha. All turned to look at Anusha who said, 'Well? I mean it!' – rather defiantly.

'Better ask your parents, this time,' said Grandad.

There followed an hour of heated argument over what the new boat should be called – which might have gone on all night if hunger hadn't forced them to go out for fish and chips.